Joyce Holms was born and educated in Glasgow. The victim of a low boredom threshold, she has held a variety of jobs, from teaching window dressing and managing a hotel on the Isle of Arran to working for an Edinburgh detective agency and running a B&B in the Highlands. Married with two grown-up children, she lives in Edinburgh and her interests include hill-walking and garden design.

Find out more about Joyce Holms by visiting her website at:

www.joyceholms.com

MISSING LINK

Always in search of a good story, Fizz Fitzgerald feels impatient when elderly Mrs Sullivan is shown into her office. Anticipating boredom, Fizz is shocked when Mrs Sullivan asks Fizz to help prove her guilty of murder. Fizz ropes in the other half of the dynamic detective duo, Tam Buchanan, who thinks that the case will prove to be a waste of time. But why is Mrs Sullivan so keen to be accused of murder? And who was Amanda Montrose, the murder victim? Lady of the Manor? Scottish gentlewoman? Or, in Mrs Sullivan's words, a 'scruffy little slut'? With at least three people who could have been Amanda's killer, it seems there is more to the Montrose murder than first meets the eye.

Books by Joyce Holms
Published by The House of Ulverscroft:

FOREIGN BODY
BAD VIBES
MR BIG
BITTER END
HOT POTATO
HIDDEN DEPTHS

JOYCE HOLMS

MISSING LINK

Complete and Unabridged

CHARNWOOD
Leicester

First published in Great Britain in 2006 by
Allison & Busby Limited
London

First Charnwood Edition
published 2007
by arrangement with
Allison & Busby Limited
London

The moral right of the author has been asserted

British Library CIP Data

Holms, Joyce
    Missing link.—Large print ed.—
    Charnwood library series
    1. Fizz (Fictitious character: Holms)—Fiction
    2. Buchanan, Tam (Fictitious character)—Fiction
    3. Law students—Scotland—Fiction
    4. Lawyers—Scotland—Fiction
    5. Detective and mystery stories
    6. Large type books
    I. Title
    823.9'14 [F]

    ISBN 978–1–84617–765–1

Published by
F. A. Thorpe (Publishing)
Anstey, Leicestershire

Set by Words & Graphics Ltd.
Anstey, Leicestershire
Printed and bound in Great Britain by
T. J. International Ltd., Padstow, Cornwall

This book is printed on acid-free paper

Prologue

Amanda is forty-five. If she puts her mind to it, which she usually does, she can pass for a woman in her mid-thirties, but today is a bad-face day. She can see her eyes in the driving mirror, narrowed, the lids drooping, fine lines gathering at the inner corners. She relaxes her expression and lifts her brows but the drawn expression returns as soon as she glances away. She is worried and unhappy but she does not yet know that she is about to die.

Her thoughts are centred largely on the dog she has just left, weak and vomiting, at the veterinary surgery. Some rubbish he must have eaten, she is thinking, a dead rabbit or possibly the horse manure he appeared to enjoy. Dirty little bugger. She'd never cared much for chihuahuas. It had been Ewan who'd talked her out of the deerhound she'd originally wanted to buy, citing the amount of exercise and grooming it would take and stressing, like the tight-fisted Scot he was, that it would cost the earth to feed. As if that mattered. It was she who footed the bills, after all, and she was far from insolvent. But Gonzo had fitted the bill adequately, completing the image she wanted to project: that of a dyed-in-the-wool Scottish gentlewoman, mistress of an estate that had been in the same family for eleven generations, and never happy without a dog around. He might not possess quite the same regal bearing as would have a hip-high deerhound but he drew less attention, which was, perhaps, an advantage she had not taken into consideration at the time.

What she had not expected was that the pup would so quickly become a substitute child to her. In fact, when you faced it squarely, he was the only living thing on God's earth she gave a damn about. If anything happened to him . . . She caught the thought and killed it. Nothing was going to happen to him. He might look like he was at death's door but the vet didn't seem to think it was anything serious. A couple of days, probably, and he'd be back to normal, galloping about the lawn in pursuit of starlings. All the same, she wouldn't be happy till she had him back home.

She looks at her watch. It is not much after five but already the streetlights are starting to come on. From horizon to horizon the sky is clogged with purplish clouds and low in the west there is a yellow tinge that promises yet more snow before the night is out.

'Christ!' she mutters aloud as she edges the Vitara through the sluggish stream of traffic. 'Still snowing in March. What a bloody country! Whatever made me think I could settle here?'

She stares out the side window at the leaden waters of the Beauly Firth and tries to recapture the thrill she'd felt when she first looked at that scene. It had been summer then, of course: late summer with the first hint of autumn in the air, and it had seemed like Paradise on earth. The heather was already turning purple on the hills

2

and wherever she stopped the car she experienced the same overwhelming tranquillity. Wood smoke lay heavy on the breeze and time seemed to move at a slower pace. People had time to talk and, without being uncomfortably nosey, showed polite interest in a visitor from down south. She'd thought it quaint, the way they'd said 'down south' instead of 'England', as though it were insensitive to refer too directly to another's bad luck.

And then Ewan had arrived on the scene, with all his charming innocence and all his wonderful collection of possibilities: the estate, the unassailable aura of respectability he took so much for granted, the seeming infinity of his trust in her. How could she not have grabbed her chance with both hands?

Let's face it, she tells herself, slowing to make the turn into the single track road leading to Breich village and thence to the estate, you knew from the beginning that it wouldn't last. You've had five good years, maybe it's time you should be thinking of moving on. Keep on presenting a moving target like you used to. It's the sensible thing to do and it's not as if you'd be breaking dear old Ewan's heart, is it? God knows he'd be just as —

Her foot hits the brake with a force that swings her against her seat belt. Hell's bells, what next?

Twenty feet ahead of her an old Volkswagen is drawn up at the side of the road, two wheels on the narrow verge but still effectively blocking the way ahead. Someone in a long waterproof coat has the bonnet up and is leaning under it, tinkering with the engine but, although he must have heard the approach of another vehicle, he does not raise his head. Amanda's thumb hovers over the horn button but she curbs her irritation. She knows it's likely that this person will be familiar to her, at least to nod to, as is everyone likely to be on this road out of the tourist season, and rudeness wouldn't fit her projected persona. She waits an interminable twenty seconds and then flicks her lights. The bastard does not acknowledge her presence by as much as a glance.

Now thoroughly incensed, she throws open the door and swings her legs to the ground. A chill little wind snatches at her coat, whipping it out behind her, and the first few flakes of snow touch her face like moths in the gathering dusk. As she approaches the parked car she is struck by a sudden inexplicable frisson of uneasiness but she barely registers the sensation. The thought that anyone would do her harm, here in her Highland hideaway where she is known and respected, is too silly to dwell on. Back home, one didn't walk down dark and wooded paths after sunset but things are different here. Civilised. Safe.

'Having a bit of trouble?' she says, veiling her annoyance with a phoney tone of concern.

The driver straightens and turns, smiling, and fear surges though Amanda's body like an electric charge. She sees the hammer. She sees the gloating, resolute eyes. And she knows she is looking at her own death.

She skitters backwards, opening her mouth to scream, but it is too late for that.

Way too late.

1

The Wonderful Beatrice, since her promotion to Office Manager, had taken to wearing suits to work, the better to annoy Margaret who felt, quite without reason, that the promotion should have been hers. In point of fact, Beatrice was still doing almost the same job as she had always done, namely secretary to whoever needed her most, but the status conferred by her new title meant a lot to her. It also gave her the confidence to speak her mind somewhat oftener than Fizz felt was strictly necessary.

'Is that all you've got to do?' she said now, coming into Fizz's office and catching her with her feet on the desk, looking out of the window.

Fizz tipped back her chair another dangerous inch. 'No, Beattie my little Jiminy Cricket, it's not all I've got to do. Not by a long chalk, I can tell you. But just look at that sun out there. Remember what it was like last August? Siberia, that's what. But this year, just when I'm trapped in this office like a hamster in a cage, the sun's melting the lampposts.'

'You were away up to Am Bealach to see your Grampa last weekend,' Beatrice stated flatly, 'and you were down the Borders fishing with Mr Buchanan on Wednesday evening.'

'It rained on Wednesday evening. That's the trouble with office hours, you can't grab the good weather when it's going. Maybe we should

5

think about starting flexitime. What do you think?'

Beatrice drew in a deep and disapproving breath and folded the front of her jacket tightly across her bosom. 'I think you should take a comb through your hair and tidy yourself up a bit, that's what I think. Mrs Sullivan has arrived for her appointment.'

Fizz allowed herself a wide and delicious yawn before swinging her feet to the floor. 'Mrs Sullivan. Uh-huh. Do we know her?'

'No, she's never consulted us before but I understand someone recommended Mr Buchanan to her. I told her he no longer worked for the firm and she asked to see you.'

Fizz was getting used to being second choice, and not only to Buchanan's clients, so she wasn't particularly hurt by this revelation. 'Who recommended Buchanan to her?'

'She didn't say and I didn't ask,' Beatrice shrugged, 'but Greenfield House retirement home was mentioned so I expect it was one of those weirdos you got involved with a couple of years back. I'll show her in and you can ask her yourself.'

'Okay. If you insist, Beattie. But keep an ear open and if you hear me snoring rush in and give me artificial respiration.'

The chances of Mrs Sullivan's business proving to be more interesting than drawing up her will were, she suspected, slight, but one could hope. The heady days when she had leapt on each new piece of legal work with a glad cry were, unfortunately, behind her and the career that had once promised everlasting satisfaction was now, by and large, nothing but a job. What a difference a year made. Buchanan had been smart to branch out into advocacy when he did. At least he had a little challenge in his life. Or would when he finally started to get some decent briefs.

She got up and went to the door to greet her new client and found herself shaking hands with a silver-haired woman who looked to be in her late sixties or possibly a little older. Fizz had never been all that good at guessing ages, particularly those of elderly persons who all looked much the same to her. Anyone between retirement and Grampa's age, which was coming up to eighty-five, she filed under 'old'. Anyone older than Grampa could only be classed as a coffin-dodger. This one wasn't all that wrinkly but her cheeks had sagged off her jawbone a bit and the way she moved indicated a severe lack of energy and possibly a bad back. It took her a minute or two to ease herself into a chair and arrange her voluminous and expensive-looking jacket, her handbag, her gloves and her gold-rimmed sunglasses.

'Dear me,' she remarked, in an educated south of England accent, 'Mr Bramley warned me not to be put off by your youthful appearance — 'a Botticelli cherub' was the phrase he used to describe you — but I have to confess to being . . . well, surprised.'

Shocked would have been the more precise term, Fizz suspected, and gave her a polite smile and her stock reply to an observation she'd long ago learned to live with.

'Appearances are often deceptive, Mrs Sullivan, as Mr Bramley may have mentioned. How is he, by the way?'

Mrs Sullivan's doubtful expression softened. 'Paul is full of life, as ever. Still running Greenfield House like a holiday camp, keeping his little coterie on their toes. They all send their fondest regards to you and Mr Buchanan.'

'It's good to hear they're doing well. I hope you'll give them my best wishes when next you see them.' Fizz toyed with her pen. 'And how did they suggest I could be of service to you?'

'Actually, I haven't discussed the details of my problem with any of them — it's not something I care to publicise too widely, just for the moment. It's an extremely delicate matter, you understand?' A sliver of sunlight edged around the window frame and tinted Mrs Sullivan's hair a pale gold as she leaned forward.

'Absolutely.' A similar, but comparatively pallid, ray of hope penetrated Fizz's boredom. She sat up. 'Anything you tell me will be totally confidential.'

'I understand that. Yes, dear, of course I understand that.' A gentle, almost motherly smile deepened the wrinkles around her eyes. 'But it's nice to have your assurance.'

'Let me get you a coffee,' Fizz said, perceiving that the interview might drag on.

'No thank you, dear. I only drink mint tea and I don't suppose you have any. I usually have a couple of packets in my handbag but I seem to have forgotten them today. What was I saying?

8

Ah, yes. What I want you to do for me is to prove me guilty of a murder.'

It was perhaps five seconds before Fizz realised she was still sitting there in her 'interested listener' pose, convinced that the words she'd just heard had a totally different meaning to the one that had sprung to mind. 'Hunh?' she said, and then collected herself. 'Prove you *guilty* of a murder . . . Right . . . Er . . . A particular murder or just any murder?'

'A particular murder, I'm afraid, dear.' Mrs Sullivan laid a blue-veined hand on the desk exposing an old-fashioned but heavy gold and pearl bracelet. 'The murder of Amanda Montrose in Inverness back in March.'

Fizz took a long look at her, searching for signs of insanity, but the grey eyes that gazed back into hers were calm and level and totally lucid. 'I see,' she said, permitting none of her sudden gleeful anticipation to show in her face. 'But of course you realise that it would be very difficult to prove you guilty of a murder you didn't commit.'

The grey eyes opened wider. 'Oh, but I did it, my dear, there's no problem about that. No, no. I'm afraid I'm guilty of the crime. Homicide. Isn't that what they call it nowadays?'

Clenching her jaw against a giggle, Fizz bent her head and drew a small, four-petalled flower on the cover of her diary. The smart thing to do was to tell this dotty old dear that she didn't handle that sort of case any more and get rid of her *tout de suite* but one could scarcely let her go without hearing what evidence she was able to produce to back up her allegation. Miracles could happen. She might be telling the truth.

'Actually, Mrs Sullivan,' she said, with what seriousness she could project, 'I can't say I'm familiar with the facts of Amanda Montrose's case but I seem to remember someone was tried and convicted of that murder.'

'That's true. That's the terrible thing about it. Some young man has just been put in jail for fourteen years for something I did.' Mrs Sullivan shook her head sharply, making her cheeks wobble. 'How can I live with that? For myself, the thought of confinement isn't really so frightening. Not at my age. I'm the last of my generation: all my brothers and sisters have gone before me and I have few friends left and little to look forward to. But just think of the terrible distress I've caused that young man — and not only him but his family, his wife or girlfriend, perhaps even children — who'll have to grow up without a father. I can't let that happen. That's precisely why I need your help.'

She gave every evidence of being sincere, almost to the point of shedding tears, and for a moment Fizz felt her scepticism waver. What if she were actually quite *compos mentis*? Appearances could be deceptive, right? Unlikely, in this case, but what was true of herself could also be true of Mrs Sullivan. She doodled another flower on her diary and thought: supposing Mrs Sullivan were thirty-five and bitchy-looking, would I take her seriously? Or if she were an old man? Or an old lady, yes, but also a tough old bird from a deprived area with a

10

previous conviction, a drink problem and needle marks on her arms? What is there about this old woman, other than her kind face and well-to-do appearance, that suggests she's likely to be innocent?

The Amanda Montrose case had been given little coverage in the Edinburgh newspapers and Fizz had barely scanned the trial reports but it ran in her mind that some degree of violence had been involved. Also, the body had taken some weeks to turn up so, presumably, it had been hidden somewhere. Both of these circumstances would imply the use of a fair amount of physical strength and, although by no means scrawny, Mrs Sullivan scarcely looked fit enough for that kind of exertion.

'Don't you think, Mrs Sullivan,' she said, 'that the police would have been the best people to deal with this?'

'Oh, the police! Don't talk to me about the police! A fat lot of good they are to anybody. I've been twice to the police and it's quite obvious they think I'm some delusional old grannie. I can see for myself that they have no intention of taking the matter any further. It's all, 'yes, yes, we'll look into it and let you know'. They're nothing but a bunch of time wasters, if you ask me. But I won't be ignored, Miss Fitzpatrick. I'm willing to spend every penny I own to have someone prove that what I'm saying is the truth.'

'I daresay the CID might want some definite proof of your guilt before reopening the inquiry,' Fizz suggested carefully, at which Mrs Sullivan reared her head back and snorted like an old

11

cavalry charger smelling the gunpowder.

'I gave them plenty of proof. Plenty! But everything I could tell them had evidently appeared in the press and I couldn't prove — not to *their* satisfaction, at least — that I hadn't read it.' Mrs Sullivan folded her hands on her handbag and fixed Fizz with a pathetic look. 'That's the trouble, you see dear, when you commit the perfect crime you don't leave any clues behind.'

Torn between hilarity and a certain unwilling deference, Fizz nodded with what she hoped looked like understanding. 'You had it all planned out in advance, then?'

'Well, no, not really,' admitted Mrs Sullivan, fidgeting distractedly with the reading glasses she wore on a gold chain about her neck. 'As a matter of fact, I hadn't meant to kill her. Violence is very far from my nature, I promise you. I feel guilty every time I swat a fly, really I do, and if I had even suspected myself capable of . . . ' her bosom heaved, 'of doing what I did, I'd have avoided that woman like the plague. But, there you are. We none of us really know the inner being, as they say, and I'm afraid I was quite swept away with . . . oh dear, one can only call it animal passion. I lost my temper. I don't believe that has ever happened to me before. Not like that. I simply saw red for a moment. There was no warning, no single moment when I decided on doing what I did. She provoked me, I had a hammer in my hand, and I hit her with it. It was all over in a second and there she was, lying dead at my feet. I can still barely believe it.'

12

A hammer, Fizz thought. That was accurate anyway. She recollected snatches of forensic evidence that had posited a blunt instrument, most likely a hammer, as the murder weapon but the rest of the story that had come out at the trial had faded from her memory. 'I think,' she said, 'you'd better tell me exactly what happened. You had met Amanda Montrose previously, had you?'

Mrs Sullivan drew a long breath and settled herself more comfortably in her chair as though she were satisfied that she now had Fizz's full and sober attention. Which was, for some reason, so.

'Oh yes, I knew Amanda Montrose.' She nodded grimly and her eyes narrowed with what would have looked like meanness in a less sweet-faced individual. 'I knew her in London when she was Mandy Knox: a scruffy little slut who had my son, William, twisted around her little finger. I knew her for what she was the minute I set eyes on her. Bleached hair, revealing clothes — a ring through her tummy button, would you believe? But William was always so ridiculously naïve and he wouldn't hear a word against her. He put all my warnings down to jealousy and, in the end, he more or less cut me out of his life altogether. I've not the slightest doubt that she made him choose between us and, of course, he chose her. As I said, she had him bewitched.'

She pressed her lips together for a moment, clearly close to tears but, just as clearly, determined not to give way to them. 'Why are men so stupid when it comes to women? Mandy was married when she met William. She left her husband and child for him but it never occurred to him that a woman who will do that once will do it again whenever it suits her book.'

'She abandoned your son also?'

'No. I only wish she had. He might have got over that in the long run.' She found a white embroidered hankie in her bag and blew her nose. 'No, she did much worse than that. She destroyed him. She introduced him to marihuana, then cocaine, then heroin. Meanwhile she was going out with other men, sometimes bringing them back to the flat she shared with William, and finally . . . finally it all became too much for him and he took his own life.'

Her voice wavered and broke on the last word and Fizz said nothing, giving her a moment or two to steady up. It was fairly obvious that, whether this story were true or not, Mrs Sullivan clearly believed it to be the truth and, hating Amanda as violently as she must have done, you could see how she might convince herself that she had caused the woman's death, simply by desiring it so powerfully.

'When did all this happen?' she asked when Mrs Sullivan had finished dabbing her eyes.

'Oh, a long time ago. William died in 1987. I think I can honestly say I'd put all that heartache behind me. You can learn to live with anything, you know my dear, if you have any strength of character whatsoever.' She shifted her position in the chair and gave a little wince as though caught by a twinge of arthritis. 'But Fate evidently

14

intended us to meet again because when I took a little Spring break in Moy this year I discovered that Mandy had married well and was living just west of Inverness, less than an hour's drive away from where I was staying. There was a photograph of her in the Inverness Courier, presenting the prizes at some kiddies' pony club competition.'

'That must have been a shock,' Fizz ventured.

'Indeed it was, dear. It brought it all back and, I must confess, all the hatred I'd felt for Mandy, and which I'd put to the back of my mind, came flooding over me, as scalding as ever.' She straightened up. 'But there was never a thought of killing her, Miss Fitzpatrick. Even in the days and weeks that followed William's funeral, even when I wanted that woman punished — and punished severely for her wickedness, murder was never in my heart. Of that I do — truly — believe I'm innocent.'

Fizz could feel herself being drawn insidiously into a dangerous acceptance of Mrs Sullivan's view of things. Daft as the whole story line appeared on the surface, there was something about the old lady's matter-of-fact delivery that precluded too confident a rebuttal. She was delusional of course, there could not be the slightest doubt about that. Sane, mature and reasonably intelligent people, such as Mrs Sullivan obviously was, simply did not bash someone with a hammer. Not hard enough to kill them. One could imagine lashing out perhaps, if sorely pressed, but a blow delivered with the sort of force necessary to smash through a cranium and do lethal damage? No, surely that would have to be delivered with intent to kill? So Mrs Sullivan was probably fantasising about that at least, if not the whole damn incident. All the same, she now had Fizz well hooked and willing to hear the rest of her crazy story, if only for the pleasure of relating it to Buchanan at a later date.

'I didn't even want to speak to the woman,' she was saying earnestly while her fingers worked agitatedly on the hankie. 'I don't think I even wanted to see her, not really, but I suppose I was inquisitive about her change of lifestyle. She was so much a city type when I knew her. Going to theatres and clubs, dining out, dashing around in her current boyfriend's fast car. I just couldn't imagine how she could have changed enough to be accepted by the local community, to be the pillar of rural society I'd read about in the paper. Her husband was some sort of local laird and owned a great deal of land in the neighbourhood — grouse moor and deer forest mostly — which had been in his family, I believe, for hundreds of years. I couldn't see her fitting in to that sort of background and I was curious to know if she were still the same wicked woman in sheep's clothing, as you might say. So, one day when I'd been shopping in Inverness I succumbed to a foolish whim and, on my way home, took a little detour that led me along the border of her estate.'

Fizz could see that speaking about the incident was going to be difficult for her. Her voice was beginning to sound somewhat breathless and unsteady and her eyes were jerking unsteadily around the room as she spoke.

'Perhaps you'd like a glass of water?' she suggested, but the offer was brushed aside by an impatient hand.

'No, thank you, dear. I'd rather get this over with, if you don't mind. If I want your help I must tell you exactly what happened that terrible evening.' She got her hands in a tight grip and stared at them for a moment as though gathering her thoughts. Then she said, 'Vengeance is mine, saith the Lord, but I wonder sometimes if, perhaps, God was using me for His own purpose that day. It has seemed to me that it was all part of some divine plan: that God wanted Mandy punished and allowed me to be His instrument. It appears so oddly coincidental that my car chose that particular spot to break down and what else could it have been but God's will that the only person who came along was Mandy? It was a quiet road, single track, and at that spot there wasn't enough space on the verge to get my car completely off the road so she had no choice but to stop.'

'Mandy was in her Vitara?' Fizz asked, a memory resurfacing suddenly about a vehicle being found.

Mrs Sullivan nodded briefly. 'I'd only been there a few seconds. My engine had run out of water and I was topping up the radiator from a can I carried in the boot. She came hurtling round a sharp bend and nearly ran into me but I didn't recognise her right away. She looked older than I'd expected her to look — one never really allows for the passage of time in those one hasn't seen for a while, does one?' She gave a little wan smile and smoothed the wrinkled skin on her hands. 'I know I look older than I did fifteen years ago but somehow I hadn't expected Mandy to look forty-five. She'd put on quite a bit of weight and she'd dyed her hair a horrible mixture of dark brown and burgundy which didn't suit her at all. Nicely dressed, though, in a suede suit and beautiful knee-high boots: so much prettier than the ghastly skin-tight miniskirts and flimsy tops she used to wear.'

There was a pause which Mrs Sullivan filled by rubbing her fingers up and down the arm of her chair and staring out of the window. Buchanan had always advocated letting an interviewee take their time without interruption but Fizz was captivated enough to prompt her just a little.

'But when you recognised her?'

'Well, I didn't, dear, as I said. Not for quite a few minutes. She got out of her little car and came up behind me. I barely glanced over my shoulder at her because I was trying to get the cap off the water can but when she spoke, asking me what was wrong, there was something in her voice that I recognised after all those years. It was like being hit by a bus, my dear.'

'Did she recognise you at the same time?'

Mrs Sullivan looked fixedly out of the window, doubtless seeing a lonely country road late on a March evening. 'Not at first, perhaps, but she must have seen the shock on my face because she gasped and said something — 'You!'

perhaps, or 'Good God!'. Something like that. I don't remember too clearly — probably don't want to remember — but terrible things were said. I remember shouting at her, I remember her screaming in my face and saying dreadful, unforgivable things about William.' She shook her head and touched fingertips to brow for a moment and then straightened her shoulders and looked Fizz firmly in the eye. 'I had the hammer in my hand — the can I kept the water in had rusted shut and there were no other tools in the car that I could use to try and open it. I . . . my arm . . . struck out. I didn't know it was going to happen. I had no intention . . . but I felt the hammer go in . . . and, oh God, the sound it made . . . ' Her voice was descending into a gurgle, as though it were being strangled in her throat, but she forced herself to finish. 'Suddenly . . . there she was . . . lying at my feet in a pool of blood.'

A sudden sob escaped her and she dropped her head abruptly, hiding her face in her neat white hankie. Although she made no further sound, Fizz could see her shoulders shaking and her fingers working overtime to dab away the tears. It was quite obvious that, whatever the truth of her recollections, she was in considerable mental anguish and if the police weren't going to help her find out whether she were actually guilty or not, somebody ought to do it.

A year ago, this was just the sort of case she'd have given her back teeth to get involved with. Even now, knowing she couldn't take time off without causing havoc with her work load and

19

inviting friction with the partners, she couldn't bear to see Mrs Sullivan walk out the door. Fortunately, an alternative was at hand.

She looked at her watch. 'Mrs Sullivan, can I ask you to leave this with me overnight? I'd like to think about what you've told me and, perhaps, talk it over with Mr Buchanan.'

'You'll . . . you'll take on my case, then?'

Fizz looked at her anxious, washed-out old eyes and was, for once, overcome by compassion.

'If I can't take it on myself I'll find someone who can.'

Someone who had the necessary contacts. Someone who had time on his hands. Someone who might have scruples about taking money from a daft old biddy but who was beginning to learn — and not before time — that man's philosophical outlook was governed by his economic needs.

In short: Buchanan.

2

Buchanan was already wishing he hadn't agreed to have his lounge redecorated. The arrangement, made so long ago, had seemed reasonable enough but now, with little money coming in and the outgoings remaining, in spite of all his scrimping, much the same as they had ever done, he was in two minds about backing out.

'See,' said Justin, who was, he stressed, no cowboy but a qualified craftsman with a City and Guilds certificate, 'it's that there great greasy stain that's the problem. All the rest's a piece of cake: coupla coats of off-white an' Bob's your uncle. But yon big blotch — kinda like a skull, when ye look at it — that's gonny take some shiftin'.'

'I know,' Buchanan admitted. 'I've painted over it four times myself but it keeps on showing through.'

He wished immediately that he hadn't said that as Justin was bound to use it as an excuse to put the price up. On the other hand, if the estimate increased to any marked extent that would be reason enough to wriggle out of the arrangement.

'Grease is hard to shift, see? We'll need to paint some sealant over it before we start, maybe two coats, and let it dry.' He ran exploratory fingers over the stained area. 'What was it? Oil of some sort?'

'Avocado, actually.' He met Justin's invitingly raised eyebrow with a shake of the head. 'Don't even ask.'

Justin had about him an air of moral rectitude and respectability totally alien to a world in which one's fiancée hurled avocados and verbal abuse at one's head prior to disappearing into the sunset without as much as a toodle-oo. Such bizarre events had never figured in Buchanan's past, either, until Fizz had popped into his life like some fiendish gremlin from the nether world, wreaking havoc with every aspect of his existence. Only those who knew her personally would appreciate the Story of the Stain in its full richness of passion, suffering and human depravity.

'Well, I could get one coat on it tonight. It'll be two days before I can paint over it but I can give it another coat on Friday. That'll give it time to dry by the time I've finished the rest of the walls and the paintwork.'

'Fine.'

Buchanan knew he wouldn't be happy saying anything else. You couldn't mess tradesmen around as though their time were less important than your own. He had agreed to Justin's estimate months ago and it was obvious the guy was working to a tight schedule — probably had to, to make a living wage out of the hourly rate he was asking. He wasn't short of work, that was certain, unlike fledgling advocates dependent on whatever briefs they could attract in a competitive field.

While Justin collected his tools from the van

he went into the bedroom and changed out of his business suit into jeans and sweater. Apart from a bowl of muesli at breakfast time he'd eaten nothing all day so by the time he'd locked Selena and Pooky into their cat basket in the kitchen and lent a hand with draping dust sheets over the furniture his tummy was rumbling audibly.

'I'm going to make myself some food,' he told Justin. 'You want something to keep you going?'

'Wouldn't say no, squire.'

'Scrambled eggs on toast okay?'

Justin appeared to sigh a little as one who had expected better, but accepted politely and went on mixing something in a bucket. Buchanan looked in the cupboard to see if there was anything more tempting he could offer but there was nothing but tinned tomato soup, which he bought in bulk as a standby, a slightly stale loaf, some muesli and an elderly lump of cheese which he only just managed to get into the pedal bin before it bit him. Even the sell-by date on the egg box was edging into the red but at least there were a dozen, which was just as well because he'd forgotten to buy any milk in which to scramble them. The end result was, however, just as good if not better than his usual effort. The mixture had gone a bit brown on the bottom while he was making coffee but the toasty flavour this imparted was not unappealing.

Justin came into the kitchen while he was scraping the toast and went over to the sink to wash his hands. 'I smell something burning.'

'No, everything's fine. All ready to serve.'

Justin was somewhat younger than Buchanan, late twenties probably: a big man, probably two or three inches over six foot and built like the proverbial brick outbuilding, and he had an appetite to match. After one exploratory mouthful he smothered everything, including several slices of bread, in tomato ketchup and demolished the lot in a matter of a few minutes. Selena and Pooky watched him, round-eyed, jostling for position behind the window of their prison.

'Needed that,' he sighed, sitting back in his chair with his coffee mug cradled in hands like two bunches of bananas. 'The wife's been on a diet for the past month and she won't have anything fattening in the house. Fruit, porridge, cottage cheese and the occasional scrap of white fish. I reckon I've lost a coupla stone more than she has.'

Buchanan eyed his bulging T-shirt and surmised that he must have looked pretty formidable a month ago. He'd probably lost weight himself recently, due mainly to forgetting to buy food while, at the same time, filling in his spare time by running round Arthur's Seat. If it hadn't been for his compulsory dinner with his parents once a month and the occasional meal he managed to scrounge off Fizz he'd be in even worse shape. 'I haven't been eating too well myself recently,' he confided, looking around the well-equipped kitchen that had been so expensively kitted out by the late unlamented Janine when they were first an item. 'I keep planning on learning to cook properly, but I never seem to get around to it.'

'You don't need to learn to cook,' Justin returned, with heartening robustness. 'All you need's a good recipe book.'

'Oh, I've got several of those.' Buchanan got up and dug his culinary library out from beneath the welter of plastic bags, string, holiday postcards, golfing tees, elastic bands, curtain hooks, fishing gut, and assorted screw nails in his kitchen drawer. Some of the books had never been opened, in others the pages were stuck together by a variety of festering foodstuffs.

Justin investigated them delicately, like a forensic scientist examining interesting traces of a little-known oriental poison. 'Plenty of stuff in there you could have a bash at. Y'don't need a PhD to shove a lemon up a chicken's arse and stick it in an oven, do you? And what about something like this vegetable broth here? It goes on about using a good stock but you could use a stock cube or a spoonful of bouillon. Don't you cook nothin' at all?'

Buchanan felt diminished in the face of such assurance. He gestured feebly at his own half-empty plate and Justin's lip curled.

'That's your best shot?'

'Well, it's a while since I've been to the supermarket. I used to buy frozen meals but I'm trying to cut down on expenses at the moment.'

'What else do you cook?'

Buchanan's mind ranged over some of his latest disasters but he felt the verb 'cook' could scarcely be applied to any of them. 'Eggs, mostly,' he admitted. 'Boiled, scrambled or fried.

Not poached. Poaching's a whole different ball game.'

'Probably had your water too hot.' Justin regarded him with deep compassion. 'What you need's a wife.'

Buchanan smiled. 'Chance would be a fine thing.'

'Nobody on the horizon?'

'Nope. I'm still waiting for the perfect woman.'

'You'll wait a long time, mate. Take what you can get and be grateful.' He looked at his watch and pushed his chair back. 'Better get a move on. The wife doesn't like me to be late for dinner. She's always starving.'

Buchanan stacked the dirty dishes and the burned saucepan in the sink while Justin collected his gear. He was heading back into the lounge when the doorbell rang.

'That'll be Fizz,' he told Justin. 'She's the only one who drops by at this time of day.'

'Girlfriend?'

'Ex-colleague. She started to work for the practice last year at the same time as I left but she'd been working part-time for us all the time she was at the Uni.'

He pressed the button on the entryphone.

'Beam me up, Scottie,' said Fizz's voice and a moment later she did her usual hop and jump through the doorway, a manoeuvre she employed to foil Selena's habit of leaping from the lintel to the shoulder of unsuspecting visitors. 'Woops! Where's your little rodent friend?'

'In her basket. I have company.' He led the

way into the lounge and introduced her to Justin who towered over her like the Jolly Green Giant.

'At last,' she cried, beaming up at him. 'I really thought that stain was going to outlive both of us. You think you can actually eradicate it without demolishing and rebuilding the wall?'

'Oh, I think so. Coupla days from now it'll be history.'

He bent over from the waist to address her as though he were in conversation with a child. Buchanan had noticed this phenomenon before, even in men much shorter than Justin, but it never ceased to amuse him. It was a response, he suspected, less to her height (which was not all that abnormal, she being at least five three or four) as to her total persona, which was that of an engaging puppy. Possibly a fluffy poodle. Interestingly enough, it was a response that was rarely apparent in those who had intercourse with her for longer than a couple of hours.

Justin gave her a guided tour of the problem wall, baffling her with the science of paint application, and only belatedly remembered his waiting dinner.

'Right, squire. We'll give that a coupla days to dry and I'll be back on Friday.'

'Roger.' Buchanan found himself rather looking forward to their next encounter and reminded himself to visit the supermarket before then.

'What a nice guy,' Fizz commented when he'd gone, 'but I thought you were supposed to be curbing your spending. You've lived with that stain for years: surely you could have put up with it till the shekels start rolling in.'

'I booked him months ago,' Buchanan said shortly. 'It wouldn't have been fair to him to cancel at the last moment.'

He dodged her predictably censorious reply by fading into the kitchen and freeing the moggies who immediately wove themselves about his ankles in expectation of the Kitty Chox which they had come to expect as a reward for suffering incarceration.

'Put the kettle on while you're in there,' Fizz called, as he was attending to their demands. 'I have a lovely story to tell you and I think it's worth at least four biscuits.'

'Sorry, we're out of biscuits and there's no milk.'

'Geez, what are you like? Make it a herb tea, then.'

There were plenty of herb teas, solely because she'd bought them herself and he didn't like them. He made a black coffee for himself and carried the lot through on the chopping board, having mislaid the tray.

Fizz had removed her Docs and was curled up in a corner of the couch reading a postcard from his parents who were on holiday in Switzerland. 'Okay,' he said, patiently. 'When you're finished reading my mail, what about your lovely story?'

She completed her perusal of the message and scanned the picture on the other side before allowing herself to be distracted, then she grinned at him.

'You're going to love this, Kimosabe. I had a visit this afternoon from a sweet old lady who wants me to prove her guilty of murder.'

Buchanan frowned at her. 'Say again. She wants you to prove her guilty?'

'You got it. She insists that she killed Amanda Montrose — you remember? That woman whose body was found in some river or other up in Inverness with her head caved in. This old dear — Mrs Sullivan's her name — she thinks she did it.'

You had to laugh, Buchanan thought. It was so damn funny the way nutters were drawn to Fizz like bees to honey. Crazy, outlandish creatures, eccentrics, deranged, demented and psychotic oddballs, warped and deviant individuals the like of which Buchanan had never previously encountered, erupted from the woodwork the minute she stuck her head out the door. Maybe they sensed one of their own kind.

'You told her to go and annoy the police, I imagine?'

Fizz shook her close-cropped golden helmet of hair. 'She'd already spoken to the police. Twice. They chased her, of course, but the thing is, Buchanan, when I listened to her talk about it I began to think she could be telling the truth.'

'How could she be telling the truth? Some low-life brothel keeper was tried and convicted of that murder, I'm sure of it.'

'Yes, you're right, but that's exactly why she's come forward to confess. She feels she can't live with the knowledge that a young man is doing time for something she did.'

Buchanan took a gulp of his milkless coffee and shuddered. 'Bleh! That's disgusting.' He got rid of the mug and returned his attention to Fizz who was evidently awaiting some comment or other. He said, 'Well, has she any evidence?'

'Unfortunately, everything she can produce has already appeared in the papers, even her eyewitness account adds nothing to the generally accepted scenario, but I'll guarantee that if you speak to her you'll be quite — '

'Me? Speak to her? No way. Why would I want to speak to her? If there were the remotest possibility that she could be genuine the police would have at least checked her out.'

Fizz swung her legs to the floor and sat forward to fix him with a hard look. Or as hard as her baby face could achieve. 'I'll tell you why you'd want to speak to her, Buchanan. Because she's got money, that's why, and she's willing to blow it all on getting put away for killing La Montrose. And money, compadre, is what you badly need right at this moment in time.'

Buchanan was horrified at the suggestion. More than horrified — shocked. He had just about come to terms with Fizz's ethics, which were, to say the least, a bit iffy. She had no compunction about stretching the truth till it was unrecognisable; she habitually used naïve people for her own advantage; she preyed on anyone who would buy her a meal or be useful to her in any capacity, especially on Dennis, the junior partner in Buchanan and Stewart, who'd been trying to get into her knickers for years. Much of this behaviour could be excused by the hard life she'd had prior to her return to Edinburgh to study Law. It was easy to understand that a young woman working her way around the world for seven years might find too sensitive a moral conscience a heavy weight to carry. As she had once pointed out, it's easy to be philanthropic when you know where your next meal's coming from. But, battening on a nutty old woman who had more money than sense? That was pretty low, even for Fizz.

'I'm not that short of money,' he said, not hiding his distaste.

She rolled her eyes around in a despairing way. 'I'm not suggesting you do anything that would endanger your chances of beatification,' she said with a sigh. 'This woman — delusional or not — is seriously unhappy and likely to remain so till somebody takes pity on her and proves, to her own satisfaction, that she could not have killed Amanda Montrose. She can well afford to pay for services rendered and you can't deny that it would be money well spent, if only for the sake of her peace of mind.'

'And, if she actually did it?'

'All the more reason to prove she did.' Fizz had the bull by the horns and was clearly convinced she was in the right. Buzzing with enthusiasm, she looked like a pretty little poppet on Christmas morning. How the eyes could deceive one.

'If there's been a miscarriage of justice somebody ought to be looking into it. Don't forget there could be an innocent guy in jail for this crime. That's what's bothering Mrs Sullivan's conscience and I don't see why we should deny her the right to clear it — one way or the other — especially since she's willing to pay the going rate for it.'

'Okay, maybe you've got a point there, Fizz.' Buchanan felt he had to concede that much or risk looking just plain mulish. 'There's always the possibility that there could have been a miscarriage of justice but it would be better if you found someone else to look into it. I don't think I'd be happy to get involved in that sort of thing.'

'Who said anything about being happy? You're not working for your doting daddy any more, Buchanan. You're out in the cold, hard world and you're going to have to learn to look after Numero Uno. Earning a crust is not synonymous with having a nice time. Sometimes you just have to get your sleeves up and get on with it, and this is one of those times. It may not be fun but if it pays your golf club fees for another year you can't complain, right?'

She was good at hitting him where it hurt. Those golf club fees were already overdue and he had been debating with himself whether he should let his membership go, at least for a couple of years, but how she knew about that was anybody's guess. He said, 'I don't know. Maybe I'll think about it.'

'What's to think about? The old dear's losing sleep over this. It's getting her down. How long does it take you to determine on which side your bread's buttered?'

Buchanan got up and, sticking his hands in his pockets, went over to stare out of the window. There was no arguing with the fact that he could use the money. Hell, he couldn't even claim to be short of spare time. All the same, the reluctance he felt at the thought of taking on such a commitment couldn't be reasoned away. When you boiled it right down it came to a choice between taking an old lady's money for nothing and getting her slung into jail for a long sentence — probably for the remainder of her life. Not a fun job whichever way you looked at it.

'The least you can do is talk to Ian Fleming about it,' Fizz nagged on. 'He's bound to know someone in the Inverness force who could tell you if there's even the slightest possibility of Mrs Sullivan being involved. Give him a quick ring.'

Clearly she wasn't going to let it go till he agreed to do something and, he supposed, bothering Ian Fleming, his tame cop, at home was the quickest way to get her off his back. With a bit of luck Ian would be able to confirm his own opinion that the case was a no-no. Groaning, he found his address book and dialled Ian's number.

'Ian? Tam here. Sorry to intrude on your evening.'

'No sweat. How're you doing?'

'Can't complain. What I'm phoning about: Fizz had a visit today from an elderly lady who claims to have killed Amanda Montrose a few months back. You remember the case?'

'Sure. Our old friend Terence Lamb's just been put away for that one. Smashed her skull open with a hammer and got rid of the body in a river.'

'No shadow of doubt about that, I imagine?'

'I wouldn't have thought so. Your old lady's raving. We get a lot of those.'

Buchanan made an I-told-you-so face at Fizz, just to keep her in the picture. 'I was pretty sure of that myself but I'd like to dig up some solid proof of her innocence just to prove to her that she's imagining the whole thing. Do you have any contacts in the Inverness team who might be willing to talk to me?'

Ian made a sort of humming noise in the back of his throat, the vocal equivalent of background music, then he said, 'Tell you who'd be the man to speak to: Charlie Vivers. He liaised with the Inverness boys on that one because he knew Terence Lamb inside out. Been chasing him for years.'

'He's here in Edinburgh?'

'At headquarters. He's with the drug squad. Decent sort. He'll tell you all you want to know.'

'Sounds just what I need. Thanks, Ian, that's another one I owe you.'

'Don't worry. They'll catch me out one of these days and I'll be hammering on your door with a bunch of your IOUs in my hand.'

'You're on,' Buchanan grinned and turned to Fizz as he replaced the receiver. 'Well, I've got a contact. Not in Inverness but over at headquarters.'

'Did Ian inquire after me?'

Buchanan tipped his head on one side and regarded her appraisingly. 'Ian won't even have your name mentioned in his presence, Fizz. You ought to know that by now.'

34

Her lower lip protruded. 'How come he thinks the sun shines out of your left ear, then? You've caused him as much angst as I ever did and he has me to thank for his last promotion as well as you.'

'Beats me,' Buchanan muttered, unwilling to get into a discussion on Fizz's idiosyncratic, not to say downright unlawful, methods of arriving at the truth of a matter, some of which had come close to costing Ian Fleming his job. 'Anyway, he's put me on to someone in the drug squad who was involved with the inquiry — liaising with the Inverness end — so, if it'll keep you quiet I'll give him a ring tomorrow.'

'Give him a ring tonight,' she demanded, scowling at him. 'He might be on late shift.'

The woman was impossible. 'Fizz,' he said. 'Enough. I've said I'll phone him tomorrow. Now will you do me a favour and get out of here?'

The scowl was replaced with a placatory smile. She knew just how far she could push her luck.

She went.

3

Fizz waited all morning for Buchanan to phone and then tried ringing his mobile which was, as usual, switched off. By the time he finally got in touch it was almost five o'clock.

'What took you so long?' she demanded.

'I was waiting for Vivers, the drug squad guy, to phone me back. He's just off the line and, I have to tell you Fizz, your Mrs Sullivan is just one of three sad people who claim to have topped Amanda Montrose, and she's the least reliable of the lot. Terence Lamb did it. No question.'

Fizz didn't know whether to be relieved or disappointed. It was what she'd have wanted to prove, okay, only not so bloody fast. 'Did he give you any evidence we could offer Mrs Sullivan to put her mind at rest?'

'I wish you'd stop saying 'we', Fizz. There's no need for me to get involved. I've done my bit, free, gratis and for nothing, and now I'm out.'

'Okay, okay. What about evidence? Did you get any?'

'Nothing that proves your client didn't do it, no, but plenty that proves Terence Lamb did.'

'That's no good,' Fizz stated baldly. 'Mrs Sullivan knows there was proof of Lamb's guilt — he was convicted, for God's sake — but she still thinks she did it. You're going to have to talk to her.'

'Nope.'

'But you must, Buchanan. She'll listen to you. She thinks I'm a daft wee lassie but you could convince her that two people can't be guilty of — '

'Nope.'

' — the same murder. You know you could and if she could be — '

'Nope.'

'Sod it, Buchanan, what would it cost you? You wouldn't be taking her money off her, you'd simply be helping her out of Christian char — '

'Nope.'

'Listen, it wouldn't take half an hour. If you come over to my place for a bite to eat we could drive over to her place and be back in time to watch the rugby at yours. Couple of cans of McEwans and a bar of chocolate, on me.'

Heavy breathing.

Strange how the thought of ready cash left him unmoved yet the offer of a home-cooked meal acted on him like a cattle prod. She could almost hear him trying to figure out some way he could claw back some advantage for himself, but evidently nothing came to mind.

'You're never going to let it go, are you?' he snarled, sullen in defeat. 'Half an hour, then, and after that you stop nagging, okay?'

'Okay,' Fizz said in the meekest of tones while grinning fiendishly at her reflection in the window. 'See you later.'

* * *

He was in a better mood by the time he arrived at her flat at six-thirty, all shaved and showered and bearing a bottle of half-decent plonk. He'd taken to wearing his hair a trifle *en brousse* at the front which made him look rather boyish and a whole lot less like the stuffed shirt he had been when Fizz first took him in hand. She couldn't help thinking, as he chatted on about his day, that she had done some decent work there, turning a spoiled, self-satisfied pedant into what was beginning to show faint signs of becoming a decent human being. There were still improvements to be made, not least on his habit of finding fault with a girl every time she used a bit of lateral thinking, but one could see light at the end of the tunnel.

'So, tell me about this copper you spoke to,' she said, when he had started on his second bowl of carrot and coriander soup. 'Was he okay about talking to you?'

'Sure.' Buchanan shrugged. 'It wasn't his case anyway. He only got involved because he was a bit of an authority on Terence Lamb who was into all sorts of criminal activity here in Edinburgh, mainly drugs and prostitution with the odd piece of GBH chucked in just to lighten the boredom.'

'Does that mean Lamb was a prime suspect right from the very beginning?'

'That's what it looks like.' Buchanan took a visibly reluctant pause from spooning soup into his mouth and resigned himself to being debriefed. 'He was well known to Charlie Vivers and his team as the manager of a string of massage parlours that were allegedly owned by this woman Amanda Montrose.'

'Go on!' Fizz choked. 'When you say 'massage parlours' you're trying to spare my blushes, right? That's incredible! Amanda was some sort of local bigwig and landowner up in Inverness, you know. Not your average madam.'

'Well, there's no concrete proof that she was involved,' Buchanan had to point out, 'but the drug squad, or at least my contact, Charlie, is pretty sure she had an interest in the business in one way or another. Lamb was certainly a long-time associate, not only of Amanda but also of her husband who was, at one time, Lamb's commanding officer in the Royal Scots. Naturally, both the husband and Lamb himself are refuting any suggestion that Amanda had any connection with the vice trade and threatening to sue anyone who implies such a thing and, on the face of it, it does seem unlikely. However, Charlie sounds convinced that they had something extremely profitable going on amongst the three of them. He reckons it's only a matter of time before he gets to the bottom of it.'

'Well, well,' Fizz commented. 'Things become interesting. And what about Amanda's murder? Do they have anything really solid against Lamb?'

'They have loads of circumstantial stuff: proof that he was in the area around the time of the murder and lied about it afterwards, some of his associates claiming that he disliked Amanda intensely, a proven propensity for violence, that sort of thing. But there was also forensic evidence that tied him to the river where

Amanda's body was found.'

Buchanan had scraped all trace of colour from his bowl. He looked into it with sad eyes but Fizz ignored him.

'What sort of forensic evidence?'

'A water weed, identifiable as coming from the river where Amanda's body turned up, was discovered on his shoes. I could manage a scrap more of that soup if there's — '

'No you couldn't. There's pudding.'

'Wow! You're spoiling me.'

'Not for nothing, amigo, you'd better believe it. Tell me more about this water weed. What's Lamb saying about it? Surely it could have been on his shoes for months?'

Buchanan sighed and looked out the window at the distant hills. 'I daresay the forensic chaps could tell how long it had been out of the water. Charlie seemed to think it was a clincher anyway.'

So did Fizz, actually, but there was no point in admitting to that at this stage in the game. 'How can they be sure of the date Amanda died? I seem to remember they were searching for her for ages.'

'Well, they can't be specific, obviously, but they must be able to pin it down to within a week or so, wouldn't you think? You can talk to Charlie Vivers yourself if you want to. He's hard to get hold of but he sounds like a nice helpful guy.'

Fizz thought she certainly would want to talk to him herself, if she were intending to take the inquiry any further, but there was no way she was going to do either till she had Buchanan committed to doing most of the work. She cleared away the soup bowls and took the vegetable lasagne out of the oven.

'Who was Lamb's defence counsel?'

'Radcliffe.'

Buchanan's expression said it all. Colin Radcliffe ranked high in the Edinburgh legal system but nobody really knew why. His average success rate was no higher than that of many other defence lawyers but it was always his face on the front page of the *Scotsman* after an acquittal, his opinion sought on every issue the media wished to highlight. In Fizz's opinion, he was nothing but an arrogant prat of the first order and she knew Buchanan agreed with her, though he would never say so behind the guy's back. Or even in front of it, probably, being gently reared.

'What sort of defence did he offer?'

'Charlie didn't go into that,' Buchanan murmured vaguely, his whole attention on the serving of food Fizz was sliding onto his plate.

'Lamb's denying ever having been in the area, I take it.'

'Uh . . . yes. Well, not for several months prior to Amanda's disappearance, that is. It would be difficult to establish an alibi since nobody can actually pinpoint the date Amanda died. Not with any accuracy.'

'So how does he explain the water weed on his shoes?'

'He doesn't. He claims he's been framed. As you would.'

Seeing that she was unlikely to get comprehensive answers to her questions till he'd got outside his dinner, Fizz let him eat and concentrated her thoughts on how to win him over to Mrs Sullivan's cause. In the end, however, it was the old lady who did that, simply by being her gentle, vulnerable, and very worried self. She was so pathetically grateful to see them that from the moment she opened her door to them she had Buchanan in the palm of her hand, though it clearly took him some time to admit that to himself.

'It's such a real pleasure to meet you at last, Mr Buchanan,' she twittered, leading them into the lounge of her large 1930s bungalow. 'My friend at Greenfield House retirement home has told me so much about you.'

'Ah, yes. Fizz tells me we have a mutual friend in Paul Bramley.'

'Well, to be truthful, I can't claim Paul as a friend. Just a friend of a friend. But I have known, or should I say, I've been aware of Paul ever since I have been visiting Miss Tweed, who used to live next door to me here. One . . . ' She hesitated and then hit Buchanan with a mischievous little smile. 'One can scarcely visit Greenfield House without being aware of Paul.'

Buchanan grinned. 'Yes. He's quite a character.'

'He thinks the world of you . . . and of Miss Fitzpatrick,' she added politely but not quite quickly enough. 'I believe you were instrumental in clearing up some problems he had a year or two ago. Miss Tweed suggested I talk to him

42

about finding a good solicitor and he told me right away that, whatever my dilemma, I could not do better than share it with you and Miss Fitzpatrick.'

'Well, I'm very flattered that he should do so,' Buchanan said, choosing an armchair facing her while Fizz settled for the banquette that ran round the window bay. 'Ms Fitzpatrick has already given me an outline of what you told her yesterday but I think it would be better if you ran through it again for me. It would be better for me to hear your story in your own words.'

Mrs Sullivan heaved a sigh. 'Oh dear. It's so upsetting to go over the whole thing again. I hardly slept last night after speaking to Miss Fitzpatrick. I simply couldn't get it out of my mind for a single second, but — no, no, Mr Buchanan — it's quite all right. I'm determined to be as much help to you as I can. But first,' she hauled herself to her feet, 'let me offer you something to drink. A coffee? A sherry?'

Buchanan declined all offers: Fizz accepted a generous helping of very good Amontillado, noting as she did so that Mrs Sullivan was no less generous with her own allotment.

'Now then, I suppose I should start with how I came to know Amanda Montrose.'

Fizz listened to the repeat performance with only half an ear, her attention wavering to a covert assessment of the room and its furnishings. There was money there, in the fine rosewood writing desk, the quality carpeting and the four good watercolours grouped beside the fireplace, but none of it was too obvious. That was par for the course in Scotland where conspicuous spending was perceived to be the badge of the nouveaux riches: lottery winners, drug dealers, dot-com millionaires, and plumbers. On a low coffee table, beside a pretty bowl of white roses, there was a studio photograph of a young man in mortar board and gown; no doubt the suicidal son. He looked sensible enough, with heavy eyebrows and a square chin, but Fizz thought she could spot a certain sensitivity around the mouth that tied in with what she knew of him.

She had taken to watching a game of rounders that was taking place in the park that lay beyond Mrs Sullivan's garden when she heard Buchanan say, 'I hope you'll forgive me, Mrs Sullivan, but I have to be frank with you or we'll get nowhere. The fact is, your story is not easy to accept at face value. With no evidence to support your confession and every indication suggesting that Terence Lamb is guilty, anyone who takes your money will do so knowing that they have almost no chance of delivering a satisfactory conclusion.'

Mrs Sullivan lifted a quivering chin. 'There has to be some evidence against me somewhere, Mr Buchanan, and if anyone were able to dig it out I am convinced it would be you. I trust you. Paul told me you were an honest man — indeed, I can see that for myself — and you are a compassionate man. I can see that too. I know you have reservations, of course you have, but I don't expect any guarantees.' She folded her hands in her lap and studied them for a moment, then lifted her head and looked intently at Buchanan as though willing him to understand. 'I'm not short of money, Mr Buchanan, but let me tell you something. When you get to my age there's only so much money you can enjoy. I have an insurance policy that will pay for any care I may need should I, God forbid, outlive my capacity to care for myself. I have no dependants and no close friends. Life, in short, has very little to offer me these days. In fact, all I want to accomplish before I die — which, one has to assume, is an event one can't put off for much longer — is to clear my conscience and make what amends I can to undo the evil I've caused. Better to pay for one's sins in this world than in the next, I'm sure you'll agree. I know, quite beyond doubt, that I am as sane as I ever was, that I did kill Amanda Montrose, and that a young man's life is about to be shattered because of my crime. Please don't ask me to live my remaining years with that on my conscience.'

Buchanan nodded, pursing his lips unhappily. For a moment Fizz was drawn to the idea of adding her own invocations to those of her client but desisted since it would probably do more harm than good. There was a short silence while Buchanan communed with his conscience.

'How would it be,' he said at last, 'if I spent a few days just looking at the facts of the case to see if there would be any point in your taking matters further? I could read over the transcripts of Terence Lamb's trial, perhaps speak with his solicitor, or with Lamb himself if he'll agree to see me. By then I may be able to give you better advice.'

'My dear Mr Buchanan, you can't know how happy that makes me.' Mrs Sullivan turned round to beam at Fizz, her face tinged with a sudden wash of colour that made her look years younger. 'Paul's advice was the best I ever had in my life. I must take him a nice bottle of wine next time I visit, to thank him for introducing me to you both. And for you, Mr Buchanan,' she added, hauling herself out of her chair and going to the writing desk, 'something in advance by way of a retainer, I think. Will a thousand pounds be enough for the present?'

Buchanan's eyes popped open and rolled round to Fizz. 'Much too generous,' he said before she could prevent him, but Mrs Sullivan was undeterred.

'Being generous, where generosity is deserved, is one of the few pleasures remaining to me. And I want you to bear in mind, Mr Buchanan, that expenditure is no object. Whatever you need to do, wherever you may need to travel, whoever you may need to bribe, there will be no quibbling when you present your account.' She topped up Fizz's glass and her own before she returned to her seat, slipping Buchanan a folded cheque on the way. 'I myself, I need hardly say, will be at your disposal throughout, and if there's anything I can tell you or help you with in any way I will be delighted to do so. Now, where shall you start?'

'There are one or two questions I still have to ask you, if you don't mind.'

She smiled, with a coquettish little flutter of her almost non-existent eyelashes that was a throwback to her youth. Buchanan had that effect on geriatric women.

'I have all the time in the world, Mr Buchanan. Ask away.'

He looked at the scribbled notes he'd been making while she talked. 'I've been wondering what you did after you . . . after you found you'd killed Amanda. You must have been very upset.'

'Upset? Indeed I was.' She glanced at Fizz as though she expected some sort of confirmation of this statement but Fizz, quite apart from being reluctant to confirm something she knew about only at second hand, was keeping her lips firmly zipped and letting Buchanan have his innings. 'I'm ashamed to say I went entirely to pieces for a while. In fact, I'm not quite sure what I did. I remember being round the other end of the car — from where I couldn't see Mandy — giving way to the most appalling hysterics. I had no idea what I should do. I simply stood there crying and waiting for someone to come along.'

She turned her face away and pressed her knuckles to her lips for a moment, visibly upset. Buchanan opened his mouth to say something, probably 'forget it if it distresses you' but Fizz flapped a hand at him and glowered him into silence.

'It's quite astonishing the way one's mind works in such situations,' Mrs Sullivan resumed presently. 'Or doesn't work, I should say. I kept thinking, it's an offence to leave the scene of an accident but I don't have a mobile and, of course, there was no telephone in the vicinity. After a while I realised that I could wait for hours till someone came along that little road and told me what to do. I don't know how long I dithered about, maybe half an hour, but eventually I started to calm down. I got into my car and drank some orange juice that was with the shopping I'd been doing in Inverness and . . . I don't know how I came to think along these lines . . . but it came to me that I could just run away.' She shook her head and added faintly, 'So shameful! I've regretted that impulse every day of the last six months.'

'It's not so hard to understand,' Buchanan said in his trust-me-I'm-an-advocate voice which was the same as his old trust-me-I'm-a-solicitor voice only more expensive. 'You were deeply shocked, confused, probably afraid of the consequences of your action. Running away would naturally be your first response.'

'I should have resisted it,' Mrs Sullivan stated firmly. 'One can never run away from one's sins. I should have driven to the nearest police station and made a clean breast of the whole thing. I would be infinitely happier in jail than bearing this constant burden of guilt. When I look back at that night I can scarcely believe I had the guile . . . the madness to do what I did.'

'What *did* you do?' Fizz asked, impatience overcoming her resolve to remain silent.

'My dear, I can barely bring myself to tell you. I tried to think if anyone had seen me driving down the road, but in the state I was in I couldn't be sure whether I had passed any other cars on my way there. So it seemed to me that the best thing I could do would be to hide all trace of the . . . the incident. I read a great many crime novels and that's what the perpetrator usually does. Fortunately, Mandy had parked her little car on the side of the road closest to the river and it was easy to run it over the edge and down the sheer drop into the ravine where the foliage hid it from view.' Her voice quavered on the last word but she raised a hand to hush Buchanan who was starting to let her off the hook again. 'No, no. Please let me finish. Mandy . . . followed the car over the edge; and if you don't believe I could do such a thing let me assure you, neither do I. I cannot imagine anything more foreign to my nature but, there you are: I did it. I imagine I must have felt driven to do it. Panic? Adrenaline? Desperation? Whatever the impetus, I can tell you it was irresistible. I don't know where I got the strength to drag Mandy to a point where she would fall straight into the river. I don't know how I managed to drive all the way back to Moy without having an accident. It seems to me now that some outside influence was guiding me every step of the way. Perhaps, as I said to Miss Fitzpatrick, the whole business was God's will. That thought is all that has kept me going for the past few months.'

That assumption didn't appear to grab Buchanan to any great extent and Fizz couldn't see it carrying much weight with a jury either. However, if it gave Mrs Sullivan a crutch to lean on there was no point in kicking it away. She

49

watched Buchanan start to close his notebook and took the opportunity to insert, 'There must have been a fair bit of blood around. Didn't that worry you?'

'Oh dear, yes, there was blood but not a great deal. After I got my car started I poured the remainder of the water over it and managed to wash most of it into the grass of the verge. It was snowing heavily by that time and of course it was quite dark so I was fairly sure the last traces would be covered before Amanda's disappearance started to cause concern.'

'As, apparently, they were,' Buchanan said, 'and any that remained would have been well rained away by the time the car was found — what was it — two or three weeks later?'

'Almost a month.' Mrs Sullivan murmured faintly. 'Mandy's body wasn't found for more than three weeks. The river was swollen with melted snow and she'd been washed quite a distance downstream, beyond the spot where the Blackwater joins the River Breich, so the police had two rivers to search before they found the car.'

'I dare say you were keeping a close eye on the newspaper reports,' Fizz ventured, at which Mrs Sullivan's pallid face drooped even more.

'Well, I was naturally taking an interest, as anyone in my position would, but unfortunately Sergeant Vivers at police headquarters seems to think that proves I made the whole thing up. Everything I can tell him has already appeared in the *Inverness Courier* and I can supply no other evidence to support my confession.'

'You confessed to Charlie Vivers?' Buchanan queried, reopening his notebook. 'I hadn't realised it was he you spoke to. Why was that?'

'Why?' said Mrs Sullivan uncertainly. 'Well, because by the time Terence Lamb was convicted I was here in Edinburgh and I didn't see the need to go all the way up to Inverness to confess when I could go to Police headquarters here in Edinburgh. The young lady at the desk said I could speak to Sergeant Vivers who had been liaising on the case with the Inverness police.' She raised her eyebrows and smiled with a touch of acerbity. 'Such a nice man, I thought him at first, very patient and understanding. He listened quite seriously to what I had to say, took down all my particulars, and said he'd look into what I'd told him and be in touch. I felt quite confident of being arrested within a few days — and, such a relief it was to have that weight of guilt lifted from me! — but a week passed, and then another week, and I heard nothing. In the end I had to telephone him again and this time he wasn't nearly so polite. In fact, he made me quite uneasy, warning me about wasting police time and more or less telling me to stop bothering him. That's when I decided to put the matter in the hands of a professional.'

'Well, I don't think I quite fit that category, Mrs Sullivan,' Buchanan said, getting to his feet, 'but if I can discover any reason that a professional should be enlisted I can at least recommend a good one.'

'Only if you deem it necessary, Mr Buchanan. I am very happy to have you act for me and I

51

hope you will continue to do so for as long as you can make any headway.' Mrs Sullivan levered herself upright and, with a special smile for Fizz, shook hands with them both. 'I feel very confident, having spoken with both of you, that you will be quite able to deliver what I want.'

Buchanan nodded. 'I'll make arrangements tomorrow to speak with Terence Lamb's lawyers and, hopefully, with Lamb himself.'

'Why would you want to speak to Lamb?'

'Because, Mrs Sullivan, if I am to prove you guilty I must also prove Lamb innocent. It would make things very much easier all round if I had his cooperation.'

'Will that take long to arrange?'

'Possibly a day or two. We'll fix something up for the beginning of the week.'

'Ah.'

Mrs Sullivan could pack a paragraph of disappointment into a monosyllable. Fizz could see that Buchanan was suitably chastened but also that he wasn't moved to offer an alternative, probably because he planned to play golf over the weekend, so she appended, 'However, we could make use of the delay by taking a run up to Inverness and checking out the scene of crime, maybe even get Amanda's husband to speak to us. What do you think, Buchanan?'

'Actually,' he began, but of course he wasn't going to say what he really thought till he got Fizz outside. However, he was saved from falsification by Mrs Sullivan whose face lit up with enthusiasm.

'Excellent,' she twittered, drowning him out.

'We can take my car and I can show you exactly where it happened. There's a charming country house hotel no distance away where my husband and I always stayed for the salmon fishing. Frightfully overpriced these days, of course, like everything else, but the cuisine is first class.'

Unaware that she had just hit Buchanan in his two most vulnerable areas, food and salmon fishing, she blessed them both with a smile and showed them to the door before he could bring himself to demur.

A woman after Fizz's own heart.

4

It wasn't, Buchanan reflected as he dropped off to sleep, as if he hadn't intended all along to visit the scene of the crime: if he were ever to be in a position to assess Mrs Sullivan's account of the murder that task was unavoidable. It wasn't even as if he'd had any real hope of being permitted to do it on his own, without Fizz peering over his shoulder and nagging him ever onwards. But *two* women hanging around his neck all weekend like a couple of albatrosses, interfering with his chances of fitting in half a day's salmon fishing or even a round of golf — it was bloody intolerable.

Fizz he could cope with. On a good day, in fact, he could almost enjoy her company — even when she was in collaborative mode, arguing with his every conclusion, annoying people he wanted to keep sweet and, like this evening, making unilateral decisions that invariably messed up his own plans. That conduct was par for the course. That was the Fizz he had learned to accept. An act of God. A force of nature. One could no more change her than one could change the weather but one could, perforce, learn to live with her. For a few hours at a time.

Mrs Sullivan, however, was a different kettle of fish. She was slow, and none too steady on her pins. She would require constant mollycoddling. Instead of getting on with the job in hand he would be reduced to taxiing her everywhere, holding umbrellas over her head, tucking travelling rugs over her knees et cetera, and on constant tenterhooks, meanwhile, in case Fizz started expressing herself in the colourful terms she was still prone to use, thus exposing their client to increased risk of heart attack. Quite apart from which, should Mrs Sullivan's account of the murder tally with the realities of the murder scene, it might be expedient to talk to Ewan Montrose and it wouldn't be a good idea to have Mrs Sullivan meet Amanda's husband face to face. That sort of thing could lead to all sorts of complications, but one could envisage huge difficulties in explaining that to the old lady. She'd have to be dumped off somewhere while he and, if unavoidable, Fizz conducted the interview.

On the other side of the scales, however, there was the promise of a couple of first-class dinners and five star accommodation and that was rather more than he would have felt justified, off his own bat, in charging to Mrs Sullivan's account. It was also something he hadn't enjoyed since the halcyon days when deluxe weekends, both here in the UK and abroad, had played a large part in his arsenal of seduction techniques. It was hard to summon up a genuine regret for the profligate days when he had felt no need to put a little aside for a rainy day but the fact remained, he was feeling the pinch now and that unquestionably made one appreciate a little luxury when it presented itself. He'd look after his money a lot better in the future, that was for sure. Probably turn into a veritable Scrooge like Fizz, who had been impoverished for so long she still couldn't spend a pound without counting the notches on it.

For a millisecond before he lost consciousness he felt a profound affinity to Fizz and all became clear: her stinginess, her lack of compassion, her huge appetite when presented with a free meal. The privations he had experienced for a few months, she had lived with for years. But all such insights had completely evaporated by the time he was awakened by the arrival of Justin and several pots of paint, practically at cock crow.

'Heavy night, squire?' Justin asked when Buchanan had dislodged Selena, like Velcro, from his white overalls and apologised for forgetting to warn him about her little foibles.

'Not really.' Buchanan found a pair of track suit trousers on the couch and pulled them on over the boxers he'd slept in. 'One of the perks of being virtually unemployed is that you don't have to set the alarm. What time is it?'

'Just gone nine. You want to move some of this furniture into the bedroom?'

Buchanan supposed he did and, together, they cleared the lounge and spread dust sheets on the carpet. Selena and Pooky retreated to the window sill from where, should the need arise, they could make a fast exit by abseiling down the ivy to the courtyard below.

'Wouldn't have taken you for a cat lover,' Justin remarked, prompting Buchanan to wonder whether to take that as a compliment.

'Yes, well, I suppose I am,' he admitted. 'Now,

I am, anyway. I'd never have thought of buying a cat but those two were more or less forced on me. Couple of damn nuisances, most of the time, but you get used to having them around.'

'They'll be company for you,' Justin suggested, looking at Buchanan in a sort of funny way so that he had to reply.

'Right. Not that I'm *short* of company but . . . '

'It's someone to come home to, yeah.'

That wasn't what Buchanan had been going to say but one could protest too much. He went into the kitchen to see what there might be to eat and found, as usual, practically nothing other than tomato soup and eggs.

'Scrambled eggs?' he called through to Justin and a minute later his glum face appeared in the doorway.

'That all that's on offer? I've had nothing but rice cakes and cottage cheese since last night.'

Buchanan opened a few cupboard doors but drew a blank. It seemed a bit early for tomato soup.

'Okay,' said Justin, looking over his shoulder, 'what about some pancakes to follow?'

Buchanan subjected the shelves to a closer scrutiny. 'Where are you seeing the pancakes?'

There was a short silence which Justin filled by shaking his head in a sad and rather pointed manner. 'You've got flour and a spare egg or two, right? Milk?'

'Sure.'

'Okay, you've got pancakes. Stand aside.'

Buchanan was only too happy to do so and,

for the next five minutes or so, was presented with a display of culinary skill that made him feel inadequate to say the least. The sight of the big man in overalls beating the hell out of pancake batter, stirring scrambled eggs, making coffee and keeping an eye on the toast, all with the casual speed and expertise one normally associated with Delia Smith, came as something of a revelation. Deep in his psyche, he now realised, had lurked the idea that one had to be a bit of a poof to enjoy cooking. Back home, the kitchen had always been the domain of his mother or of the daily help and neither he nor his father, still less his brother Paul, would have dreamed of boiling a kettle, nor would they have been encouraged to do so. Men were the breadwinners and the whole point of a woman's existence was to minister to their needs. An old-fashioned and traditional point of view, perhaps, but then his mother was an old-fashioned and traditional woman. Which was probably why her sons were so helpless.

'Time I changed my ways, obviously,' he admitted as he and Justin started work on the creamiest scrambled eggs he had ever tasted. 'I've always eaten out before, or brought home a carry-out, but that works out pretty expensive when you're doing it seven nights a week and when there's almost no money coming in you start to notice it.'

Justin's glance was not overtly sympathetic. 'Spoiled rotten, you are,' he mumbled through a mouthful of toast. 'You've got a good cookbook there: *Cooking for Guys*. Why don't you use it?'

'I don't know.' Buchanan thought about it. 'I never have the stuff. You know what it's like: you get halfway down the list of the ingredients and suddenly you hit soft brown sugar or soy sauce or half a nutmeg or whatever and have to pack it in.'

'Half of those things aren't necessary. You can use demerara or Lea & Perrins or whatever and it won't make much difference. Anyway, a fiver'll buy you all the staples you need. I'll write you out a shopping list.'

It felt to Buchanan a bit like he was being hustled into doing something he hadn't quite decided on doing but on the other hand he knew it was something he should do, whether he wanted to or not.

'I'm going to Inverness on business for a couple of days,' he said, 'leaving about four this afternoon, coming back late on Sunday, so I'll leave you a key.'

'I wouldn't bother. Suits me to cut away early for the weekend. Couple of days at the beginning of the week'll see the job finished.' Justin scraped his plate clean and got the pancakes out of the oven. 'Got a spot of syrup, squire?'

Buchanan didn't go in for such exotica but found an inch or two of marmalade in a forgotten jar and made do quite happily with that. When they had finished Buchanan stacked the dishes in the sink, as was his habit, but Justin tsk-tsked briskly and had them washed, rinsed and on the drainer in moments. Buchanan could hardly fail to be impressed by the ease and speed with which he executed every task.

The very thought of doing the washing up weighed on Buchanan like a yoke, expanding in his imagination to a chore of vast magnitude and indescribable boredom yet Justin's deftness exposed the procedure as the work of two or three minutes.

'Right,' said the maestro when he had run the dishcloth over the cooker and the working surface. 'Better get started.'

Buchanan left him to it. He had little to do today other than study the transcription of the trial evidence against Terence Lamb but he knew he could finish that in a couple of hours so he had a long bath, packed his overnight bag, did his bit of homework, and was waiting at the window when Fizz and Mrs Sullivan arrived to pick him up in the latter's car. He wasn't overjoyed at the thought of crawling up the A9 at thirty miles an hour with a geriatric at the wheel but Mrs Sullivan turned out to be a fast, competent driver, if a trifle heavy on the brake, and they made good time.

'Not far now,' she said, as they left Beauly behind. 'The Montrose estate, Breichmenach, is just down that wooded glen where the sheep are. I could show you the . . . the place where it happened now, if you like, or we could leave it till tomorrow.'

'Let's do it now,' Fizz responded, without as much as a glance over her shoulder at Buchanan, who was sprawled sideways in the back seat. 'We might as well get ahead with what we can while the going's good. It could be raining tomorrow.'

'For myself,' murmured Mrs Sullivan, 'it's a

chore I would prefer to have done with as soon as possible. Naturally, I haven't been back there since it happened and I'm not sure just how traumatic an experience it will be. One can only prepare oneself as best one can and hope it won't be so terrible in reality as it appears in one's imagination.'

Buchanan started to say, 'I'm sure there's no real need for you to — ' but she raised a hand from the wheel to stop him.

'No. You're very kind, Mr Buchanan, but it's something I have to do. It's all part of my penance, you see. I want to do it. You do understand, don't you?'

Buchanan understood perfectly, his own conscience being of the super-tender variety, but such self-flagellation left even his own sensitivity somewhat in the shade. He could see the increased tension in Mrs Sullivan's shoulders as they left the main road for a tree-lined byway that wound its way steadily into the hills. For the first half mile or so it bordered a fast-flowing river that had carved its own gouge in the surrounding rock but, as the road climbed, the river below was for the most part concealed in a deep, thickly wooded gorge.

After about ten minutes Mrs Sullivan's foot eased on the accelerator and the portion of her face visible to Buchanan in the driving mirror began to show distinct signs of distress. With their speed dropping virtually by the minute they crawled forward and drifted to a halt a few yards short of a sharp bend. No one said a word as they got out of the car and walked on, Mrs

61

Sullivan leading the way with her head up and her hands clasped tightly in front of her waist.

Rounding the corner behind her, Buchanan felt as though he had walked into a film set; a scene that had been waiting there, still and vacant, for the entrance of the players. The evening sunlight lay, thick as honey, on the greenery that pressed close on both sides and the smell of warm earth, in the absence of even the slightest movement of air, was like the smell of summer itself. Nothing stirred, no sound penetrated the wall of leaves or climbed from the torrent far below. Then a blackbird on some high branch burst into song and the spell was broken. Mrs Sullivan stood rigidly in the middle of the road, seemingly transfixed but, as Buchanan moved to take her arm, she nodded towards a part of the grass verge that was slightly wider than the rest.

'There is where I parked my car.' Her voice shook. 'I didn't have much choice because there was steam pouring out from under the bonnet and I was afraid to drive on.'

'That in itself must have been unnerving for you,' Buchanan said, 'happening so unexpectedly on such a quiet road.'

'Yes.' She leaned against him a little, evidently glad of his support. 'But in fact it wasn't so unexpected. The same thing had happened once before, on the drive north actually, but that first time I was on the main road and a lorry driver came along and gave me a can of water. There was a fault of some sort in the engine. I'm referring to my old car, of course, not the one I have now.'

Fizz was standing at the edge of the road, leaning over the stretch of barrier that offered some protection on the bad bend and trying to see down into the gulf below. 'So,' she said, turning, 'Amanda came round the corner and stopped . . . where? On this side of the road?'

'Just past the end of the barrier.'

'Okay, so she got out and walked over to you. Ten or twelve paces. Didn't you hear her coming: turn round to see who it was?'

'No, dear, I didn't hear her getting out of the car. There was snow on the ground so I expect that muffled the sound of her footfalls. Indeed, the wind was so boisterous, howling down the glen and whipping the trees and bushes about, that I didn't even register the sound of the car's approach. She would have slowed down for the bend, I imagine, and then, of course, I was making a good deal of noise myself, trying to hammer the cap off the rusty old water can I'd been given, a few days previously, by the lorry driver I told you about.'

'You weren't aware of her, then, till she spoke? Is that the case?'

Buchanan was of the opinion that Fizz's style of questioning could be a fraction gentler under the circumstances. He could sense Mrs Sullivan's shoulders rigid with tension beneath his arm and suspected she was finding it difficult to hold herself together.

Her voice had regained a little strength, however, when she replied, 'That's right. I just turned and . . . and there she was behind me.'

'And all the argy-bargy started straight away?'

Mrs Sullivan appeared to wince at the choice of phrase but a touch of asperity appeared as she said, 'Yes. And then I struck her down.'

'That's quite straightforward, then,' Buchanan intervened, keeping his tone neutral and giving her shoulders a small squeeze. 'I imagine the car went over about here where the ground slopes?'

'Just to your right, I think. I only had to push it a few yards in all and it went quite easily over the grass. Surprisingly easily. It went straight to the bottom and there was no sign of it from above. I looked to make sure.'

'No wonder it took the police so long to locate it. They'd have to work their way up the river for the whole length of the ravine.' Fizz leaned dangerously over the chasm, one arm hooked around a skinny sapling that would not have supported her for a second had her feet gone from under her.

Mrs Sullivan drew an unsteady breath. 'I wonder,' she said, 'would you forgive me if I had a little sit down in the car for a few minutes while you complete your survey? It's all been a bit . . . '

'Of course,' Buchanan said. 'Would you like me to walk back with you?'

'No, thank you. There's not the slightest need. And please do take whatever time you need, I'll be just fine on my own for a while.'

Buchanan waited till she was out of earshot before he sent Fizz what she customarily referred to as One of his Looks. 'You were a bit tough with her, Fizz. She's not some dyed-in-the-wool career criminal who's in the habit of being snarled at.'

'Who's snarling? If we can't ask her some straight questions we're not going to get very far, are we?' She propped her behind on the barrier and laughed at him. 'If she turns out to have caved Amanda Montrose's head in with her itty-bitty hammer I'm going to wish I had a photo of you cuddling her like she was your long lost grannie. The more I see of her the more I start to wonder if she could be as nutty as marzipan. All this talk about God's will. I'm waiting to hear her say God told her to do it.'

'You don't believe that for a minute, Fizz, and neither do I.' Buchanan stuck his hands in his trouser pockets and sat beside her in a spot where he could feel the sun on his back. A thrush had joined the blackbird in its evensong and there was a loud thrum of bees in the wild cherry trees behind the barrier. He wondered whimsically if the scene would return to its silent vigil after he and Fizz had departed.

'I'll tell you what I believe,' Fizz said. 'I believe that if she didn't do it, she was awfully lucky.'

'Lucky? In what way?'

'Well, if you'd planned to do away with an old enemy and wipe out all trace of the crime you could scarcely have picked a better place than this as the venue. Quiet road: very little chance of being seen or interrupted. A long narrow stretch incorporating a blind corner: easy to block the road at a point where an approaching car doesn't expect you and too far for said car to reverse to a turning spot. Handy access to a gap in the trees through which to push a small car over the cliff and into one of the most impenetrable stretches of the river. No distance at all to transport a body to a point where two rivers join and thus double the time for the police to locate the deceased.' She gave him a sideways glance, bright and challenging as that of the blackbird that was sussing them out from the far side of the road. 'What d'you think, Kimosabe? Was she lucky? Or smart?'

Buchanan took his time about answering. Fizz's reasoning was unavoidably compelling but the idea of Mrs Sullivan performing the whole horrific train of actions she had described to them was simply a non-starter. Try as he might to picture her swinging a hammer with such hideous force, manhandling even a small car over the brink, or transporting a limp and bloody corpse some three miles or more, his imagination was not equal to the task.

'There are other possibilities,' he said, not really knowing what they might be but convinced that, however unlikely, that had to be the case. Then he thought of one. 'What you have to bear in mind, Fizz, is that Mrs Sullivan need not have been the person who chose this venue. Suppose she's imagining everything she's told us or — okay then — if she's just plain lying to us for her own reasons. In either case, she's simply making use of the facts that are there already. It was the real killer who decided that this would be the best place to commit a murder, and for the reasons you've just pointed out. The venue was probably described in the local papers, all Mrs Sullivan had to do was write herself into the scenario as the perpetrator.'

'If that's the case, I bet she's been here herself just to get her geography right. Which means she was lying when she told us she hadn't returned to the SOC.' Fizz tipped her head back and looked up through the leaves at the cobalt blue of the summer sky. 'I reckon she's a lot wilier than we've been giving her credit for.'

'That's possible,' Buchanan had to grant her, although he had strong reservations even about that. 'No doubt time will tell.'

Fizz smiled her pixie smile. 'If we give her enough rope, perhaps she'll hang herself.'

5

Fizz was still asleep when Buchanan knocked at her door. Normally she was up with the lark but no doubt the thick curtains in her bedroom, plus the soporific effects of the five course meal she'd succumbed to the night before, had something to do with her sloth.

'Fizz? Are you in there?'

'What's up?' she croaked, swimming up from a great depth.

'What's up? It's nine-fifteen, that's what's up. I thought you'd died in your sleep.'

'Well, I haven't so sod off.'

'Okay, but I'm seeing Ewan Montrose at ten-thirty so if you want to come with me you'd better stir a leg. We leave at ten.'

Fizz's vision was still a bit wonky but her feet were already on the floor. 'Just let me grab a bite to eat first. Go down and order me everything on the menu while I get dressed. Ten minutes.'

'Order it yourself. I'm not getting myself associated with your gluttony.'

'Bastard.'

She had planned to have a long, luxurious soak in the bath this morning, thereafter anointing her hair and body with a selection of the unguents so generously supplied by the management and possibly enjoying a morning cup of coffee on her balcony in the comfort of the thick towelling robe and matching slippers she found hanging behind the bathroom door. Instead it was a quick sprint through the shower and a hasty descent to the breakfast room in time for fresh strawberries and cereal, scrambled eggs with lamb's kidneys, two chocolate croissants and a large quantity of coffee. She felt somewhat bagged-up afterwards, as she knew she would, but the habit of stoking up with free food whenever the opportunity arose was a hard one to break.

Buchanan was waiting for her out front on the terrace looking like an advert in a sportswear catalogue. He kept going on about being utterly impoverished but in Buchanan-speak that translated as not being able to afford a new Boss suit every few months plus at least two exotic holidays a year plus God only knew how many expensive nights out in the average week. His two-year-old walking trousers and lightweight cashmere sweater would pass muster under the closest inspection but to him they were ready for Oxfam. Fizz had no patience with such people but she was grateful to them none the less since she still bought most of her clothes in charity shops. After a lifetime of five pound bargains it was hard to get used to high street prices.

Buchanan straightened from his supporting sundial as she approached.

'Where's Old Mother Hubbard?' she greeted him.

'Still in her room, I imagine. Obviously, we don't want her anywhere near Ewan Montrose so I encouraged her to have breakfast in bed and a lazy morning. She seemed quite happy with that idea.'

'I imagine she would be.' Fizz took in the wide sweep of sunlit lawn, the rose gardens, the woods beyond and the backdrop of spectacular mountain peaks. 'There are worse places to chill out. Still, I expect we'd better be on our merry way.'

Buchanan appeared to be in no great rush, nor did he drive the few miles to Breichmenach estate with anything approaching haste, a fact which led Fizz to suspect that he had revised his prediction of their ETA since speaking to her; either that or he'd exaggerated it in order to rush her along. Probably the former, she decided, since he firmly believed that he'd be struck down by a thunderbolt if he meddled with the precise truth.

The estate was something of a disappointment. There was, admittedly, plenty of it but it was in poor shape: the woodland virtually unmanaged, the gardens scrappy, and too many acres given over to grouse moor. The lower hills which, at this time of year, should have been green with saplings and mature trees, were cropped to the bare earth by deer and scarred by the rough tracks needed to transport lazy hunters to where they could scarcely fail to bag a stag.

The house itself was no showpiece either although it had probably possessed a certain rugged beauty at one time. One could spot the original building in the centre of ugly Victorian extensions but the overall effect was gloomy and brooding like a Vogon spaceship come to rest among the empty hills. Backed by a solid phalanx of Scots pines, it was a memorial to some previous owner's wealth and social standing rather than a comfortable country home. It was built on three floors in an odd mixture of styles, with the entrance situated at the top of a semicircular staircase that arched over the ground floor to the floor above and, apart from two imposing bays to either side of the doorway, the windows were small and curtainless, giving the impression of mean, piggy eyes.

There was no one around but when the car stopped at the foot of the staircase they could hear the slow clop of a horse's hooves and a moment later a woman appeared from the far side of the building leading a dun-coloured palomino. She was perhaps in her late thirties, tallish and no lightweight, with breasts that bulged out of a low-buttoned man's shirt and thighs that tested the seams of her riding breeches to destruction.

Buchanan got himself smartly out from behind the wheel so that he was in a position to say 'good morning' to her as she passed by. Her response was unenthusiastic.

'If you're looking for Ewan he's down at the stables. You'll see the horse boxes from the corner there.'

'Thank you.' He reached a hand to scratch under the horse's forelock. 'That's a fine animal you have there.'

Actually he couldn't tell a good horse from a broken-down hack, as Fizz well knew, nor, since a particularly traumatic ride a couple of years back, was he overly fond of the species, but he was a master of the opening gambit. The woman's sullen expression lightened imperceptibly.

'She's one of our best brood mares.'

'You breed horses here? I hadn't realised that.'

'On a small scale. Just palominos.' The horse nudged her impatiently between the shoulder blades making her take a step that took her well into Buchanan's personal space, but she made no move to retreat and neither did he. 'You'll see most of them in the stables this morning because the annual village fête is being held in the paddock this afternoon.'

'Really?' Fizz inserted, feeling this tête-à-tête had gone on long enough. 'That sounds interesting. Is it open to the public?'

'Of course.' The woman's lustrous brown eyes flicked momentarily towards her and then returned to Buchanan. 'Two-fifty to get in, proceeds to the new village hall. It's nothing special, more of a cattle show actually, but come if you want.'

'We may do that,' Buchanan told her, giving her his sexiest smile, and she finally tore herself away, ambling off down the drive with her broad arse rolling in a swagger closely mimicked by the horse.

Following her directions they discovered the stables in a matter of minutes and here everything looked comparatively spic and span. There were twelve wooden horse boxes, each with a head nodding over the half-door:

palominos all and ranging in colour from russet through gold to dark cream. A couple of yearlings were fenced into an open-fronted shed beside which a stocky chap in dungarees was forking manure into a trailer. He looked up just as they turned the corner of the yard and his eyes widened in somewhat comical dismay.

'My God! Is that the time? Mr Buchanan, nmph?' The question mark was indicated by a strange nasal sound tacked on in lieu of words. He rushed over to them and, after a cursory cleansing on his trouser leg, offered a hand to Buchanan who shook it, removing most of the residuary manure before Fizz had to do likewise. 'I thought we'd have everything squared away here well before now but we've had quite a morning of it what with bringing all the horses in and getting the low pasture cleared up for this afternoon. Nmph? Never mind, that's the worst of it done now and Marcia can handle what's left. Come into the house and let me get you something to drink while I wash my hands.'

He stripped off the boiler suit and threw it over a fence, revealing jeans and a check shirt that were not noticeably cleaner. Fizz thought him not bad looking, though a bit long in the tooth for her tastes, his gingery hair thinning slightly at the crown of his head but rising up in a wave like a tsunami at the front. His wife had been something like ten years his junior, she calculated, if the newspapers had got their facts right, but they'd only been together for five years so neither had been in their first flush of youth when they'd tied the knot.

They followed him, at a brisk pace, into the house via a big farmhouse kitchen complete with Aga and through a series of dark and panelled passageways till they emerged into the sunlight of a cobbled-on sunroom of incongruously modern design but some considerable luxury and with a view that needed only a stag or two to be completely over the top.

'There you go,' he barked, waving an arm that encompassed the overstuffed cane suite, the piles of glossy magazines, the hothouse plants and the panorama as far as the horizon. 'Make yourself at home and I'll be with you in two minutes. What can I offer you, nmph? Coffee? Tea? A beer, maybe?'

They settled for coffee and he disappeared at what appeared to be his customary forced march, his footsteps echoing like machine-gun fire all the way down the corridor. Fizz fell into the soft clasp of a three-seater sofa which squeaked plaintively at the assault. 'Not quite what one would have imagined, is he?'

Buchanan walked over to the glass wall and looked out, sticking his hands in his trouser pockets. 'What would one have imagined?'

'Well, something a bit flashier, maybe. Haven't you checked out the press photographs of Amanda? She was a foxy lady. No day-old chick, maybe, but classy, you know? Designer clothes. Hair. Make-up. Jewellery. The lot. I'd expected more of a trophy husband, hadn't you?'

He shrugged without looking round. 'I don't know that I'd given it any thought. Maybe Ewan

74

would clean up reasonably well. Imagine him in a dinner jacket.'

Fizz tried and failed. 'I bet he doesn't own one,' she said. 'He could pass muster in a dress kilt, maybe, with one of those wee bum-freezer jackets, but even then he'd need a few weeks in a charm school, not to mention a decent haircut, before you could take him out in public. I wonder what Amanda saw in him. Maybe he has a — '

'Money, maybe,' Buchanan cut in as though he suspected she were about to say something crude, which was, in fact, the case. 'Social standing. Peace and quiet.'

Fizz snorted. 'Plenty of peace and quiet in this neck of the woods, I'll give you that, but I don't see peace and quiet being at the top of Amanda's wish list. That's not the way she's painted by the media — not by the *Inverness Courier*, anyway. And why would she want to live here in the first place, an hour's drive from anything resembling a metropolis and the nearest Harvey Nichols at the other end of the country? Either the local paper has the wrong end of the stick or she's a woman of strangely catholic tastes.'

Buchanan declined to offer an opinion on this, merely making the obscure little growl at the back of his throat that was intended to indicate that he had his own thoughts on the matter but wasn't disposed to share them. Just one of the zillion things about him that got straight up Fizz's nose. She gave up on the discussion and contented herself with admiring his bottom till Ewan reappeared.

'Sorry about that,' he said, pushing magazines aside to make room for the tray of coffee things he was carrying. 'Don't know where the time went this morning. One minute it's seven o'clock and the next — nmph? — there you are walking into the yard!'

Buchanan turned from the window. 'It's a lot of work for two people — what, ten-fifteen horses? — or do you have more help?'

'Just Marcia, most of the time, though Oliver helps sometimes. He's supposed to be the gardener/handyman but he's fairly flexible, thank God. There's not usually so much to do but we're getting ready for our once-a-year day in aid of Breich village improvement fund.' He gave a droopy little smile as he passed Fizz her mug. 'Can't say I feel much like acting the genial host this year but it's been a family tradition for generations and there's simply no way of getting out of it.'

'It can't be easy for you,' Buchanan said, sounding genuinely sympathetic.

'Oh, I'll get through it. Probably won't be so bad once it gets going. It's a very jolly occasion, usually, and draws most of the farmers in the district as well as a fair percentage of locals from as far away as Fort Augustus. Amanda used to love meeting our neighbours and presenting the prizes. She'll be missed by everyone this year.'

Fizz could well imagine Amanda queening it like mad in designer tweeds and Gucci shoes, mixing with the local gentry and being gracious to the hoi polloi. Then again, maybe she was doing the woman an injustice.

76

'But you're not here to listen to my woes, nmph?' Ewan said with forced brightness. 'Tell me, how is it that I can be of help to you?'

Buchanan sat up and put his mug on the table. 'As I mentioned when I phoned this morning, I'm acting for a lady who believes that she's responsible for your wife's death. She may be delusional or she may be telling the truth but unfortunately there's no proof either way. If she's genuinely guilty, an innocent man has been imprisoned unjustly, if she's innocent it's necessary to put her mind at rest.'

'No problem,' Ewan said right away, his mouth stretching in one of his low-wattage smiles. 'Tell her she's in the clear. This chap, Terence Lamb, is as guilty as they come. Not the slightest doubt in my mind, nor in anyone else's.'

'That's certainly the way it looks from the transcription of the trial. However, there's enough grey area to make a second look worthwhile.'

'Grey area?' Ewan lifted his brows politely but Fizz sensed a faint annoyance in his tone, which was perhaps understandable in the circumstances. He'd obviously thought the whole business was done and dusted and would hate the thought of having to go through all the trauma of another trial. 'Surely there's no shadow of doubt, is there? I would have said the evidence was damning enough by any standards. The jury had no hesitation in coming to a unanimous decision and I'm sure it must have been quite clear to the meanest intelligence that

Lamb was lying in his teeth throughout the entire trial.'

'Lying about what?' Fizz intruded, earning herself a pinched look from the man who was getting paid to ask the questions.

'Well, lying about how and when he managed to get water weed from the Breich river on his shoes, for a start.'

'How did he say it got there?' said Fizz, to show Buchanan how chastened she was.

Ewan took a moment to cast his mind back and then shook his head. 'I don't believe he was able to come up with anything approaching a convincing explanation, not till the closing day of the trial when he appeared to be claiming that the real killer had framed him.'

'Did he have anyone in particular in mind?' Fizz wondered.

Buchanan was starting to breath audibly, always a bad sign, but she was too curious to care.

'Practically everyone concerned with the case, if I remember correctly.' Ewan counterfeited another smile. 'Myself excluded, I'm happy to say, although I've no idea why. The spouse is always the prime suspect, nmph?'

Fizz was about to give her opinion on that but Buchanan fired her a don't-even-think-about it look and said quickly, 'Were you on friendly terms with Terence Lamb?'

'When our paths crossed, yes, I'd have said both Amanda and I were on friendly enough terms with the fellow. He was in my company for a time, but perhaps you knew that, nmph? The

78

Royal Scots. We were in Belfast together and, actually, he took a bullet in the leg that was meant for me and would probably have killed me. The poor chap was seriously wounded in a bomb blast that night, so I felt I had to do what I could for him after he was invalided out. He helped out around the estate for a while but Breich was no place for a man like Terence. Nmph? It was too quiet for him here, not enough action, he said, so after about a year he took off for Edinburgh and got himself a job as a security guard.'

'But you still saw him from time to time?'

'Two or three times a year, maybe, not more than that. He'd show up for the summer fête more often than not — he'd be here today if he weren't in jail.' Ewan's almost childishly earnest face darkened a little at the thought but whatever memories it conjured up for him he pushed aside. 'He wasn't a bad soldier but he couldn't get used to civvy life. They tell me he went downhill very rapidly after he settled in Edinburgh. Got in with a bad crowd. Drugs. Prostitution. That sort of thing. Very sad.'

Fizz was desperate to refer to the allegation that Amanda too had been involved in the vice business but she knew Buchanan would choke her if she did. She had to keep reminding herself to bite her tongue and preserve the illusion that she was only there as an independent witness.

Buchanan stretched out his long legs and wrapped both hands around his coffee mug. He said, 'There was some question about his being here around the time of Amanda's death.'

'That's true,' Ewan nodded, apparently more than willing to be as helpful as he possibly could. 'I saw him fishing the Blackwater around that time and stopped to have a few words with him but by the time he was charged with Amanda's murder I couldn't remember exactly when that was. Some time in March, certainly, but I couldn't even make a guess at the date, not with a man's freedom hanging on my answer. One day's much like another here, nmph? I only know it's Sunday when I hear the church bells from way over at Breich.'

'And there's no question of his having picked up the water weed while he was fishing the Blackwater?' Fizz suggested.

'Apparently not. I understand the same weed exists in both rivers but there is a clear genetic difference between them. In fact, the forensic chappies claim to be able to pinpoint which stretch of the river is particular to that specific gene pattern and they're sure the weed on Lamb's shoes came from the point where Amanda was discovered. Incredible, isn't it, nmph? The wonders of modern science.'

Everyone agreed that science was wonderful and seconds of coffee were dispensed, Ewan getting the last dribble out of the pot.

'Had Lamb been fishing the Breich at that time?' Fizz asked while Buchanan was helping himself to half the sugar bowl.

'No chance. The Breich isn't much of a salmon river and where it crosses our land — which is the only stretch Lamb had permission to fish — it's too inaccessible because

80

of the narrowness of the gully and the state of the undergrowth. Even if you could work your way along to a half-decent pool the overhanging trees would make casting impossible. One of these days I'll scrape enough money together to get it cleared.'

Buchanan smiled in a chummy way. 'I imagine this place is a bit of a money sink. What's the grouse shooting going to be like this year?'

'Better, I think.' Ewan brightened a little at that and waved a hand at the distant moors. 'We got a great burn going early in the year and the new heather got away to a fine start so, with a bit of luck, we'll have good sport to offer by mid-August. Some fair heads among the stags too. Are you a sportsman yourself?'

'I don't shoot,' Buchanan said, 'but I enjoy having the occasional tussle with a salmon when the opportunity arises.'

'Then feel free to have a cast or two in the Blackwater while you're here. I don't know how long you'll be in the neighbourhood but the upper stretches, just below the end of the woods, are in nice condition just now. Oliver took a twenty-four pounder there the day before yesterday. It was a bit on the red side but we sent it away to be smoked and it'll be fine.'

'That's extremely kind of you.' Buchanan looked surprised and pleased by such generosity, just as if that hadn't been what he was angling for all along. 'I may have an hour to spare before I turn in tonight.'

'Then I wish you luck,' Ewan said warmly. 'Early morning seems to be the choice time at the moment but tomorrow's Sunday and we can't have you breaking the law, can we, nmph?'

Everyone smiled politely at this flash of wit and Buchanan stood up, evidently of a mind to quit while he was winning. As Ewan walked them to the car he was full of bonhomie, pressing them to come to the fête, promising to look out for them and assuring them that he was at their disposal should they feel the need to consult him again.

What a nice guy, Fizz found herself thinking as he waved them goodbye from the foot of the steps, and then wondered: a bit *too* nice?

6

Mrs Sullivan was comfortably ensconced in the garden when they got back, stretched out on a sun lounger with the current edition of *Homes & Gardens* and a surprisingly large whisky and ginger ale. She was wearing a longish beige dress which even Buchanan could tell was beautifully tailored and had draped a turquoise silk scarf around her throat in that casually stylish way most women never quite bring off.

The effect was strangely at odds with the picture he had formed of her, which was that of a rather dowdy and not too sharp-witted old dear, and he found the transformation more than a trifle unsettling. Had she been cozening him, at first, into a false sense of her potential or was this just one of those mutations that all women seemed able to bring about to suit the occasion? She looked entirely different in her new guise: even her plump and almost vapid face had taken on a new alert expression and her eyes seemed to focus on his with a quite piercing directness.

It occurred to him that, whereas he had, till now, seriously doubted the reliability of her confession, this new Mrs Sullivan had something about her that challenged his conviction. He could not have said what that something was, precisely, but suddenly he was no longer sure that murder was entirely beyond her. And would he, he wondered, have taken on the case had he suspected she was guilty? Probably not. There was a hell of a difference between putting a dizzy old lady's mind at rest and getting involved with a full-scale enquiry into a miscarriage of justice. Maybe this was the time for a fast exit. He glanced at Fizz to see if she gave any sign of noticing the change in their client's persona but she appeared oblivious to anything but the gin and tonic Mrs Sullivan had ordered her.

'He seems a really nice guy,' she was saying. 'Not what I'd have considered Amanda's type — not from what you and the papers say about her — but you can never tell what people see in each other, can you?'

Mrs Sullivan diluted her drink with a spot more ginger ale and raised her eyebrows. She seemed almost to be suppressing a secret excitement and what appeared to be a smile was clearly tugging at the corners of her mouth. 'What type is he?'

'Well, a bit of a country bumpkin,' Fizz told her. 'A bit like an overgrown schoolboy playing at soldiers. Gruff voice, keeps going 'nmph?' all the time like he was saying 'got it'? Reasonably pleasant to look at but fattish around the middle and losing his hair on top. Not particularly brainy, or if he is he hides it well under an assumption of naïvety.'

'It's probably not an assumption,' Mrs Sullivan opined, her smile widening into a cheeky grin. 'He'd have to be pretty naïve to marry a witch like Amanda. I don't doubt for a minute that she preyed on him just as she preyed on William. She would certainly be attracted by the social position he could give her here — a big fish in a small pool — but I doubt very much if her husband gained very much out of the alliance. If they were together for five years, as I'm told, I'll wager he regretted it for four.'

And if that were true, Buchanan thought, one would be wise not to lose sight of the fact that Ewan had as valid a motive for getting rid of her as anyone else. He said, 'The single most unavoidable fact you have to take on board is the presence of that specific water weed on Lamb's shoes. It places him, beyond question, at the scene of the crime and at a time consistent with the estimated date of Amanda's death. Until we deal with that anomaly it's going to be uphill work proving his innocence. He doesn't appear to have any explanation to offer and neither do you.'

She pursed her lips, deepening the surrounding wrinkles, and gave her head an impatient little shake. 'Someone put it there, of course,' she said, sounding more trenchant than Buchanan had previously seen her. 'I don't know who would want to frame him but it's quite evident to me that the most obvious explanation has to be the true one. It's simply a matter of finding out who would benefit by Lamb's imprisonment.'

The most likely beneficiary had to be the person who committed the crime of which Lamb was accused, but if Mrs Sullivan wasn't admitting to interfering with the course of justice — and how would she even come to *know* Terence Lamb? — then the killer had to be someone else.

'You'd never come into contact with Terence Lamb at any time, I take it?' he asked, just to be sure, and her indignant expression was all the answer he needed.

'Of course not. I've never seen the man in the flesh and, if you ask him when you see him next week, he'll tell you the same thing. I wasn't even aware of his existence till I read the report of his arrest in the *Scotsman*.' She heaved herself up in her chair and rearranged her cushions with somewhat over-animated efficiency. 'And, if I had planted damning evidence on that poor man, what reason could I possibly have to refrain from telling you about it? Tell me that. It's a great pity you don't trust me to tell you the truth Mr Buchanan as, I can assure you, I have no intention of confusing the issue in any way.'

Buchanan smiled at her placatingly. She was undoubtedly in a very strange mood: like a bottle of champagne, shaken but still tightly corked. This might not be the ideal time to jerk her lead but he was going to have to make a few things clear.

'Unfortunately, Mrs Sullivan, in order to get at the truth it's necessary to treat every bit of evidence, from whatever source, with scepticism. What you believe to be indisputable fact may, from a different point of view, have other interpretations. You didn't expect this investigation to be fun — did you? — and I'm afraid there's no way I can do my job properly without asking personal questions and taking nothing you or anyone else tells me at face value. You may not like it but it's part of the price you have to pay.'

She didn't like being lectured but she made no reply, contenting herself with tipping her chin at no one in particular and staring into the middle distance.

'We'll have another go at Ewan this afternoon,' Fizz announced blithely, as though she hadn't been following the exchange, 'and we'll also try to find out what the hired help have to say about Terence Lamb and how often he turns up at the estate. There's a woman who helps with the horses and also a gardener/handyman called Oliver who wasn't around this morning. Maybe they'll be more interesting than the boss fella.'

'I really don't see why I shouldn't come to the fête with you,' Mrs Sullivan said, casting a speaking glance at Buchanan over the rim of her glass. 'No one would have the least suspicion that I am your client and what if they did? As far as any of those people are concerned I'm just a deluded old woman.'

Fizz shook her head. 'It's when you turn out *not* to be a deluded old woman but the killer of Ewan's wife that the shi — the sh — that we'd be in trouble.'

Buchanan was pleased to see that she was making an attempt to clean up her language but he had a funny idea that Mrs Sullivan was aware of what she had been about to say and was more amused than shocked.

'Oh, I daresay you know what you're about, the two of you. I'll just take a walk round the garden and write a postcard to Miss Tweed since

I missed visiting her this weekend. I've probably had enough sun this morning anyway and, I must admit, I do enjoy a little nap after my lunch.'

She probably slept like the dead, Buchanan thought about an hour later, particularly if the bottle of wine she'd shared with Fizz over lunch had the soporific effect on her it would have had on him. Even Fizz, who had consumed, uniquely for her, no more than her fair share of the Chablis, was sleepy-eyed as they drove back to Breichmenach estate. Buchanan tried to broach the subject of Mrs Sullivan's suddenly altered persona but she refused to be intrigued.

'Well, of course she's different,' she said, through a yawn. 'You don't expect her to scruff around in her everyday gear in a country house hotel like that one, do you? All the other guests are dolled up like something out of *Vogue*.'

'It's not just the clothes, Fizz, it's the way she looks at you. It's as if she was asleep before and has now got all her senses about her. She looked . . . I don't know . . . animated . . . switched on. Didn't you notice the air of confidence she's developed?'

'Everyone has an air of confidence when they're all dolled up to the nines.'

'Okay, what about the booze, then? Didn't you think that was a bit out of character?'

Fizz pushed out her lips as though she were blowing a kazoo while she considered this, then said. 'Maybe. Just a fraction. But, hell, a double whisky and some wine with her lunch doesn't make her an alcoholic. She's on holiday after all.'

She turned her head to give him a hard look. 'I wish you wouldn't do that. It really gets on my tits.'

'Do what? What did I do now, for God's sake?'

'That noise you make when you think you know better than me but can't be bothered arguing about it.'

'I don't know what you're talking about. I never opened my mouth.'

'You do it without opening your mouth. That growl.'

Buchanan had no recollection of ever making such a sound but there was no point in either denying the accusation or apologising. She'd only find something else to complain about. For a person who looked the very picture of sunny congeniality, she was a complete nark.

For all that they were late in arriving, lunch having been a leisurely indulgence, there was still a queue at the parking area, which was an adjacent field. Already there were a surprising number of vans and trailers, Landrovers and horse boxes in situ and more people milling about than would have been expected from the apparent population of the surrounding area. Fizz was unimpressed by the spectacle, having grown up on a sheep farm and having attended, she claimed, a hundred better organised events from Balmoral to the Borders, but Buchanan found the holiday atmosphere rather engaging.

The rough pasture where the main events were taking place was divided into two sections: one for a cattle show and the other for various stalls and amusements. From one side they could hear the echoey, amplified voice of a presenter interspersed with bursts of genteel applause, and from the other came the skirl of a pipe band, the intermittent crack of air rifles, and the screaming of happy kids. There were the usual coconut shies and fortune tellers, a bouncy castle and a few stalls selling refreshments, horse and dog requirements, farm produce and local crafts, but the majority of interest was centred on sheepdog trials which were being held on the hillside bordering the paddock.

Buchanan was fascinated by the level of communication between man and dog and remained watching while Fizz went off in search of a White Elephant stall. With only one contestant left to compete and the current top score beatable only by a record time the excitement in the crowd was almost tangible. The five sheep being harried, coaxed and guided around the course were clearly under the influence of one mean-looking ewe who had her own ideas about how she wanted to spend her afternoon and these did not coincide in the slightest with those of the brown and white border collie who had her sussed from the first blast of his master's whistle. She took off at every angle but the right one, she stood her ground tenaciously till the dog was virtually within nipping distance, she returned his malevolent yellow gaze with knobs on; and her adherents followed her with blind confidence, wherever she went.

Precious seconds ticked by while master and dog, between them, divided the mini-flock into two groups, cut one out of its group, put it back in, turned them this way and that in a complicated dance that edged them towards a tiny fenced fold at the foot of the hill. The dog rushed and stopped, stood like a statue or crept forward on its belly, never relinquishing its dominance, never taking its baleful eye off the touchy ewes. Closer and closer to the fold they edged, the sheep hovering, uncertain, making small abortive escape attempts, all of them anticipated by the dog and foiled within a few paces. With seconds remaining, the shepherd moved round them and opened the gate of the pen. Slowly the dog crept forward and the sheep sidled towards the opening. Then the warrior queen made a break for it, spooking the other four who scattered, but the dog was after them like a bullet, halted them in their tracks and dropped, panting into the grass while the five of them walked calmly into the enclosure as if that's what they'd intended to do from the outset. An explosion of applause burst from the crowd as the commentator announced a winning round and Buchanan found himself grinning as proudly as if he'd accomplished it himself.

Throughout the tussle Buchanan had been aware of a woman in front of him taking photographs but had registered her only as an annoying head that got in the way at crucial moments. Now he realised that the camera was a professional looking model and that the woman was also carrying a notebook and pen, marking her, in his own mind at least, as a reporter.

'Excuse me,' he said as she started to move

away and she turned to him with the hopeful smile of one ever on the lookout for a scoop.

'Am I right in thinking you're from the local paper?'

'I'm from the *Inverness Courier*, yes. Chloe Miller.'

'I wonder if I could have a few words with you.' He got his wallet out of his back pocket and found one of his new business cards.

She scanned it and wrinkled a very attractive, if slightly snub, nose. 'An advocate? What . . . Ah, it's something to do with the murder, is it? I thought that business was a thing of the past.'

'Well, it is and it isn't.' Buchanan waggled an equivocal hand. 'Look, could I buy you a coffee or whatever and pick your brain for half an hour. I just want to hear what your thoughts are on the matter of Terence Lamb's guilt.'

She meditated briefly, looking at her watch and swithering, and then nodded. 'Just half an hour then. I have to interview some people and there's no telling when they'll disappear.'

'Half an hour,' Buchanan assured her. 'I'll set my timer.'

She had a lovely smile but he would have been unsure whether to class her as pretty or not. She wasn't really his type but her face was bright and vivid with dark eyes and arched brows and it was set off quite charmingly by one of those geometric hairstyles of the variety Buchanan would always associate with old photographs of Mary Quant. Maybe she was a little on the thin side but her skinny arms and legs gave her the engaging appearance of a young colt, an impression borne out by the way she moved over the ground in a progression of wobbly strides.

The refreshment tent was almost full and redolent with the smell of trampled grass and spilled beer. The counter was lined with tweedy types, all of whom appeared to know each other well, and their loud-voiced conversation and roars of laughter vied for supremacy with the taped pipe music someone had thought necessary to the ambience of the place. They found a table as far away as possible from the speakers, both electronic and human, and Buchanan got straight to the point.

'I'd be interested to know what you think of Terence Lamb's conviction, Miss Miller.'

One eyebrow slid up under her fringe. 'You mean, am I glad about it or do I think it was unsafe?'

'The latter,' Buchanan said, and then, 'Perhaps I should have explained my interest first. I'm acting for a lady who claims Lamb is innocent and that she herself committed the murder.'

The second eyebrow joined the first but there was no amusement in the dark eyes beneath, only a sudden, very close attention. She seemed very young, probably in her early twenties, but she was right in there like an old trouper. 'Really,' she murmured, her hand drifting towards the notepad she had thrown down on the table. 'What's her name, this woman?'

'Forgive me, but I'd rather not say at this point. I'm just making a few preliminary inquiries to see if there's any possibility she could be speaking the truth. What do you think?'

'I'd say it was highly unlikely,' she said sombrely and then flashed up a whimsical smile. 'But what a lovely story it would make.'

'Wouldn't it?' Buchanan returned her smile and covertly examined the ring finger of her left hand which was agreeably naked. 'I've read all of your reports in the *Courier* — at least, I assume they were all yours.'

'Yes, they let me handle it from the start,' she said, displaying a muted sort of enthusiasm as though she were hugely proud of her work. 'I'm not on the staff there — just a stringer — but they use a lot of my stuff. Fortunately for me, I live just down the road in Breich and I knew all the people involved so I was able to talk my way into the job. I wouldn't normally have been given that kind of opportunity but the editor was absolutely great about it. I'm hoping I could be offered a staff job on the strength of my coverage.'

'You deserve it,' Buchanan asserted, maybe a little over-generously. 'I found the pieces very interesting, especially your take on Amanda. Maybe I was reading too much between the lines but I got the impression that you weren't one of her greatest fans.'

Her eyes lifted to him shrewdly. 'You noticed that? It wasn't supposed to show — at least I don't think it was. Maybe it was a Freudian slip. But, yes, I did dislike Amanda pretty comprehensively.'

'May I ask why?'

'Why? Because she was a two-faced, conniving

woman. A social climber. Scruff in toff's clothing. Sweet as banoffee pudding to your face but ready to rifle your pockets should you drop dead.'

This was delivered in a neutral tone and with a face devoid of expression but Buchanan was left in no doubt that she meant what she said.

'Any special incident you'd like to share with me? Just as an example.'

She looked at her watch and then glanced evasively around the room. 'It's a bit soon to be speaking ill of the dead. People around here are trying to forget the whole thing ever happened and there's no point in opening up old sores, is there? I mean, your client is probably hallucinating about being involved and, even if she isn't, Terence Lamb richly deserves to be behind bars whether he killed Amanda or not. He's the lowest of the low. Let's just let sleeping dogs lie.'

'I hear what you're saying,' Buchanan said, 'but being a lawyer I can't go along with the idea of punishing a guy — however depraved — for something he didn't do. Besides, my client is tortured by the idea that she took a life and I feel it's important for her to know the truth — especially as she's almost certainly innocent.'

She shrugged. 'I don't know anything that would help to free Terence Lamb. If I did I would probably take it to the police.'

'Naturally. I appreciate that. All I'm after, really, is some idea of what the situation was like up at the big house before Amanda's murder. Were they happily married, Amanda and Ewan?'

'Sure. Like Bill and Hilary Clinton.' She

quirked up one corner of her mouth to show she was being facetious. 'They both had their eyes firmly on the main chance. She got to be the lady of the manor: he got her money to keep the estate tottering along. She got a brainless lapdog of a husband who let her do whatever she chose to do without complaint, he got as much sex as he could handle and the wherewithal to lord it over the rest of us locals.'

Buchanan rather thought she was looking at him closely as she said this but decided that it was because he was beginning to get through to her. She was becoming prettier by the moment and he was no longer certain that she was not his type. At one time his type could have been classed as tall, elegant women with loose morals and sophisticated tastes. Now he was beginning to wonder if all he required of a partner was the requisite number of limbs and no penis. Heigh-ho, he thought briefly, for the halcyon days when he had never been without a girlfriend. The last few years had witnessed a serious drop in the number of candidates and, of those he had managed to attract, none had lasted beyond the second date, a circumstance he could blame only in part on Fizz. Certainly she had been responsible for the departure of more than one, but not intentionally, he was certain. As far as the others were concerned, they either took against him for no reason or accused him of being a philanderer: nothing being further from his nature. Hope, however, sprang eternal.

'What about Terence Lamb? You knew him too?'

'Sure.' She seemed more comfortable with that subject. 'He was an ex-soldier, you know. Same battalion as Captain Ewan Montrose. They were together in Northern Ireland ten or fifteen years ago and went through some sort of bonding experience there. Lamb claimed he saved Ewan's life but he was always full of bullshit like that and it's not easy to check out that sort of thing. Anyway Ewan gave him a job of some sort up at the big house and he used to walk down to the pub in the village every other evening for a few drams.'

'How did he get along with the locals?'

'Not a great favourite with any of them. He was loud-mouthed, once he had a couple of drinks inside him, and got very abusive if anyone argued with him. There were a couple of near-punch ups, both caused by his attitude to women, but I don't think any of the locals were entirely confident about taking him on.'

'What was his attitude to women?'

'Slimy,' she said tersely and checked her watch again. 'Sorry, but I really have to get back to work now. Time's getting on and I have people to talk to.'

'I'm really grateful to you for your help.' Buchanan got up and held her chair back for her. 'I don't know how I'll be placed this evening but, if I can get away, would you let me buy you a drink?'

She busied herself by slinging her camera bag onto her shoulder and pocketing her notebook. 'Give me a ring,' she said, producing a card that identified her as a freelance journalist. 'I'm

7

The sheepdog trials had finished by the time Fizz found her way back to where she had left Buchanan and the stewards were marking out the vacated slope with markers for a hill race. She looked for him, in a desultory sort of way, around the cattle pens and the pipe band but was soon distracted by the clay pigeon shooting where, after seducing her two male opponents into a false estimation of her capabilities, she won a grotesque glass bowl and the sort of applause usually reserved for child prodigies.

Ewan Montrose flashed in and out of the scene, dressed in a faded army kilt and a khaki shirt with the sleeves rolled up above his elbows, but he was always too busy to buttonhole, rushing to get somewhere or in close conversation with landed-gentry types, of both sexes, in shooting waistcoats and long-skipped deerstalkers. He appeared well-liked, judging by the body language of his chums, and there was a lot of backslapping and air-kissing going on as though, maybe, he hadn't seen these people since Amanda's funeral. A lot of the time he was attended by a chap with a hard, muscle-bound sort of face who topped him by half a head and whose biceps, exposed by similarly rolled-up sleeves, looked ready to burst through the stretched skin. This guy, one assumed, would be Oliver: nominally the gardener/handyman but allegedly ready to turn his hand to anything. Fizz could well believe it.

She was in no particular hurry to quiz Ewan any further — if she couldn't wangle another trip north to assist Buchanan in that undertaking she'd start to worry about losing her touch — but she was suddenly consumed by a desire to discover if Oliver was as tough as he looked or just a big teddy bear in a crocodile's hide. She trailed him for ten minutes before he abandoned Ewan, who was talking to the winner of a red rosette for a stringy Blackface ram her grandfather would have had butchered for the freezer.

There weren't many places where one could take the weight off one's feet but the hay bales that some farmer was using to form a temporary enclosure for his lambs offered a respite for those with not-too-tender behinds. Oliver sat himself down, crossed his legs and, with a fine disregard for fire precautions, lit up a fag.

Fizz approached obliquely and mimed sudden recognition. 'Oh . . . hello. You must be Oliver, I think. I missed meeting you when I called on Ewan this morning. I'm Fizz Fitzpatrick. Perhaps Ewan mentioned that Tam Buchanan and I are making some inquiries . . . '

'About Amanda, aye, I heard.'

He didn't offer to shake hands, nor did his expression encourage Fizz to believe that he had been living for this moment, but she gave him a shy smile and one of her best wow-aren't-you-gorgeous looks, and laid claim to the adjacent hay bale. 'I expect it's a bit of a wild goose chase, this whole inquiry, but Buchanan is a total softie and he's set on proving to this old lady that she has nothing to worry about. You'd think it would take you about five minutes to set her straight but she's convinced that someone framed Terence Lamb for the killing and we're finding it impossible to turn up any evidence to the contrary.'

He exhaled a plume of smoke, most of his attention on a skittish pony that was giving its young rider a hard time. 'Aye. I can believe that.'

'I suppose you must have known him pretty well,' Fizz persisted.

'Slightly. Only slightly.'

'But, Lamb worked at the estate for a year, Ewan tells me, so you must have seen quite a bit of him.'

'He kept himself to himself.' Oliver's head was still turned away from her in real or pretended concern for the child who, in fact, now had his mount well under control.

'Did you get along with him?'

'Not much. He was an arrogant bastard.'

'How about Amanda? Did she get along with him?'

He shifted his attention to the glowing tip of his cigarette, examined it closely for a few seconds, took a deep drag and said, exhaling the words like a smoke signal, 'Far as I know she didn't see much of him. Probably couldn't have cared less about him one way or the other.'

Fizz shifted her position on the hay bale so that the sharp stalks punctured her bum in a different pattern. 'He found country life a bit of a bore, Ewan said, but he still came back on quite a regular basis. Why was that, do you think?'

'It was just for the salmon fishing. Ewan let him have a go on the Blackwater any time he liked.'

'Did he drop by the big house to say hello to Ewan and Amanda if he was in the area?'

His eyes had never once met hers since the moment she sat down and now they were fixed on the hill-runners knocking their pans out on the sun-baked hillside. 'Oh aye,' he said easily but with a brevity that didn't escape Fizz's notice.

'Where did he stay? In the village?' she asked and had to wait while he inhaled again for a reply.

'They let him crash in his old bedsit above the garage. It's been empty since he left.'

Fizz found that interesting to say the least. For a guy who was as unlovable as everyone said he was, Lamb had done pretty well out of the Montrose family. One would have thought that the offer of permanent employment would be payment enough for a bullet in the leg, but Ewan had continued to pamper the guy even after he moved out. Something he had glossed over rather smoothly when questioned.

'Was Ewan aware how Terence was earning a living in Edinburgh?'

He flicked a glanced at her, so briefly she almost missed it. 'The massage parlours, you mean? I've no idea.'

'Were you?'

There was a short silence while he very carefully ground out the stub of his cigarette against the sole of his boot. 'I had my suspicions. He never said as much, but you could tell by the way he talked sometimes that he was into something sleazy.'

'But you never mentioned it to Ewan?'

'Nup. None of my business.'

The bleating of the lambs behind her, which was of a volume totally at odds with their size, was beginning to get to Fizz. She wondered if she could entice Oliver into the beer tent but thought she might lose him altogether if she gave him the opportunity to remember a pressing engagement elsewhere. She said, 'Did he go down the village much?'

'Just for the occasional pint in the evening.'

'Did you go with him?'

'No,' he said shortly, prompting her to ask, 'Why not?'

For the first time, he turned to face her and she could see by the grim set of his mouth that he was fed up with her questions. Even in a good mood, as he had appeared before her arrival, he was far from comely: riled, he was downright scary. Like a warning hooter, a lamb baaed loudly at her back, making her jump.

'Because he couldn't keep his filthy hands off my girlfriend, that's why. Foul-mouthed, dirty-minded bastard, that's what he was but if I'd broke his jaw it would've cost me my job. As far as I'm concerned hanging's too good for the bastard.'

'So,' Fizz ventured, sweetly, but getting ready

to duck, 'maybe you know of someone who might have had it in for him?'

'Half the village,' he snarled, lurching angrily to his feet. 'Better be going. The boss'll be looking for me.'

'Nice talking to you,' said Fizz politely but he didn't return the compliment.

She watched him melt into the throng, blasting a passageway through the queue for the toilets en route, and felt reasonably contented with the results of her interrogation. Oliver might consider himself a match for any baby-faced, straight-out-of-uni solicitor but he still had a thing or two to learn. He had communicated a lot more than he thought he had: enough, perhaps, to imply that there was more going on at Breichmenach estate than met the eye. She doubted if Buchanan had achieved as much in the course of the afternoon.

Buchanan, however, appeared to have sunk into the ground. She checked out the show ring and the beer tent, the angling stall and the dog show and finally ran him to earth in the audience of the Highland dancing competition.

'Hey,' she said, surprising him with a swift poke in the ribs. 'If I didn't know you better, amigo mio, I'd think you were trying to avoid me.'

'Would I ever?'

'Yes.'

'Will you look at those kids. Aren't they amazing?'

He indicated the current competitors, a bunch of tinies who were prancing about like fleas, and

Fizz looked obediently, though it was a sight she had seen many times in the past. They were cute little things, unbelievably minuscule, with hands poised like twigs in the position called *caber fèidh*, the stag's antlers, and itsy feet that seemed virtually repelled by the platform. Enchantment was writ large on the faces of the crowd but Fizz could only remember the battle of wills she'd fought, and eventually won, when her grandfather had tried to enrol her for pre-school dancing lessons. Some kids were born to dance: others were simply not.

'Charming,' she said dutifully, and in the same breath, 'found anyone worth talking to?'

'Yes, actually,' he said, allowing her to drag him away from the racket of the fiddle music which accompanied the dancers. 'I ran into the reporter from the local newspaper. We didn't get much opportunity to talk but we may have a beer later.'

They walked over to the show ring where, the most interesting classes having been already judged, the crowd was thinning and some of the seats were becoming vacant.

'*May* have a beer?' Fizz asked, 'Depending on what?'

'Depending on whether I deliver Mrs Sullivan to be interviewed. That's the bargain.'

'A-hah. And would you consider doing that?'

'I'm thinking about it. There would have to be all sorts of guarantees first: no publication till we've closed the case et cetera, but it'll depend also on what Mrs Sullivan wants to do.'

'What's the harm in it?' Fizz argued. 'It's not

like Mrs Sullivan can tell her anything she doesn't know already, is it? And maybe she'd come out with something the reporter can prove to be impossible, thus solving our case for us with no sweat expended.'

'I don't know that it would be wise to take the risk of exposing Mrs Sullivan to media interest. I'd have to be sure the right safeguards were in place — and sure, also, that we'd get something worthwhile in return.'

'What's your feeling about that? Does this reporter know anything we don't?'

'Possibly. Nothing was hinted at, exactly, but . . .'

He seemed at a loss for words.

'Your antenna was twitching?' she offered and he looked at her with, one would have thought, unnecessary suspicion.

'You could say that. And you? What have you been up to?'

'Well, I won this priceless artefact in the clay pigeon tournament and I also had a very interesting conversation with Oliver, the so-called gardener/handyman.'

He looked at her over the top of his sunglasses. 'You think he's more than that?'

'Let's say he's big and tough and the kind you'd want on your side in a pub brawl.'

'You'd know about that,' he said. 'But being big and tough does not, of itself, imply any lack of moral fibre. In fact — I'm no expert on the subject but one would imagine a certain robustness might be considered an advantage in a gardener/handyman.'

Fizz pressed her lips together, reminding herself of her vow to stop using bad language. 'It wasn't just his appearance that interested me, it was the way he answered my questions: thinking before he spoke, saying as little as possible, telling me only what I could have found out from other sources.'

'Hmm.' Buchanan started to growl at the back of his throat and then stopped himself abruptly and said, 'You don't think he might just be naturally slow?'

'Not a chance. Sharp as a tack. But he did let out one little fact that he didn't intend to share with me.'

Buchanan took off his sunglasses entirely. 'What was that?'

'He hates Terence Lamb because he's a sleazeball and kept touching up the girls — Ollie's girl in particular. He said — listen — he said that if he'd punched Terence it would have cost him his job.'

'Cost Terence his job?'

'No, that's the point. It would have cost Ollie his job — which means that Terence was more important to Ewan than Ollie. Even *after* he'd left his job at Breichmenach and gone to Edinburgh.' She waited for his response. 'Interesting?'

They'd reached the show ring where a skinny woman with a geometric haircut was photographing a farmer with a Charolais bull. Buchanan led the way into the back row of benches and got them installed behind a landed twit with a sunshade. They could see little of the ring from there but Fizz was barely interested in the proceedings anyway so she made no complaint.

'What d'you think?' she insisted. 'Are you getting bad vibrations, coz I sure as hell am. There's more going on up at the big house, Horatio, than we have dreamed of.'

He replaced his sunglasses and looked at her through them with what could pass for faint acceptance. 'You could be right, Fizz, but then again Oliver might have been exaggerating.'

'I don't think so. He'd have loved to settle Terence's hash and, believe me, he didn't look the type to hold his hand without the threat of some very serious reprisals. He knew which of them was for the high jump if things got physical.'

Buchanan didn't answer but at least he appeared to be thinking about it. He put his elbows on his knees, leaning over and studying his shoes for a while, and she gave him peace to get on with it while she tried to see what was going on in the ring. It was still hot, as it had been all day, but a sluggish little breeze had appeared as the sun got lower in the sky and it was pleasant enough just sitting there and relaxing. She was on the point of dozing off when she felt a hand lightly touch her shoulder and Ewan's voice said,

'Ah, there you are, Miss Fitzpatrick . . . Mr Buchanan. I did spot you earlier but — pressure of work, you know. Keeping the visitors happy et cetera. Have you enjoyed your afternoon?'

'Very much,' Buchanan said, getting up and

stepping over the bench to shake hands with him. 'I hadn't expected quite such a sizeable event. You must have garnered in every family in the district.'

Ewan looked more than a little smug. 'I'm pleased to say we have a wider catchment area than that. The good weather has helped this year but we always get a good attendance. There's not a lot of excitement to be had around these parts, even at the height of summer, nmph, so the locals have to make the most of what's on offer.'

He glanced down at his feet as he spoke and Fizz suddenly realized that he had a tiny dog with him, on the end of an extendable leash: a bald-looking, shivering little rat with bulbous eyes and legs you could have flossed your teeth with.

'Gonzales,' Ewan introduced it, slightly sheepishly as behoved any red-blooded man caught in charge of such an abortion. 'He was Amanda's dog. She absolutely adored him and he's quite lost without her, poor mite.' He bent down to pat the thing's head and essayed a whimsical smile. 'We comfort each other.'

Fizz recalled some mention of a dog in the newspaper reports she'd swotted up on, but she'd pictured something more utilitarian than Gonzales. 'Of course,' she nodded. 'Amanda had just taken him to the vet's when she . . . when she was stopped on the road.'

'That's right. He'd eaten something pretty vile that day and was a pretty sick little chap. We thought we'd lose him too for a while but he pulled through in the end. There's not much of him, as you can see, nmph, not much back-up he can call on in an emergency, so to speak. Never mind, he's fine now.'

Buchanan offered the dog his fingers to investigate but it was too nervous to be interested and danced away sideways to the extent of it's leash, so he said, 'Was there any suggestion that he might have been poisoned? I'd imagine that Amanda's killer, knowing of her affection for her dog, could more or less bank on her taking him to the vet and could then estimate the time of her return along that quiet road.'

Ewan nodded. 'That was suggested, yes. It's a theory that ties in with the known facts but unfortunately the vet was unable to prove that the poisoning was deliberately induced or accidental. However, it would have been perfectly simple for Terence to slip something into a titbit or even into the dog's meal. He was certainly here around that time.'

'Staying . . . ?' Fizz gave him time to answer, but when he ignored the monosyllable she added, ' . . . where?'

'Eh? Oh, up at the house I imagine, in his old quarters above the garage.'

'That was very generous of you. Was that where he normally stayed when he fished the river?'

Ewan put on a bland expression which suggested to her that Oliver had told him about being asked the same questions earlier. 'Not really generous, Miss Fitzpatrick. The flatlet's not up to much and hasn't been used by anyone else since Terence went to Edinburgh. When he asked permission to stay there for the odd night there really wasn't any reason to refuse.'

He caught sight of an acquaintance a few seats away and waved enthusiastically.

'My goodness. Andy McFarlane. Haven't seen him in years.' He turned briskly and offered Fizz his hand. 'Do forgive me if I rush off. So many people to say hello to, nmph? Do drop by again if you need any more information. Always happy to see you, Mr Buchanan.'

He shot off to see his friend at a speed that had Gonzales's legs whizzing faster than the eye could follow in an effort to keep up. Buchanan also made preparations for departure.

'We should be getting back,' he said, picking up his jacket and slinging it over one shoulder. 'Mrs Sullivan will be waiting to hear what progress we've made this afternoon.'

'What's your hurry? You haven't had a go at the clay pigeon shooting yet.'

'It's almost five,' he said mulishly. 'Mrs Sullivan will be bored, all on her own, and besides, your arms are getting a bit red. You should get out of the sun.'

Fizz wasn't worried about sun damage as her skin was pretty well weathered from long periods in warmer climes than Scotland's, but it occurred to her that Mrs Sullivan would probably want an aperitif before dinner and one couldn't have her drinking alone.

8

Mrs Sullivan was, very evidently, far from bored. She had discovered two kindred spirits in a corporate banker and his wife from Somerset and had spent, she declared, a highly satisfactory afternoon in the course of which she had enjoyed entertaining conversation, learned to play gin rummy, received good advice on her investments, and won seventeen pence. She was, however, just as eager to debrief her two agents as Buchanan had predicted and listened to the chronicles of their labours with close attention. When they had finished bringing her up to date she seemed well content with the way things were progressing.

'This business of the chihuahua being poisoned,' she said with an expression of acute chagrin. 'It's all nonsense. I didn't even know Amanda owned a dog and, even if I had, I would never do such an abominable thing to a dumb animal.'

'Maybe someone else did,' Fizz murmured, half asleep in the bee-loud sunshine.

Mrs Sullivan speared her with a sharp glance that struck Buchanan as slightly out of character — or at least, out of the character he had assumed her to be.

She said, with quite an edge to her tone, 'Why on earth would someone do that, may I ask? No one had any reason to lure Amanda to her death other than the person who killed her, and I've just stated that I didn't do that. You're not, I sincerely hope, about to suggest that some other person had decided to kill her and chose — by some amazing coincidence — to do the deed on the same day as I did it?'

Fizz's lids opened with a jerk, the white of her eyes very blue and shiny, and she said, 'Oh, sorry. I wasn't thinking what I was saying. Ready for my siesta, I suspect.'

Immediately Mrs Sullivan became the motherly figure she'd always been. 'Go and lie down for a while before dinner, dear. You've probably been in the sun too long. I believe your shoulders are quite red. I'm going to drive down to the village to buy a can of hair spray before the shops shut so I'll see if they have some kind of after-sun cream that would take the heat out of the burn. Do you care to come with me, Mr Buchanan?'

Buchanan thought it might be a good idea to have some time alone with her to discuss the implications of giving Chloe an interview, so he waited while she went up to her room for her car keys and then accompanied her around the back of the hotel to the car park. She was chatting on about the times she'd stayed at the hotel with her husband, reminiscing about places they'd visited locally and people they'd met, when she stopped abruptly in mid-stride and looked about her with a puzzled expression.

'Is something the matter?' Buchanan inquired.

She remained frozen for another second and then clapped a hand to her cheek. 'Good God,

113

my car's been stolen!'

Buchanan's first thought was that she was making a mistake. There was an attendant in the kiosk at the entrance and he must have been aware who owned what car: it would be virtually impossible for anyone to drive away in a vehicle that was not his own. He said, 'Where did you leave it?'

She pointed to a slot currently occupied by a BMW. 'Right there. I parked it right there yesterday evening after dropping off you and Miss Fitzpatrick with the luggage.'

'You're absolutely sure?'

'Absolutely.'

'In that case we'd better have a word with the attendant.'

The guy saw them coming and must have realised all was not as it should be because he got out of his booth and came to meet them, hitching up his pants and tucking his shirt tidily into the waistband. 'Help you with something, sir?'

Buchanan, having been accused once too often of chauvinism, allowed Mrs Sullivan to speak for herself and she said, a little shakily, 'My car is not where I left it.'

The attendant nodded his head in greeting. 'Mrs Sullivan, the dark blue Hyundai, right?'

'That's right,' she said, suddenly starting to become more angry than shocked. 'It's gone.'

'Right over there by the hedge, ma'am.'

She spun round to follow his pointing finger and her jaw sagged. 'That's not where I left it. Why was it moved?'

A hint of amusement came and went swiftly in his eyes. 'That's where it's been all along, ma'am.'

'That's ridiculous. I left it over there on the far side.'

He smiled the sort of smile she must have hated: the sort of smile he kept for geriatrics. 'It's easy to make mistakes. It's such a big car park and all these bushes and hedges are confusing.'

'I'm not in the least confused,' she retorted, but the irritation in her voice wasn't matched by the little uncertain frown gathering her brow. 'I'm perfectly sure I left it where that BMW is now.'

'Never mind, we've found it now,' Buchanan inserted, noting that the attendant's car-side manner was beginning to show it's superficiality. 'Let's just be glad it wasn't stolen.'

She huffed and puffed about it all the way over to the car.

'I don't believe for a moment that man was telling the truth. I'm perfectly sure in my own mind that he moved my car to give the place to one of his regular guests. Just look. That BMW is in the shade, whereas we will be hot and stuffy till we're halfway to the village. Besides, that slot is not only closer to the hotel, you can even take a shortcut through the shrubbery to the side entrance. It's quite outrageous. I shall speak to the manager about it when we get back.'

Buchanan wanted to tell her to let the matter drop before she embarrassed herself further but he couldn't think of a way to phrase the advice without giving offence. However, time — or, more likely, self-doubt — had worked its magic by the time they arrived back at the hotel and she passed by the manager in the lobby without buttonholing him, which was something of a relief. Even more significantly, she made no reference at all to the matter in front of Fizz and, in deference to her feelings, neither did Buchanan. Nonetheless, he lost no time in bringing his confederate up to date with events as soon as they were alone together.

Predictably, her chief aim being to keep him from chucking in the towel, Fizz took the whole thing with a pinch of salt. 'Well, so what?' she said lightly. 'I bet you've done that yourself in a busy car park. It doesn't mean you've got Alzheimer's.'

'But she was adamant that she'd parked on the near side of the car park. She wouldn't let it go. And the fact that she didn't tell you about the incident — I don't know about you, Fizz, but it makes me suspect she was ashamed of it.'

'Well, of course she'd be embarrassed. She'd be worried that we might think she was losing her marbles, whereas it was a perfectly natural mistake.'

Buchanan was far from convinced. Furthermore, he found the manner in which Mrs Sullivan could morph between a well-sussed senior citizen and a total liability extremely unsettling and wished to God the real Mrs Sullivan would stop messing about and step forward. It would be interesting to discover which persona she'd present to Chloe this evening.

Apropos that arrangement, he asked Fizz, 'What are your plans for the evening?'

'Oh, I dunno.' She rolled her head lazily to and fro on the back of her arm chair. 'I thought I might help you to quiz this reporter guy.'

Buchanan had tried strenuously to avoid the use of the personal pronoun when referring to his new contact. He was well aware that he was being irrational but he didn't want Fizz even to be aware of Chloe till he had established whether or not he was in with a shout. Now, however, she had him cornered and it would be just too childish to flannel.

'Not a guy,' he said shortly and fished the business card she'd given him out of his wallet.

She sat up to take it from him and frowned at it. 'Age?' she demanded: a one-woman Gestapo.

'Early to mid-twenties.'

'Married?'

'Who knows.'

'I'd better sit in. You're too easily distracted.'

'Now you're being silly. There's absolutely no need for two of us to pick her brains. You know how I feel about overkill: it just puts people on their guard and you get damn all out of them.'

'It's not as if it's the first time you've spoken to her,' she mentioned, with a sweet reasonableness that warned him she was settling in for a war of attrition.

There was only one way you could hope to win such a war against Fizz and that was to blitzkrieg her, right at the beginning, and with such extreme prejudice that she knew you meant business. Otherwise she could nag on and on till

117

you were ready to give her all you possessed if only she'd shut up. Buchanan hated to be put in the position of acting like a tyrant but on this occasion he felt he had little choice in the matter, since Chloe's cooperation could prove vital to the case. It was a short but bloody battle, pretty brutal on his part, tenacious on hers, but in the end he forced her to accept his terms: she could be present at the interview but was forbidden to draw attention to herself in any way, to open her mouth unless directly addressed, and to consume anything even remotely alcoholic.

Buchanan was perfectly content with this agreement for almost ten minutes after it had been signed and sealed and then began to wonder if he had conceded rather more than he had intended. Fizz, even bound and gagged, could be a disruptive influence at any interview, constantly raising her eyebrows at his choice of approach, and conveying her disapproval by as little as a blank-faced glance out of the window. And what about his intention of keeping her away from Chloe? What the hell had happened to that?

He had got himself into a perfectly foul mood by the time Chloe arrived but the sight of her, cool and elegant, in a short, mint green dress and very high-heeled sandals, did wonders for his *joie de vivre*. The four of them retired to the sun parlour which faced the wrong way for the magnificent pink and gold sunset and was therefore virtually deserted.

Chloe settled herself into the corner of a

couch next to Mrs Sullivan, consented to a small glass of white wine, and crossed her slender brown legs in a manner that riveted Fizz's attention, not to mention Buchanan's.

'So,' she said, 'shall we start at the beginning, Mrs Sullivan? Suppose you tell me everything you can remember about that tragic evening and we'll see if it ties in with the known facts. That way, should there be any discrepancy, we can set your mind at rest about your own culpability.'

Mrs Sullivan's chin came up a little at that but she was in her grannie persona and merely smiled. 'There's no question about my culpability, Miss Miller, but I may perhaps be able to convince you of that.'

She launched into her now familiar account of her alleged crime and Chloe listened carefully, asking the bare minimum of questions and making only the occasional scribble on her notepad. As far as Buchanan could perceive, the second account was exactly as he had heard it the first time and delivered with the same, undeniably persuasive, conviction. It was quite evident, when she had finished her story, that Chloe was, if not completely won over, at least profoundly impressed. It was quite clear that she'd expected to interview some colourful old eccentric who could possibly be used to bring a touch of humour to a rehash of the Amanda Montrose case but Mrs Sullivan's certainty and self-possession had quickly demolished that idea. Her expression, as she glanced momentarily at Buchanan, was totally nonplussed.

'I must say, Mrs Sullivan, I'm very impressed

by what you've told me. You certainly have a comprehensive grasp of all the facts, as far I'm able to confirm them, and your knowledge of the topography around the scene of crime is spot on. The catch is, as I'm sure Mr Buchanan has already pointed out to you, all that information has already appeared in print and the fact that you are familiar with the scene of crime doesn't prove that you were there at the time Amanda met her death.' She frowned down at her almost pristine notebook and flicked it dismissively with one plum-tipped nail. 'You must try to remember some significant detail that was not in the general domain. Something more precise about the way Amanda was dressed, perhaps, or some item in her car that only the police know about.'

Mrs Sullivan looked disappointed, but not oppressively so since she had to be aware that Chloe was having difficulty in maintaining her scepticism. She made an expressive motion of her hand. 'Mr Buchanan and I have been down that road, Miss Miller. I'm afraid I took very little note of Amanda's appearance, or indeed of anything else. My recollection of the whole incident is clouded by my utter panic at what I had done: in fact, it's a miracle that I've retained the details I've just related to you. I fear there's nothing more to be dredged from my memory.'

'You never know what may turn up,' said Chloe, stretching out a hand to touch Mrs Sullivan's arm. 'I'll certainly keep looking out for anything that might jog your memory and I'll contact you if I find a possible lead — through

Mr Buchanan, of course.' She threw Buchanan a smiling glance, presumably to assure him that, now she'd assayed her half of the bargain and found it pure gold, she was happy to comply with all the conditions they'd agreed upon. However, a certain current of impatience, emanating from Fizz's corner of the group, reminded him that there was still the small matter of the quid pro quo.

He said, 'You must already know a lot more than we do about the Montrose family and their staff. It seemed to Fizz and I — rightly or wrongly — that there's something just a touch iffy about Ewan's choice of associates. Terence Lamb is one case in point and his gardener/handyman is another.'

'What have you on Oliver?' Chloe asked with quick interest, and for a moment she seemed to wear the same expression of intense concentration as Buchanan had witnessed on the sheep dogs that afternoon. The expression 'newshound' came and went in his mind in a split second, but it left an after-flavour that gave him pause.

He shook his head. 'We don't have anything on the guy: just a gut feeling, that's all. Fizz thought him more of a minder than a gardener and he was also suspiciously cagey about answering questions. Is he another of Ewan's ex-comrades-in-arms?'

'No,' she said, with every appearance of complaisance. 'He came with the Amanda package.'

'What's that?'

'Amanda arrived on the scene about five years

121

ago, complete with Oliver, wardrobe and enough money to drag Breichmenach estate out of the red. Before her arrival the place was quietly disintegrating because Ewan had neither the money nor the drive to do anything positive about saving it. Enter Amanda and in under a year she had the gardens more or less under control, the roof mended, the stables constructed and a viable horse breeding programme in operation. Say what you like about her, she knew what she wanted. Ewan was once again part of the huntin'-fishin'-and-shootin' scene and his beautiful lady wife was the first VIP you thought of to open the new tourist attraction or whatever.'

'Beautiful?' Mrs Sullivan asked, somewhat pointedly, and Chloe smiled.

'Something of an exaggeration, perhaps, but I daresay some people thought her pretty enough. When you have as much money as Amanda had you can do quite a lot to improve on what God gave you.'

'Where did her money come from?' Buchanan said.

'That's a good question. Maybe she'd married it. I've discovered that Amanda's past is pretty much *terra incognita*. I've traced her as far as Brighton, where she was on the committee of the local Arts Society and President of a couple of other charity organisations. But she was resident there for only a couple of years and there's a gulf of at least ten years between that point and the period Mrs Sullivan has just been speaking about, when she was married to William.'

'I think it's quite clear that she had something to hide,' Mrs Sullivan said. 'There were probably other victims of her selfish and immoral way of life. She was an evil woman, Miss Miller. I've told Mr Buchanan that and I think this attempt to cover her tracks is proof that I'm not exaggerating.'

'If that's true, Mrs Sullivan,' Chloe said, possibly in a mistaken attempt to comfort her, 'there could be plenty of other people who had a motive to kill her.'

There was a moment when Buchanan thought Mrs Sullivan was about to bite her nose off but before he could intervene she gave Chloe a frosty little smile and said, 'I've not the slightest doubt of that, my dear, but I got there first, more's the pity.'

Buchanan caught the eye of a passing waiter and circled a forefinger to order another round of drinks. Outside, the sky had faded to a translucent greenish blue against which the mountains were silhouetted like ramparts. He could still pick out individual plants in the rockery that bordered the foot of the lawn, at least fifty yards away, but the sun was well down already and it would soon be fully dark.

'There was, I believe,' he said, 'some suspicion that Amanda and Lamb were co-partners in the prostitution racket he was running in Edinburgh.'

Chloe zipped her notebook and pen into her bag before she answered. 'I heard that rumour, yes, but I never managed to establish any proof of its authenticity — and you can believe me when I say, I tried. It would have made the kind of story that would have paid my mortgage for the rest of the year. But no, I'd be risking prosecution if I even hinted at that in print. Even Terence Lamb continues to deny it.'

'He could be lying,' Mrs Sullivan said. 'Maybe Ewan Montrose has some sort of hold on him.'

'I'd be more inclined to think that if pressure had been brought to bear it would be the other way round.'

Chloe didn't appear to be going to elaborate on that remark so Buchanan asked, 'You suspect Lamb had something on Ewan?'

'Well, let's face it, Tam,' she said, using his given name for the first time, making him twitch guiltily and bringing a glint to Fizz's eye, 'he was allowed to crash in the chauffeur's flat above the garage whenever he chose to do so, he was given free access to some of the best salmon fishing water north of the Spey and nobody ever said a dicky bird to him for causing friction in the village and rolling home drunk and noisy at all hours of the night. He had a special relationship with Ewan, that's for sure, and I doubt if it was based entirely on the fact that they were old army chums. Ewan's not a bad guy but I just don't see him as quite that generous.'

'Even to someone who'd taken a bullet for him?'

'That's the story Terence puts about and it may be true but, then again, who can prove or disprove it? Terence certainly had a bit of a limp but he could have acquired that from falling out of his pram. I tried to research the claim once or twice but I don't have either the contacts or the clout to get into army records. Maybe you'll have more luck, and if you do, I'd appreciate it if you'd share it.'

The look she exchanged with Buchanan was clearly intended to be warm and friendly but it was like a woolly mitten on an iron fist. He'd have put a fiver on her having been voted The Girl Most Likely to Succeed when she left school, but the jury was still out on whether that was a good point or a bad one. She might be a bit over-ambitious but she had terrific legs.

He walked with her to the car park, using the opportunity for private conversation to establish communication links. 'I'll probably be up and down between here and Edinburgh till I get this business sorted out, so I'll keep in touch with you and maybe we can get together and compare notes from time to time.'

'That would be fine, Tam. I have a note of your telephone number so I'll give you a buzz if I come across anything that could be of interest to you.'

'Excellent.' He watched her, with a twinge of conscience, drive away down the drive with, probably, close to the legal limit of alcohol inside her but comforted himself with the thought that she didn't have far to go. The booze hadn't loosened her tongue much so it was unlikely to interfere too much with her driving.

Fizz, waiting for him in reception, was of the same opinion.

'Not giving away any more than she has to, is she? I wonder why not? You think she's another one with something to hide?'

'Like what?'

'How do I know? I'm just making the balls, it's up to you to fire them. It's your case after all.'

'Oh, is it? Well, it's nice to hear you admit that.'

'What a grouch you're getting to be. Come and buy me a huge amount of intoxicating liquor before I die of dehydration. Mrs Sullivan's retired to her room so we have the whole night to ourselves.'

'Count me out,' said Buchanan firmly. 'I'm getting up at the crack of dawn to have a bash at landing a salmon.'

'Oh goody. I'll come with you.'

Buchanan was too tired to fight. 'I thought you would,' he muttered, and went to bed.

9

Fizz had never been all that keen on fishing for salmon, probably because she had never been fortunate enough to hook one, but she perfectly understood, as would any angler, that actually landing a fish was not what it was all about. Ninety-nine per cent of the time the enjoyment came from communing with nature: from watching the sunrise or the sunset or the wildlife, from smelling the gorse or the dew-damp earth or the dark-brown musky scent of the river, from listening to the birdsong and feeling the sun on your face and letting your thoughts dwell on happy things.

All that, however, could be achieved without standing up to your bum in icy water and if she missed out on the ultimate thrill of besting the king of fish in its own domain so, almost always, did Buchanan.

She sat on a rock for a while, watching him setting up his salmon rod and choosing his fly, but when he waded out to midstream and started lashing the water to a foam she became quickly bored and decided to try working her way downstream to where the Blackwater met the Breich to see if she could get a closer look at the place where Amanda's body had turned up. This seemed like a good idea at the time, and remained so for maybe half a mile, but then the undergrowth became a thicket and the going got rough. She picked her way through the brambles for a bit longer, getting ever more irritated by the scratches and entangling branches, but finally she was brought to a halt at a spot where the walls of the ravine closed in, narrowing the river to a five yard-wide torrent and leaving no footing above the waterline. Up ahead, she could see the river widen again but even that section was choked with overhanging willows and scrubby bushes and looked pretty well impassable.

It looked, at close quarters, like a small tributary of the Amazon, and only confirmed what she'd suspected earlier: the police had taken so bloody long to find the body because that's what the killer intended. They'd have had to use boats a lot of the time, where the bank was blocked and, with the river swollen with melted snow, that would have been no easy task. Whoever had dumped Amanda's earthly remains where they did must either have been very familiar with the terrain or had researched every detail of the killing in advance. Mrs Sullivan claimed to have let the corpse slide over the brink of the ravine only yards from where the car went down, the torrent below carrying her victim downstream beyond the confluence of the two rivers, but a smarter killer would not have left things to chance. He or she would have made sure that Amanda's body ended up precisely where it would be extremely difficult if not impossible to locate, precisely as — coincidentally or not — it did. In fact, a less accessible stretch of terrain would have been hard to find anywhere in the country.

She shifted her scrutiny to the nearside bank and was just in time to see a flash of colour disappear among the trees above her head. Sugary pink. Not a colour worn much by men: not in this neck of the woods, at any rate. So: a woman. And a woman who didn't want to be seen.

Without pausing to think she called, 'Hi! I didn't see you there. Isn't it a lovely morning?'

Nothing moved for a moment, then a figure took shape like a wraith in the shadow of a bushy rowan. It was Marcia, welling out of a sugar-pink vest and looking just a little too surprised.

'Oh, it's you, Miss Fitzpatrick! Good morning. You're out early.'

'So are you. It's the best time of the day, don't you think?'

Marcia's face, as she watched Fizz scrambling up the bank towards her was about as welcoming as a clenched fist and her body language was claiming she had other things to be getting on with, so Fizz said, 'Buchanan's fishing that big pool up at the dog-leg. I suppose I ought to be getting back to him now in case he's ready to pack up.'

There had been a time — quite a long time, in fact — when she'd have kept Marcia's kind of woman well away from Buchanan. He was all too susceptible to sultry glances and pouting lips, and while Fizz had no objection to him looking, she had never been quite comfortable with the idea of his doing anything more than that. Why that should be, she had no idea, since she herself had no designs on the man. Not permanent designs, anyway, and Buchanan was a permanent sort of guy. All his liaisons in the past, as far as she had been able to ascertain, had been entered into with expectations of their developing into a lifetime relationship, marriage, two point four children and all the trimmings. Such a scenario was anathema to a girl like Fizz, who had been footloose and fancy-free for much too long to tie herself down, especially to someone as strait-laced and law abiding as Buchanan. That being the case, she had decided to let him make his own mistakes in future. Consistent with her own requirements, naturally.

'I'm going that way myself,' Marcia claimed, abandoning her escape plans as Fizz had calculated she would, and they picked their way out of the thicket and onto the fishermen's path that crested the embankment. Marcia didn't offer any explanation as to why she had left the path in the first place and Fizz, not wishing to put her on her guard, forbore to ask.

It was now going on for seven o'clock and there was enough heat in the sun to disperse the pockets of mist that had hovered over the low-lying areas an hour ago. Huge, jewel-coloured dragonflies were darting about looking as if they'd been spray-painted in ruby red, emerald green or sapphire blue and the surface of the river was hazed with hatching flies. It seemed almost a pity to sully the morning with the drudgery of quizzing Marcia but, Fizz reflected, that was part of what she was here for.

She tried to sound as if she were making casual conversation as she said, 'Have you been working at Breichmenach long?'

'A few years.'

'Like it?'

'It's okay.'

'What's Ewan like to work for?'

'I've had worse bosses.'

'How about Amanda? Did you like her?'

'What I saw of her. She didn't come round the stables much.'

Two whole sentences, Fizz thought. Now we're getting somewhere. 'She didn't ride?'

'No.' Back to square one.

'Not much of a country girl, huh? More of a city type.'

'I wouldn't say that.'

'No? What would you say?'

Marcia raised her heavy-lidded eyes from the path and gave her a long look, but said only, 'I never really knew her well enough to judge.'

'Oh, come on,' Fizz said, and laughed to show she was just joshing. 'You lived and worked within spitting distance of her for ages. You must have some idea of what sort of person she was.'

'I hardly saw her. She had her own interests.'

'What sort of interests?'

Marcia's steps quickened almost imperceptibly, giving Fizz cause to suspect that she was impatient to reach Buchanan and thereby instigate a change of subject.

'Oh, I don't really know,' she said. 'Committees and such like, I suppose.'

'Did she go away on trips sometimes or was she mostly at home?'

'She and Ewan were in the Seychelles last

131

October.' This was divulged with the willingness of a witness who knows damn well it's not what you wanted to know and was followed in the same breath by, 'Oh, there's Mr Buchanan now. It doesn't look as if he's caught anything.'

Fizz had, by that time, more or less given up on her anyway. She wasn't going to give much away but whether that was due to her natural sullenness or because she had something to hide was anybody's guess. No doubt Buchanan could get more out of her later. If he could keep his mind on the job.

He was standing in the shallows with his arms folded, apparently talking to himself but as Fizz descended the bank the trees thinned and she could see Ewan Montrose sitting on the rock she herself had recently vacated. He looked, to Fizz, more like a passing tramp than the proprietor of a country estate but that was probably due to the fact that he hadn't shaved yet and that his overalls were a dingy and faded grey.

Marcia hopped down the final two feet of embankment, all awobble, and undulated across the gravel towards them. 'Good morning, Mr Buchanan. No luck yet?'

Buchanan returned her greeting with the disinterested smile he used when he was interested as hell. 'Too bright this morning, I think. There's not much moving in there.'

'I was just suggesting he try up at the bridge,' Ewan said to Fizz, 'but as Tam says, a bit of cloud cover would make all the difference. The weather forecast's for showers later but the wind's still coming from the east so I doubt if we'll see much in the way of rain.'

'Unfortunately, I'm not going to be able to hang around for long,' Buchanan said, ignoring Marcia's flesh with a fixedness that fooled Fizz not at all and probably Marcia likewise. 'Mrs Sullivan wants us to be on our way immediately after lunch and there are one or two people I'm hoping to speak to before we leave.'

'Anyone I can help you contact?' Ewan asked.

'Not unless you have any allies in the CID who'd be willing to give me a few minutes.'

'Oh, that's no problem. All the officers on the murder squad were extremely considerate and sympathetic. Some of them even attended Amanda's funeral. The man you want to talk to is Inspector Haig, who led the inquiry. Hell of a decent bloke. He'll put an end to your old lady's imaginings if anybody can. Bring the two of them together if he'll let you and he'll close your case for you in minutes.'

'But maybe you don't want to close your case so quickly,' Marcia suggested, drooping her eyelids at Buchanan in a look that would have stripped paint. She moved round him to sit on everyone's favourite rock, consequently — and quite unintentionally Fizz was sure — giving him a better view of a cleavage like the Cheddar Gorge.

Her remark struck Fizz as being somewhat insulting: implying, as it did, that Buchanan would make more money by swinging the lead. However Buchanan translated it differently.

'It does give me an opportunity to escape from the big city for a while, that's true,' he said, with the kind of smile he didn't make use of very often — not in Fizz's presence anyway — but which made him look almost tasty. 'But, to tell you the truth, I'll be very happy to see the end of it. I have a suspicion that it's one of those cases that's going to end unhappily whatever I discover. It'll take something very convincing in the way of proof to persuade Mrs Sullivan of her innocence and, should the facts indicate that she's telling the truth, there won't be much job satisfaction in providing the evidence to put her behind bars for what would probably be the rest of her life.'

Marcia stirred restlessly. 'You surely can't believe there's a grain of truth in her claim?'

'Guilty till proven innocent, nmph?' Ewan answered her, grinning insanely at his own wit. 'It's certainly a novel situation but, as you say, a difficult one. My own mother was a little delusional in the last few years of her life. Thought people were watching her from aeroplanes, which was upsetting for all of us, especially as her retirement home was close to Prestwick airport. There was no way she'd abandon the idea, whatever we did to reassure her. Sad to witness that sort of thing, isn't it?'

'I'm not entirely sure we *have* witnessed it,' Fizz put in, just to stir things up a little. 'Mrs Sullivan is not by any means starting to lose her marbles, not by a long shot. She may be elderly but she's sharp as a tack and when you're talking to her she comes across as entirely level-headed. It would be just too easy to dismiss her story as a delusion.'

'But it has to be a delusion,' Marcia retorted. 'Every shred of evidence points to Terence Lamb as being the guilty party. You must know that.'

Buchanan nodded. 'That's true, as far as it goes,' he said, 'but Lamb is still protesting his innocence and, to be frank, I find myself wanting the answers to one or two questions that were never asked during his trial.'

'Really?' Ewan's face was arranged to depict only faint amusement but his eyes were intent. 'What questions would you have asked, nmph?'

Buchanan picked up his salmon rod from the rocks where he had laid it and started to take it to pieces. 'I'd have liked to know what Lamb's motive was for killing your wife. That area wasn't fully explored, was it?'

'Oh, I think it was,' Ewan said, glancing briefly at Marcia who didn't notice it, being engrossed in arranging the hem of her skirt to better effect. 'They'd never really taken to each other right from the beginning, you know. Tell you the truth, Terence wasn't easy to get along with — short-tempered, aggressive — and Amanda wasn't at all in favour of having him around the estate. It was actually she who suggested he might be happier someplace where there was more for him to do. Suggested it quite firmly, in fact. I don't think Terence had ever forgiven her for that.'

'Hardly a reason to kill her, however,' Buchanan said reasonably, but Ewan answered only with a shrug.

It was Marcia who said darkly, 'You don't know Terence.'

'No,' said Buchanan, 'but I'm looking forward

135

to remedying that in the near future. I'm told he was a well-known character in Edinburgh — well known to the Lothian and Borders police, anyway.'

'Exactly,' Marcia said. 'There was an officer from the Edinburgh drug squad here, helping the police with their inquiry. He told me Terence was trafficking drugs in a big way — '

'Allegedly,' Ewan put in with a twinkle.

' — and the police also suspected him of being involved in several muggings.'

'And of running a string of brothels, I believe,' inserted Fizz, determined to keep the cat among the pigeons. Buchanan's style of interrogation, which was invariably low-key and unthreatening, was all very well but she herself believed in getting down and dirty.

'So it would appear,' Ewan said smoothly, 'although it has to be said that no clear evidence exists to prove that he was personally involved.'

'Or Amanda either,' Fizz continued for him, and saw his face flush with angry colour.

'That lie,' he said through clenched teeth, 'was nothing but a rumour put about — I believe — by a local journalist who was simply trying to make a story more interesting. Totally outrageous.'

'Chloe Miller,' Fizz supplied.

'Precisely. Chloe Miller. An illiterate, spiteful, opportunistic little tramp who doesn't mind whose reputation she sullies as long as it gets her into print. She has caused endless trouble for Amanda and I over the years.'

'Any idea why?' asked Buchanan mildly.

Ewan sucked in a calming breath and looked

away across the river. 'Oh, trivial things, that's all. Just trivial things, nmph? She lives in the village and — well, if you've any idea what village life is like you'll know that there are always little feuds going on. Small matters like who's invited to sit on a committee and who's left out. I've forgotten what first got up Chloe's nose, but it wasn't worth remembering, I can assure you.' He made a great show of looking at his watch. 'Good Lord, it's after seven. Time we attended to the horses, Marcia.'

Marcia bounced obediently to her feet and smiled at Buchanan. It wasn't much of a smile, in fact it barely creased her cheeks, but it was packed full of implication. 'Will you have to come back to Breichmenach to complete your inquiries, Mr Buchanan, or will you have done all you can do by this afternoon?'

'Hard to say, at the moment. I have people to talk to in Edinburgh next week and it'll depend on what transpires from those conversations.'

'Well, you'll be very welcome any time you care to drop by,' Ewan said, waving his arm in the general direction of the house. 'Maybe we'll be able to fit in a few casts together, see if we can get you a fish.'

'Very kind,' said Buchanan and everyone smiled and waved and went through the usual parting motions like the best of pals.

Fizz waited till the other two were out of earshot before she said anything and then she murmured, 'I wonder how Amanda felt about having a slag like that hanging around her husband day in day out.'

137

Buchanan looked up from an appraisal of his fly case and gave her a hard look. 'What grounds do you have for calling her a slag?'

'Oh, come off it, Buchanan, she's gagging for it.'

'I doubt that very much and, even if she were, that doesn't make her a slag, does it? You're assuming the worst just because she's a foxy lady.'

'Foxy? You think? She's forty if she's a day.'

'I didn't notice any wrinkles.'

'In my experience,' Fizz said sweetly, 'you don't get wrinkles on a balloon.'

Buchanan pressed his lips together, making the muscles stand out at each side of his mouth. He was still sorting out his fly case and giving the task most of his concentration. 'Do you have anything against the woman, Fizz, or are you just being catty?'

'Just keeping your mind on the job, that's all. You'd be wasting your time with Marcia anyway. She's just checking out her pulling power. I reckon there's more going on between her and Ewan than meets the eye.'

He raised an eyebrow. 'I assume you have grounds for that suspicion also?'

'Sure I have,' Fizz stated, gaining his undivided attention at last. 'I thought you might have noticed that when she and I got here she said good morning to you.'

'Uh-huh. I noticed.'

'But she didn't say good morning to Ewan, did she? Now, I may be a nasty distrustful person but that says to me she'd *already* said good morning to him and if she had — mark this — it must have been helluva early in the morning and before he'd even shaved. I don't think it would be too wild a flight of fancy to suspect they'd shared a bed.'

Buchanan thought that over. 'It's a possibility, Fizz, no more than that. It's also possible they'd run into each other up at the house as they set out on their walks, or perhaps they had some early chores to do before they left.'

'They had still to see to the horses, or so Ewan claimed, and that would surely have been their first job of the day. Anyway, it's something we should bear in mind. If they'd had something going on before Amanda's death they'd both have to go on our list of suspects.'

'They were on it already,' Buchanan said tersely, and slung his fishing bag over one shoulder. 'And, by the way, don't think I missed the significance of their both choosing to walk the riverbank at the crack of dawn. It's very likely they were keeping an eye on both of us.'

They started down the path in the direction of the road where Buchanan had parked Mrs Sullivan's Hyundai, each of them pursuing their own train of thought. It seemed to Fizz as though their weekend's work had produced very little in the way of hard facts. If this had been a normal case she would have been tempted to focus her attention on Ewan Montrose. Not only was he the husband of the deceased — always the most likely person to have done the dire deed — but he could tick all the necessary boxes: means, motive and opportunity. Who stood to gain by the death of his rich wife? Who else knew exactly where and when to lay an ambush for Amanda? Who knew the river Blackwater better than he? Who — almost certainly — was pretty damn cosy with the voluptuous Marcia? The trouble was: most of those boxes could be ticked by Oliver, Marcia, possibly Chloe Miller, and even by Mrs Sullivan herself.

It was still hard to picture an old lady committing such a crime — one which, Fizz was certain, had to have been premeditated. Such direct and bloody violence was rarely associated with female killers who, for the most part, preferred to be elsewhere when their targets actually fell victim to the poison or wonky steering or explosion or whatever death had been arranged for them. Taking a hammer to somebody's skull was more of a guy thing, one would have thought, but you could never be sure. It was perfectly possible for Mrs Sullivan to drive up to Breichmenach, spend a few days picking out the perfect spot for her needs, and arrange a certain set of circumstances that would entail Amanda being at that spot at a time when she could be halted with little fear of another car coming along at the wrong time. That might not be the way she was claiming it had happened but, if she were involved at all, that's the way it panned out.

What it all boiled down to was perfectly straightforward: she was either making up the whole story from start to finish or she was guilty — not just of a crime of passion — but of a vicious and pre-planned murder.

10

The remainder of the morning was, for Buchanan, considerably less interesting. He did manage to secure a brief and hurried interview with the inspector who'd been in charge of the Amanda Montrose case but it afforded him little new information other than the predictable fact that the Inverness-shire police were confident that they'd got the right man for the killing. Inspector Haig, for all Ewan's rave review, was notably less accommodating than Sergeant Vivers had been and dismissed Mrs Sullivan as a crank without wasting a moment on reflection. As far as he was concerned — and who could blame him? — the case had been brought to a satisfactory conclusion and he now had more to do than help some nutter put a blot on his career by proving he'd made a mistake. Buchanan had expected nothing better, in point of fact, but one had to go through the motions.

He drove the Hyundai back to Edinburgh, Mrs Sullivan choosing to ride in the back with Fizz, so he had peace to sift through the information they'd managed to bring to light over the weekend, and it seemed to him that the old lady's money had been well spent, in terms of work done and facts gleaned. Unfortunately, he was no closer to establishing whether she was guilty or barking mad. Or, for that matter, both. On the one hand it did appear that there could be something going on at Breichmenach estate which the inhabitants didn't want to advertise, and which might or might not be connected to Amanda's death, but on the other hand Mrs Sullivan's loss of memory and eccentric manner had to be viewed as suspect. He wanted to believe her innocent but if she were innocent she was going to have to face the fact that she was delusional, and that was going to be hard for her to swallow. It was also going to be hard on the person who had to break the news to her but maybe, if it came to the bit, he could get Fizz to do that. Or maybe not. Fizz, at her most sympathetic, would probably phrase the information something like: Turns out you're nuts, Mrs S. Life's a bitch, huh?

As he half-listened to the two of them conversing sleepily on the back seat and tried, between-time, to make some sense out of the weekend's findings, he was entertained by recurrent images of Marcia in her pink vest: a vision which, while not akin to his usual fantasies, certainly made the miles slip by unnoticed. Longish in the tooth she might be, chubby she certainly was — by today's standards at least — but she was one hell of a woman. When you pictured her alongside Chloe they made about as striking a contrast as you could imagine but it had to be admitted that both had their points. Marcia might be dynamite in the sack — though Buchanan had to admit he had been fooled by that come-and-get-it approach before — but Chloe was dynamic, interesting, challenging, and that too was nice.

Lost in his own thoughts, he only vaguely registered Mrs Sullivan saying, 'My word, isn't that the loveliest thing you've ever seen?'

'What?' said Fizz's voice, sounding vaguely puzzled.

'Your bracelet, dear. How delicate the links are and the design of the clasp is so intricate. Let me have a closer look.'

Buchanan found himself intrigued by this comment because he was familiar with the bracelet in question. He had himself given it to Fizz for Christmas and, although he'd thought it quite pretty at the time, he'd chosen it because, while she might not appreciate it as an object of personal adornment, she could pawn it easily if she were ever in dire straits. He had been quite surprised to see her wear it from time to time and to have Mrs Sullivan's approval added to Fizz's seemed quite an accolade for his taste in costume jewellery.

Fizz, however, was less flattering. 'It's nothing special.'

'Oh, but it is. Look how the stones refract the sunlight. Look how the colours change as you turn it round.'

There was a long silence during which Buchanan tried to see Fizz's face in the driving mirror and eventually found her looking bemused and faintly worried. She seemed to be watching Mrs Sullivan as though the latter was still examining the bracelet and this was confirmed a good five minutes later when she said, 'Yes. Quite fascinatingly beautiful.'

'I'm glad you think so,' Fizz returned, and the

subject was dropped.

Peace reigned for some considerable time thereafter, a peace broken only by contented sighs from Mrs Sullivan, but a small uneasiness had taken root in Buchanan's brain. He had nothing substantial on which to base any misgivings, other than Fizz's perplexed expression, but he could almost feel her confusion wafting over the back of his seat like perfume. It was clear she found something bizarre in Mrs Sullivan's intense interest in her bracelet — so did he himself for that matter — and he could only hope to God that the old lady wasn't having another of her senior moments. It was beginning to get seriously alarming, the way she kept ricocheting between the rational and the slightly loony.

His suspicions were even further roused when, just after they'd passed Pitlochry, she started to sing. Not loudly or drunkenly: in fact you couldn't even make out the words, but the effect was extremely unnerving simply because it was so out of character. In either of her two personas, the Sweet Old Grannie or the Retired Teacher, she was invariably prim, with a marked sense of her own dignity. Such antic behaviour as this, which might have passed unremarked in Fizz or her cronies, sat on her like a kiss-me-quick hat on the Archbishop of Canterbury.

Fizz, this time, wouldn't even meet his eyes in the mirror, but started talking about various walks she'd done in the neighbourhood, and in such effervescent tones that Buchanan knew she was troubled. But that only seemed to make matters worse because, instead of diverting, or even drowning out Mrs Sullivan, the old dear went on singing throughout her spiel. This went on for some considerable time but just as things were becoming totally manic Mrs Sullivan spotted a McDonald's sign.

'Oh, stop, Mr Buchanan, please. There's a McDonald's up ahead at that service area. Let's have a hamburger.'

'A hamburger?' Buchanan uttered, shocked into incivility.

'A hamburger,' said Mrs Sullivan robustly, 'and chips. And a nice mint tea to follow; I have some sachets left.'

Buchanan took the slip road without attempting further argument, comforting himself with the thought that at least he might have the opportunity for a quick word with Fizz while Mrs Sullivan powdered her nose. Annoyingly, however, they both stuck together like Velcro and Fizz maintained such a cheerful aspect throughout their repast that he was left in no doubt that she was trying to make him think the whole affair was a figment of his imagination.

He had a coffee while they both fell on their food like ravening beasts — surprising behaviour only in Mrs Sullivan's case — and then got back on the road. He was curious to discover what further behavioural peculiarities he might be called upon to witness by the time they reached their destination, but both his passengers disappointed him by dozing off just south of Perth and remaining semi-comatose till he drew up in the mews outside his flat.

He was a little doubtful about letting Mrs Sullivan drive herself home from there but she now seemed totally *compos mentis* and assured him with great confidence that her nap had quite refreshed her and she was in top shape. She offered Fizz a run up to the Royal Mile, which she accepted with alacrity, but Buchanan intervened, claiming he wanted to swap notes with her and would see she got home safely.

'Okay,' he said, when they'd arranged to meet the following evening and finally taken their separate ways, 'let's go. We've got lots to talk about.'

He could see by her face that she knew she was on a sticky wicket but she must have been able to tell by *his* face that he wasn't going to be conned, because she said right away, 'Lots to worry about, huh?'

'What do you think?' he said. 'You were in a position to see her properly. Was she acting as strange as she sounded?'

He heard her sigh as she followed him up the staircase but he didn't hear her reply as Selena was waiting on the ledge of the fanlight and hit him like the seven-fifteen from Central as he crossed the threshold. By the time he had dislodged her from his sweater, greeted Pooky, awarded them their Kitty Chox, and returned to the lounge, Fizz had removed her boots and stretched out on the couch.

'Make mine a G&T,' she said cheekily. 'A large one.'

Buchanan was not inclined to refuse her since the thought of a Glenmorangie had been looming large in his imagination for the last half hour.

'So,' he said when they were settled down with their drinks, 'what about our client?'

'Oh, it's *our* client now, is it? When she's on the ball she's *your* client but as soon as she starts looking like she's away with the fairies she's *ours*.'

'Okay, *my* client. I couldn't tell what was happening between you two but it sounded a wee bit peculiar.'

She waggled a hand, palm down. 'Peculiar? I don't know. It's easy to leap to conclusions. She was certainly fascinated by my bracelet. I mean, really fascinated. Sat looking at it for ages, turning it around to catch the light till my arm was dropping off. I thought that was odd — not crazy, exactly, but a little excessive. But she seemed to me to be in an odd mood all the way from Inverness. Difficult to describe, actually, but . . . just *odd*. Sort of like a kid in a sweetie shop: happy-looking. Relaxed. Interested.'

'You think she had been drinking . . . or taking drugs?'

'That's the first thing I thought of. There was no smell of alcohol on her breath, I checked that, but she could very well have been at the mind-altering substances. She certainly had all the symptoms but, on the other hand, she could have been just very happy.'

'Or just very short of marbles.'

'Or she might be on some sort of medication for depression. Half the population of the western hemisphere's on Prozac these days.'

Buchanan found himself more than willing to believe any excuse Fizz could come up with. From hating the very idea of taking on the case he was now seriously against the idea of giving it up, as he would be bound to do if his client proved to be mentally unstable. Not only were the money and the working conditions attractive, the work interesting, and the side benefits considerable, but he had formed an unwilling respect for Mrs Sullivan and wanted to see her happy.

'We have to give her the benefit of the doubt,' Fizz argued. 'There's no way we can ask her to get a psychiatrist's certificate of sanity or even undergo tests. In any case, I don't see how any doctor could tell if she was having crazy turns unless she owned up to it, which she won't.'

Selina had stolen onto Buchanan's shoulder and was rubbing her cheek against his jaw to show that there were no hard feelings about being cared for by a neighbour for the past two days. He raised a hand to pat her and considered the problem for a few minutes and then said, 'I don't see what we can do but keep a close watch on her over the next few days and see if she does anything more convincing one way or the other. I'd like to have a good look around her flat for signs of substance abuse but there's little chance of that opportunity arising.'

'I could easily — '

'No, Fizz. Please don't even think about it. When I see Sergeant Vivers I'll ask him if he had any suspicions about Mrs Sullivan's habits. He ought to be able to spot a junkie with one eye closed after twenty years in the drug squad. I'll try to get an appointment with him tomorrow after I've had a word with Terence Lamb.'

'I thought I might sit in on that conversation,' Fizz said, eyeing him over the rim of her glass. 'A woman's touch, y'know? It would help to establish the truth of what we heard from Chloe — that his attitude to women leaves much to be desired.'

'Is that germane to the case?'

'It might be, since the victim was of the female persuasion.'

'Okay, you can come along but leave the talking to me.'

'I live only to do your bidding, O beloved of the gods.'

There was a time, he reflected, when he wouldn't have trusted her to keep her mouth shut in such a situation, but she was changing: becoming recognisably more sensible and less of a loose canon. Besides, he'd be glad to have her opinion on Terence Lamb.

He was not prepared, however, for the picture she made when he picked her up at the office the next day. Her business suit was a sober charcoal grey but the skirt barely skimmed her knees and there seemed to be — for such a small person — an extraordinary length of leg between the hem of her skirt and her three-inch heels. He was aware that she had modified her take-it-or-leave-it approach to fashion since joining the firm but he rarely saw her within office hours, and she invariably reverted to her jeans and Docs on the stroke of five. This new Fizz was an improvement, he supposed, but it depressed him nonetheless as the loss of her riotous mane of hair had depressed him. It seemed that the old Fizz was fading away like a dream and, although he had deplored almost everything about her, he had loved her too, in a way. Not the way a girlfriend had once accused him of loving her — that was ludicrous — but as a unique personality, a person so sure of herself that she regarded the opinions of other people with total indifference. Now he could see she was beginning to conform to the standards expected of a professional woman and he was saddened to think he may have played a part in bringing that about.

Terence Lamb was already in the interview room when they were shown in and his eyes went immediately to the sheer black stockings and sexy shoes,

'Well, well,' he said, ignoring Buchanan completely, 'things are looking up. You can pay me a visit anytime, flower.'

Fizz acted deaf, took a seat opposite him, and looked him over with the expression of someone clearing a choked drain. Buchanan had the distinct impression that, even had her legs not been hidden by the table, she would have crossed them anyway as she always did, and to hell with him.

He shook hands with Lamb, locking eyes with him for a moment to let him see he wasn't happy with his attitude, and then took his notebook and folder out of his briefcase.

'I imagine your lawyer had already outlined

my reasons for asking for this interview,' he said, finding Mrs Sullivan's photo among his other papers. 'This is the lady in question. Perhaps you've seen her before?'

Lamb took the photograph and held it carefully by the corners. His hands were big but long-fingered and sensitive, a good match for a face that came as a surprise to Buchanan, who had half-expected a brute. This guy was anything but brutish. In fact, his narrow features and sombre grey eyes gave him the look of an ideal butler; a blond, slightly superior, twenty-first-century Jeeves. He was about Buchanan's own age, give or take a couple of years, but looked flabby and unfit for a man in his early thirties and his skin had already taken on the greyish prison pallor.

It was obvious that he was doing his best to find some recognisable detail of the face in the photograph so Buchanan didn't feel the need to suggest looking for family likenesses.

'No. She's a stranger to me, but she looks sensible enough — bloody smart, in fact — so if she says she did away with Amanda Montrose, she probably did. Why the hell won't somebody take her seriously?'

'Well, that's what we're trying to do, Mr Lamb, and with your help we may very well succeed. I hope you'll feel able to be totally frank with me because if you are innocent as charged someone else is lying and the only way we're going to be able to sort out the sheep from the goats is to compare your version of events with all the others.'

'Believe me, mate,' Lamb said, eyes wide and ingenuous, 'when you're faced with a life sentence you forget about being coy. Like you say, we're both on the same side and I've got nothing to hide anyway, so ask away.'

'Okay.' Buchanan sorted out the list of questions he had prepared, conscious as he did so that Lamb was filling his eyes with the vision of Fizz. A small smile played about his mouth, regardless of the fact that her blank eyes stared straight through his and out the back of his head to the horizon.

'Let's start with your friend, Ewan Montrose. You and he served together in Northern Ireland, I understand.'

'The Royal Scots. Based in Crossmaglen.'

'And you somehow took a bullet that would have killed him?'

'Right.' His eyes tilted up at the corners as he grinned, destroying the complaisant image and replacing it with the sly, lascivious look of a minor fiend. There was something not quite right about the expression but, Buchanan's attention once alerted, it soon became clear what it was. Lamb had, at some time, undergone plastic surgery on his mouth and possibly on his eyes.

'Not intentionally — between us three, like,' Terence leered, 'but quite profitably, as it turned out. Ewan was about to step through a doorway but I pushed him aside and went first. Bloody near cost me my leg but it bought me six weeks in a private clinic and a cushy berth for a year or so after I was discharged. I'd have been in

152

hospital anyway, but Ewan's the old-fashioned kind, y'know: debt of honour, blood brothers and all that garbage.'

'I understand you took more than one would that night.'

'Right. An IED exploded before the lads could get me away and I took the full blast. Nothing life-threatening — just flesh wounds — but I was cut up pretty bad. Had to have a bit of plastic surgery where it showed but I've still got the scars all over my body.' He sniggered. 'Ewan used to cringe like a big lassie every time I took my shirt off.'

'But you only lasted two years in that cushy billet.' Fizz mentioned. 'What went wrong?'

Lamb fingered a swastika-shaped gouge in the table top. 'Nothing went wrong. I quite liked it there: the company, the fishing. Great in the summer, but the winters were dire. I just got bored, I suppose. You can't retire at twenty-nine, can you?'

Her expression showed little empathy. 'So you headed for Edinburgh and opened a chain of massage parlours.'

'Not all at once. Just a couple a year for the past three years.'

'Profitable?'

'Can't complain.'

'But, of course, they were actually brothels under another name.'

Lamb gave no evidence of being insulted by this allegation. 'As far as I'm concerned they were massage parlours. All my girls were trained masseuses. What they did on their own time was

153

none of my business and I certainly didn't charge for it.'

Buchanan considered accepting this claim at face value but he was quite sure a high percentage of immoral earnings found their way into Lamb's exchequer either as rent for premises supplied or under some other guise. Not much of it would appear on his books, that was certain.

He said, 'How did you get along with Ewan's wife? Did she resent you?'

Terence spared a lingering glance at Fizz as though to remind himself of her charisma and then met Buchanan's eyes and shrugged. 'I got along just fine with Amanda. No problem.'

'Was there . . . forgive the intrusion, but was there ever anything between you?'

That struck him as amusing. 'Me and Amanda? No way. Not that I didn't fancy her, I don't mind admitting it, but Amanda was the original Ice Woman. Siberia. Try anything on with that lady and you'd've been risking frostbite — and in a very painful place.'

He leered across the table at Fizz who continued to stare through him with no expression on her face whatsoever.

Buchanan re-shuffled his papers and said carefully, 'I'm sure you'll have heard the rumour that Amanda was your business partner. I know you've denied it more than once but if I'm to overturn the verdict against you . . . '

He broke off as Lamb emphatically shook his head.

'No way. Neither Amanda nor Ewan knew anything about the massage parlours. When I decided to move to Edinburgh I originally planned to start my own security firm and as far as either of them knew, that's what I did. They gave me a cheque when I left — a sort of golden handshake — and it happened to be Amanda who signed it. Could've been either of them — they had a joint bank account for that sort of thing — but it was Amanda on that occasion and, of course, somebody managed to find out about it. Looked bad, I'll admit that, but Amanda never knew what I actually spent it on.'

'How much was it for?'

The tip of Lamb's tongue emerged to moisten his lower lip before he said, 'Ten thou.'

Buchanan blinked. 'Ten thou? That's extraordinarily generous, surely?'

'A drop in the ocean to Amanda. She was rolling in it.' Lamb leaned back in his chair and smiled smugly. 'Old Ewan was on his uppers when she came along: trying to keep Breichmenach House from falling down with bugger all other than his army pay. Everything he's got now he owes to Amanda.'

'But having got it,' Buchanan wondered, 'could Ewan have been considering moving on to fresh fields and pastures new?'

Lamb's evil grin spread across his features. 'Moving on — to Marcia, you mean? The delectable Marcia? Well now, I've wondered about those two myself. She puts it about a bit, does Marcia, I can vouch for that personally, but if old Ewan's getting his share of that he's being very canny about it and she's saying nowt. I bet he is though, don't you?'

The question was addressed to Fizz who declined to offer an opinion.

'Doesn't say much, does she?' Lamb asked Buchanan. 'But she's a real doll, if you like them young.'

Buchanan ground his teeth. He'd dealt with Lamb's type a hundred times and knew that open confrontation only complicated matters but, all the same, he could feel the skin of the man's throat beneath his hands.

'Okay,' he said, drawing Lamb's eyes back from Fizz to himself. 'Just one more thing. The matter of the forensic evidence found on your shoes. I see from the trial transcript that your advocate was unable to offer any explanation of how it got there. Any further thought on the matter?'

'Only that some bastard put it there,' Lamb said, and the muscles about his mouth twisted viciously with the words. 'I was up at Breichmenach around the time Amanda was killed — whenever *that* was! She'd been dead so long by the time they found her that they can only give an approximate date. What good's that? Doesn't mean a damn thing, does it, but they managed to make it look like I was in the area the same day! Okay I went up there for a couple of days in March but I was fishing the Blackwater at least a mile upstream from where she was found, never went anywhere near that gully. Nobody in their right mind would fish there. If I ever find out who pinned this thing on me I'll gut the fucker.'

'So, who framed you? You must have some idea.'

Lamb shook his head wordlessly, too angry to speak.

'Come on, Terence,' Buchanan nagged. 'Who had it in for Amanda? Who knew you'd been in the area and were the best person to frame? Who had access to your shoes? You must have some ideas. Ewan? Oliver?'

This evoked no reply other than a deep-throated growl. Lamb's rage was an almost palpable thing reaching across the desk and Buchanan was hastened in his departure by the thought that maybe he'd been wrong in bringing Fizz along. He zipped his papers back into his briefcase but before he could make his farewells Lamb leaned forward and addressed Fizz.

'You've got a great face, babe,' he said, eliciting not the slightest response. 'I could put you in the way of making a lot of money, you know. You're sitting on a fortune.'

Fizz's eyes refocused on his as she pushed her chair back from the table. 'Money can't buy happiness, Mr Lamb.'

He grinned like a wolf. 'In my business it can.'

Buchanan reluctantly offered him his hand and got Fizz the hell out of there. The air outside seemed infinitely fresher than it had done half an hour ago.

'You tolerated that extremely well, Fizz,' he had to say but she merely tilted her baby face up to his with a smile.

'What a wanker,' she murmured sweetly. 'If he was trying to make me blush he was about twenty years too late.'

157

11

Fizz had not originally intended to accompany Buchanan on his promised visit to Mrs Sutherland in the evening. What changed her mind was not, as Buchanan alleged, the thought of the Amontillado, but a desire to re-open the question of the water weed on Lamb's shoes. If Lamb was telling the truth about being framed — and his rage had appeared very convincing — somebody had planted that evidence. Yet Mrs Sullivan denied having done so. This anomaly opened up a whole new avenue of possibilities. Either Mrs Sullivan was, for some unfathomable reason, lying or Lamb was lying or Amanda's actual killer was neither of them but some unidentified third person. A bit problematic whichever way you looked at it.

When they drew up outside Mrs Sullivan's house they could see her sitting in a corner of the back garden keeping watch for them down the path at the side. Her bungalow was the last house in the street and had a bigger plot of land than the others as well as a pleasant outlook over the park. Edinburgh house prices were shooting up these days and solid old pre-war properties like this were changing hands at outrageous prices, so the old dear wouldn't have to worry about being able to afford a nice retirement home if it came to the bit.

She beckoned them in without rising from her

chair. 'Forgive an old lady for not getting up, my dears. All our gallivanting about has left me a little tired today, but I've been impatient to see you and to hear the results of your talk with Terence Lamb. You did see him, I hope?'

'Oh yes,' Fizz assured her, dropping into an overstuffed basket chair beside her. 'We spent half an hour with him, which was about twenty-five minutes longer than anyone would want to.'

Mrs Sullivan sighed and compressed her lips. 'I'd heard he was an unpleasant person. I do hope you weren't distressed.'

'I'll get over it.'

The only remaining chair was a sun lounger which, even in the upright position, was so low that Buchanan's knees were folded up to the level of his armpits. It wasn't easy for him to maintain his dignity but you could see he was trying. He said, 'You're quite right, Mrs Sullivan, Lamb is a totally despicable character but I have to say he comes across as pretty genuine when he claims to have been framed for Amanda's murder.'

'Well, of course he does, poor man.' Mrs Sullivan agreed. 'He wasn't involved with it in any way.'

'The thing is, you see,' Fizz pointed out, 'the thing that puzzles me is that, if neither you nor Lamb introduced the water weed evidence, someone else must have done so. That means we're now looking for someone who had something against Lamb and wanted — or needed — to have him out of circulation for a long time.'

'Yes, of course, I quite see that.'

'Which means, and I'm sorry about this, that I have to ask you again: are you willing to swear that you had nothing to do with it?'

Mrs Sullivan sighed deeply and twisted the marriage ring on her wrinkled finger. 'My dear Miss Fitzpatrick, if only I could convey to you just how much I wish I *had* faked the evidence. It would be so much easier to prove my guilt. I could almost wish I had lied to Sergeant Vivers when he asked me about it only, of course, I'd have had to back up my claim by telling him how I'd gained access to Terence Lamb's shoes and I'd no idea where he lived or, indeed, who he was.' She looked away across the hedge to where a bunch of kids were screaming around with a football. 'It's just terribly unfortunate, for both Terence Lamb and myself, that this person should throw a spanner in the works. If it hadn't been for him — or for her — the police would have kept on with their investigation till something turned up that would have pointed to me. I'm sure I must have left some evidence somewhere. The police are so clever nowadays it doesn't seem possible that I could have committed the perfect crime.'

'Well, it seems you have, Mrs Sullivan,' Buchanan said, amusement flickering behind his eyes, 'but we'll keep foraging around for some sort of lead, at least for a few days. I'm seeing Sergeant Vivers later on this evening so I'll try to persuade him to take another look at the evidence.'

'Well, I do wish you luck, Mr Buchanan, but I

have to say that I didn't find him an easy man to influence.' She turned to Fizz and laid a light hand on her arm. 'My dear, if you would be so kind, I've left some refreshments on the table in the kitchen and I'm sure you and Mr Buchanan must be in need of them. What will it be, Mr Buchanan? Coffee? Tea? Or something a little stronger?'

Buchanan having plumped for coffee, Fizz started across the grass to the back door and noticed, halfway there, that the glass in one small panel was broken. Someone had nailed a piece of wood across it, a shoddy solution that struck her as out of place in Mrs Sullivan's well-tended home. She went ahead with Buchanan's coffee and carried it out together with the tray of sherry and biscuits Mrs Sullivan had prepared.

They were discussing Amanda's association with Mrs Sullivan's son when she got back and she was in time to hear Buchanan say, 'It might help if we were able to speak to someone who knew your son and his wife at that time. Can you give me a list of any friends of yours or of theirs who could talk to me about them?'

Mrs Sullivan sat up and moved some magazines from the garden table to make way for the tray. 'Thank you, Miss Fitzpatrick. That was most kind. Do help yourself, Mr Buchanan. I baked these this afternoon. Now then, what friends can I suggest? Dear me, it's not so easy as one might think.' She sipped thoughtfully at her sherry. 'I never came into contact with their friends, although goodness knows they seemed to have a great many. And my friends . . . well

161

there wasn't anyone I felt I could confide in. It's a strange thing but after my husband died I realised that most of our circle consisted of colleagues of his and their wives. Without him, I really had little in common with any of them and I allowed our friendship to dwindle away. I made new friends, naturally, but one tends not to share one's woes with new friends. Still, some of them must have met Amanda. I'll look through my address book and see if it jogs my memory.'

Buchanan nodded and helped himself to a biscuit and Fizz, spotting a gap in the conversation, said, 'I see you've lost a panel in your back door, Mrs Sullivan.'

'Oh, those children!' she exclaimed, with mild irritation. 'They're forever tramping down my bedding plants to get their balls back. Every day we have words about it. It's the price one has to pay for having such a pleasant outlook over the park. The man's coming tomorrow to mend it.'

'Were you here when it happened?'

'No dear, I was in town having my hair done for our trip to Inverness.'

'So how do you know it was the kids who did it?'

She gave a short laugh. 'Because the cricket ball was lying on the floor under the table when I got back. The little monkeys! I should have confiscated it instead of throwing it back over the hedge.'

Buchanan got up and went over to have a closer look at the damage. He said, 'I expect you took a look around to make sure nothing was missing?'

'No, no, no dear. It wasn't a break-in or anything like that. I'd have noticed. Goodness me, there were plenty of valuable objects lying around for anyone who wanted to take them. My gold fountain pen. The silver photograph frames. I even keep a dish with a few notes and coins on the corner of the dresser, just in case I have to pay for something at the door. Besides, the boys would never do anything like that. They're little ruffians but there's no harm in any of them.'

Buchanan stifled a sigh. 'It still doesn't look very secure, Mrs Sullivan. You took a chance leaving it like this while you were away from home. It's an invitation to a burglar. Anyone could kick the board free and slip a hand in to open the door from the inside.'

'I had no choice but to leave it,' she said with a touch of militancy. 'Just you try to find a joiner on a Saturday! I had to hammer that board on myself but it seemed quite secure to me.'

'Well, if you'll give me your hammer and nails I'll try to make it more so. Better safe than sorry.'

It took him a good ten minutes to fix it to his satisfaction and by then they were running late for their date with Charlie Vivers. Fizz had barely time to swallow her second glass of sherry in one gulp before they were scooting across town to Vivers's local where Buchanan had arranged the rendezvous. For all that, they were first to arrive and had waited quarter of an hour at an outside table before Vivers strolled up wearing a beat up brown leather jerkin and jeans.

He was short and thick set with a gut that was starting to hang over his belt and the sort of face

163

you end up with when you've smoked too much and drunk too much for the past forty years: high-coloured, coarse-skinned and disillusioned. Buchanan made the introductions and then went in to the bar to get the drinks.

Vivers started to make small talk while they waited for him to return but it was quite apparent to Fizz that he was battling a strong desire not to laugh. Eventually, she couldn't resist saying, 'What's so funny, Charlie?' and his face cracked into a wide grin.

'Your mate, Ian Fleming,' he said, shaking his head in mock reprehension. 'He has a crazy sense of humour. The way he described you . . . well, I didn't expect to be meeting a very amiable young lady, let's put it like that.'

Fizz could well imagine how Ian Fleming would have described her: he'd probably advised Vivers to make his will before leaving home. Pity he didn't warn him about the sheep's clothing.

'Yes,' she said shyly, wishing she still had a long curl to twist around her finger, 'He's very naughty, isn't he? He's played tricks like that on me, lots of times.'

Buchanan, at that moment arriving back with the drinks, gave her a raised eyebrow as though he had detected a bum note in her tone, but she just gave him a 60-watt smile and let him worry.

Charlie made a large hole in his malt whisky before saying, 'I don't know why you're wasting your time with that daffy old woman. Christ, I wish I had a pound for every one of those I've had to listen to over the years.'

'Well, one of the reasons I'm dealing with her,'

Buchanan said, 'is because I'm being paid to do so. I also rather admire Mrs Sullivan and I don't like to see her being tortured by what is very probably an illusion. But the third reason is that it's just possible that the Inverness-shire CID got it wrong and put an innocent man in jail for life.'

'Well, I wish you luck, Tam, but I'm as sure as I can be that you're wasting your time. There's not a chicken's chance in Somalia that your client's telling the truth. I talked to her for three-quarters of an hour, believe it or not, which is longer than I'd have given most cranks I can tell you, and didn't get a word of sense out of her. Oh, she'd done her homework all right. Ten out of ten for the facts. I think she may even have visited the SOC, but she couldn't tell me a thing other than what had appeared in the papers.' Vivers sank the remaining third of his whisky and reached into a pocket for a packet of Embassy. 'Quite a lot of them are like that. I can't figure out what makes them do it. Some of them probably want their fifteen minutes of fame, some of them just associate so closely with the killing that they really believe they did it. It's a funny business.'

Buchanan caught the eye of a waitress who was clearing the table next to them and signalled another round. 'I'd be interested to know why you gave Mrs Sullivan more time than you normally would,' he said. 'Was it because you found her story, in spite of everything, just a fraction believable?'

There was a tiny pause while Vivers lit his cigarette and savoured his first drag. Then he

165

smiled, almost bashfully, making his eyes crinkle up round the corners. 'You want the truth, Tam? Well it turns out that beneath this crusty exterior there beats a heart of pure mush. I was taken by the old dear, like you were. She's a real sweetie, isn't she? Like the dear old grannie you might have had if your grampa'd been a bit more choosy. I knew she was nuts from the word go, sure I did, but I was sorry for her. Same as you. Didn't want to hurt her feelings.' He accepted delivery of another malt and gave it his immediate attention. 'It was a mistake, of course, it always is in these cases. She was on the phone every other day after that, wanting to know what progress I was making, pestering me to talk it over again, suggesting possible lines of inquiry. I couldn't get rid of her.'

'Apparently Inspector Haig also had people claiming responsibility,' Fizz remarked, and saw by the faint twisting of his lips that she'd said something he didn't like. What was it? The mention of other nutters? Or the reference to Inspector Haig?

He swallowed his bile and said, 'One was a down-and-out looking for a lodging, one was a care-in-the-community case who claimed Amanda Montrose was in the pay of a foreign power. You get all sorts.'

While Fizz tried hurriedly to phrase another sentence with the name Haig in it, just to observe the effect, Buchanan beat her to the draw.

'But, when you interviewed her, you didn't have any doubts about Mrs Sullivan's sanity, did you?'

'Well she wasn't making a lot of sense, let's face it.' Vivers picked a piece of cigarette paper off his top lip and regarded it for a moment as though it were a valuable piece of evidence. 'I'm not saying I thought she should be in a strait-jacket but I certainly had serious doubts about her current state of lucidity. I remember wondering once or twice if she'd been smoking pot.'

Buchanan's face showed he didn't like that. Too close to the truth maybe. 'Pot?' he said. 'At her age?'

'Sure, at her age,' Vivers grinned. 'What age is she? Sixty-five? Seventy? That would make her thirty-something back in the Swinging Sixties. Plenty of those hopheads are still on the weed — if they haven't moved on to something stronger by now. Keeping me in a job, they are.'

He slugged back the dregs in his glass and let Buchanan wave to the waitress again for a refill. At the rate he was putting it away, which was faster than even Fizz could keep up with, their tab was going to raise Mrs Sullivan's eyebrows. Those malts were doubles and they were already putting a shiny glaze over Charlie's pouchy eyes. Another few cc and he'd be an open book.

While his attention was on a passing stretch limo full of screeching party girls, Fizz exchanged a meaningful glance with Buchanan who indicated that he'd seen what she had seen and had drawn the same conclusions. She gave him a few minutes to relax and then said, 'Did you make any inquiries into Mrs Sullivan's background?'

Vivers tipped his head on one side and regarded her with a look she was familiar with: a sort of besotted, who-could-expect-any-hint-of-brains-from-such-a-poppet look. 'Listen pet, when you're in the middle of a murder inquiry you don't have time to waste checking out the loonies.'

'But, you weren't actively involved with the case, were you Charlie? You were really just roped in because you were familiar with Terence Lamb and his modus operandi.'

'That's right,' he said, with a marked crispness of tone and took a large slug of his newly-arrived malt. 'But I was instrumental in bringing the case to court. You didn't read *that* in the papers, did you? All down to the brilliant Inspector Haig, wasn't it? The murder had Lamb's fingerprints all over it but Haig would never have seen that if I hadn't been there to point them out to him.'

'What fingerprints?' Fizz probed.

Vivers waved a slightly uncoordinated hand, narrowly missing Buchanan's bottle of tonic water. 'Just over a year ago Lamb's girlfriend, Colleen Wilson, was found in a rubbish skip down by Leith docks, her head beaten in with a hammer. Lamb was in Aberdeen at the time, with six friends — including a Justice of the Peace — willing to swear he hadn't been out of their sight for three days. We couldn't make a case against him but I can tell you this: there were rumours that the dead girl had made unspecified threats to Lamb the week before.' He locked eyes with Buchanan and shook his head lugubriously. 'I knew that guy, Tam. There were things he did I couldn't even tell you about in front of this little girlie here. Women were just objects to him. Just toys to be used and thrown away.'

His voice drifted into silence and he sat staring into his whisky for a moment while Fizz, and probably Buchanan, waited for him to be a little more indiscreet. Then he said, as if to himself, 'Fishing? Terence Lamb keen on fishing? Pull the other one. If he was making such frequent visits to Breichmenach House it wasn't salmon he was after, he was getting his leg over Amanda Montrose — or talking business with her — or both.'

'You believe the rumours about their being business partners?' Buchanan prompted as Vivers's concentration began, visibly, to drift away.

'Bloody sure they were. I've been trying to prove it for years. And not just in the brothel business: they were into hard drugs, skunk, cocaine, heroin. Peddling the stuff round the universities and the clubs, paying their girls in fixes too, like they all do.' His mouth turned down bitterly. 'I've seen some of those lassies coming out of Touch-and-Go and his other places toked up to the eyeballs. Some of them barely out of their teens.'

'Did you have any evidence at all to prove Amanda's involvement?'

Vivers looked sick. 'Nothing that would stand up in court, no, but we've witnesses who've seen them together in Edinburgh more often than would be likely for social reasons. Sneaky, hole-and-corner meetings in a car over at the shopping mall at Cameron Toll but nothing lovey-dovey going on, just po-faced conversation. Also, when you start looking into her background it turns out to be very obscure. You go back a few years — ten or twelve — and you get into a real cat's cradle of leads that go nowhere. We're pretty sure she was in Greece for several years before that — ' he grinned suddenly, his face wrinkling deeply at each side of his mouth, ' — not in London, as our aged friend insists — but you could lose a supertanker in Greece without the slightest effort. God knows what she was up to there or what name she was using. Oh, I know what you're going to say: that her past isn't necessarily murky just because it's difficult to track down. Damn right, and don't I know it but, when it's Amanda Montrose's past you're dealing with, you can bet your life it's no accident you're getting nowhere.'

He made to lift his glass to his lips again but, after a brief skirmish between discretion and the allure of free booze, he changed his mind halfway and lit up another fag instead. 'It's not just the young lives these people destroy, the families they break up. It's not just the terrible things their victims are forced to do for the price of the next hit. The whole drug scene is built on a foundation of violence and corruption. Damn near every crime in Edinburgh, from shoplifting to GBH, has drugs at the root of it. These people, the Terence Lambs of this world — aye, and the Amanda Montroses too — the more of

170

them that get a hammer through their skulls the better for all of us.'

He stretched an arm, made a show of checking his fancy watch and tossed back the remains of his drink. 'That's me. I'm away home to the wife. Its been nice talking to the pair of you but — listen, Tam — you're on a wild goose chase if I ever saw one. Do yourself a favour and quit while you're winning. You can't prove a negative.'

Buchanan got to his feet to shake hands. 'I'll give it serious thought, Charlie, but if I need to talk to you again . . . ?'

'Happy to help. You can catch me here every night about this time. I usually drop in for a quick one when I come off shift.'

He gave Fizz's cheek a quick pat — too fast for her to snap at his fingers — and headed off down the street with the slow and careful stride of a man pissed as a newt but hoping no one would notice.

'Well,' Fizz remarked, watching his retreat, 'I'd say that was worth a few drinks, wouldn't you?'

'Quite enlightening,' Buchanan admitted. 'He was a lot more forthcoming than I'd expected him to be. Ian Fleming must have given us a good reference.'

'Maybe,' Fizz said, thinking this was highly improbable. 'Or maybe he'd secretly love it if we proved his pal Haig had made a boo-boo. He's pretty pissed-off at not getting his fair share of the glory, did you notice?'

Buchanan raised his eyebrows but avoided admitting he'd missed the inference by saying, 'He certainly likes his drink. It's not hard to see why he suggested meeting at his local instead of at police HQ.'

'Or why he's so willing to be helpful.' Fizz finished her G&T — her third, but small ones — and looked pathetically at Buchanan.

'Three's your limit, Fizz, you know that,' he said, which was rubbish. 'Let's take a walk round the Meadows. I feel like stretching my legs.'

It crossed Fizz's mind to buy another drink for herself, just to let him see that she could do as she pleased, but she'd never bought her own booze in her life and didn't want to start any more bad habits.

12

The sun had sunk below the level of Arthur's Seat as they walked round from Tollcross to the Meadows but there were still people playing pitch and putt on Bruntsfield Links and the usual bunch of joggers, footballers and cricketers on the Meadows, squeezing the last unforgiving minute out of the day. Cherry petals littered the grass and piled up, like drifts of pink confetti, in the gutters and everything glowed green and gold and rosy in the evening light.

'We should do this more often,' Fizz said, swinging her arms energetically. 'We should bring a couple of your golf clubs and have a game of pitch and putt.'

Buchanan looked at her. 'Don't you have any other friends to do things with?'

'Sure,' she said and took his arm, hugging it close and hanging on it heavily, smiling up at him with fiendish glee, 'but I like you best Buchanan.'

'Get off!' He shook himself loose, only partly feigning a very real alarm. It might be just a joke to Fizz but there was something very potent in the feel of her soft breast against his elbow; and the smell of green apples that emanated from her hair had always had a localised effect on him similar to that of an electric cattle probe. Neither of which was exactly distasteful in itself but one had to bear in mind that what one was dealing with here was a woman whose name was Tribulation and that giving way to unchaste thoughts about Fizz was analogous to using a hair dryer in the bath.

He said, 'I don't know how you feel after talking to Charlie but I'm depressed as hell.'

'Why?' She stared at him. 'You think he's right about Mrs S being a crank?'

'No, not that. I mean, she may well be a crank — she probably *is* — but there's a lot more to this business than we've even suspected. I'm starting to think there could be some seriously nasty forces at work behind the scenery.'

'Really?' Fizz considered that for a moment. 'You're thinking about Terence Lamb's activities, are you?'

'I don't know what I'm thinking about,' Buchanan admitted, 'but there are things that give me twinges. That smashed pane in Mrs Sullivan's back door, for instance. It could, of course, have been the kids like she says it was, but you're forever telling me that coincidences like that hardly ever happen, and for once I tend to agree with you. To me the business has more the look of someone using the park's proximity to make the damage look innocent.'

'Yes, okay, I thought that too but I can't imagine why anyone would want to break into her home. To search for something? What could they be searching for?'

Buchanan shook his head without answering. The possibilities were few and Fizz could identify them as easily as he.

'They could have been trying to check up on

her,' she offered, confirming his opinion of her shrewdness. 'Maybe trying to confirm that she's who she says she is. Or . . . ' One hand floated out in front of her as though she were feeling her way through a fog. 'It could be that they were after something specific . . . something she's not telling us about. You'll have to confront her with this, Buchanan. She could be holding out on us.'

She hardly needed to point that out since he had come to that conclusion before they had even left Mrs Sullivan's garden, but it was something he had decided to do, if possible, without Fizz's assistance. If Mrs Sullivan had been withholding information he'd have to rap her over the knuckles and that was best done on a one-to-one basis. There was also a slightly better chance of getting her to confide in him if she didn't have a capacity audience.

'I don't believe she's been lying to us,' he said, turning into Middle Meadow Walk which would take them back to his car. 'You could tell she was confident that there was nothing sinister in the broken glass. If she does have something that someone else wants I'll lay you ten to one she isn't aware of it. However, I'll talk to her tomorrow, if I feel I can do it without putting her in a panic, and see if she can suggest anyone who might have an interest in her belongings.'

They walked on in silence through the trees, entertained by the music of a lone piper whose wife, no doubt, had refused to let him practise indoors. After a while Fizz returned from wherever her train of thought had taken her.

'Looks as though there could've been quite a

few people willing to carry out a little carpentry on Amanda's skull,' she said, with her usual delicacy of phrasing. 'Not just her husband or her husband's fancy woman, or even the likes of Oliver, they're easy to put under the microscope, but what if she fell foul of one of her druggie contacts — a supplier, maybe, or even one of her customers. She could have been carrying a fortune in heroin, or whatever, and somebody killed her to get it. Or maybe it was one of Lamb's 'masseuses' who'd taken all the abuse she felt like taking. Or even, when you think about it — '

'Don't, Fizz. Please don't think of any more possibilities, things are depressing enough without listing dozens of possible perpetrators, none of which we have the remotest chance of identifying.'

'We could always suss out the massage parlours,' Fizz submitted but he shied away from that idea as she could certainly have foretold he would.

'No chance, Fizz,' he said strongly, still traumatised by his last encounter with Edinburgh's vice scene, which was a good eighteen months ago at least. 'I absolutely refuse to go near one of those places ever again and it's no use your volunteering to talk your way in because you wouldn't get over the threshold. Women — non-participating women — are taboo.'

'Really' she said, innocently. 'You appear to be very au fait with the pros and cons . . . to coin a phrase.'

Buchanan refused to dignify that thrust with an answer. 'So don't get any ideas about taking unilateral action along those lines,' he added as though she hadn't spoken, 'because it'll get you nowhere.'

'No, I guess not,' she said and sighed gustily. 'I don't suppose it would be a very profitable exercise anyway.'

Buchanan was glad to hear her give up the idea so easily because, at one time she'd have been straight in there, welcome or not, lying herself black in the face and risking consequences that were too horrific to contemplate. He took this as a sign that she was growing up at long last and learning some common sense. Which was good news.

★　★　★

Fizz had no intention of sussing out Touch-and-Go until at least eleven the following evening so there was no real reason why she shouldn't accompany Buchanan to his 7 p.m. meeting with Mrs Sullivan. However, it was easier to opt out of the arrangement altogether than to invent some reason for being unavailable for the remainder of the evening. She had no trouble in cancelling her tryst since Buchanan made it quite clear that he didn't want her company anyway and, while his preferences would not normally have carried any weight with her, humouring him saved having to think up an excuse that would satisfy him without raising his suspicions.

She spent the evening shortening an old skirt to an indecent length and selecting a top which, with the top three buttons left undone, looked suitably slaggish. There was a bitterly cold wind whistling up the High Street as she emerged, which was an excuse to cover much of her ensemble with a coat, but she was shivering by the time she reached the unobtrusive doorway that led to Terence Lamb's centre for sport and recreational activities.

Somewhat surprisingly, Touch-and-Go occupied premises on the first floor, above a second-hand dealer (Marshall and Gregg, suppliers to the impecunious elite), a closed-down grocer's shop and a grotty newsagent's with a sleeping cat in the window. Access was by a shadowy stair at the side, no doubt a boon to the less intrepid client, but the windows above were framed in ruby red neon lights that spelled out the name and left little doubt as to the services on offer. Behind the lights, shiny gauze curtains hid such naughty goings on from the eyes of the world, but from across the road Fizz could see the occasional shadow pass unhurriedly by.

She hung around for a few minutes so that any punters who had just arrived would have moved on into their private cubicles or whatever. She had very little idea of what the place might look like inside but she supposed there would be a reception area of some description and she had no intention of penetrating any further than that if she could help it.

Just as she got herself psyched up to make her entrance a lone male came round the corner and paced slowly towards the doorway. She could tell immediately where he was headed because of the way his head kept turning nervously this way and that but he kept going straight past the entrance till he came to the next corner. Then, after taking a good look round, he turned back. This time there was a strange little hesitation in his step, almost a stumble, right at the crucial moment but he didn't turn in, just walked on about twenty paces and paused. Fizz found herself grinning as she watched him jittering from one foot to the other. He bent to retie a shoelace. He turned up the collar of his jacket. Then, in a sudden access of courage, he turned and made purposefully, but still nervously, for the foot of the stairs. There he paused for a last quick look around. For a second, just as he pushed open the door, Fizz was sorely tempted to yell, 'Oi, you!' but the moment passed.

She gave him five or six minutes and then followed him up the stairs. At the top there was a single door, painted rose red with the panels outlined in black. Above the bell was a computer-printed card bearing the name of the enterprise and the invitation to press and enter, which seemed apt, given the circumstances. She slipped her coat off and did both.

An eye-watering blast of cheap perfume slapped her in the face like a wet towel as she stepped through the doorway into much the sort of reception area as she had imagined, only a good bit bigger. There was room for a reception desk on one side and, on the other, for a long banquette seat where sat five youngish women in pink, medical-type overalls. Everything was peach and pink, the vinyl painted walls, the bedroom-quality carpeting, the satiny cushions trimmed with fake swansdown, the lampshades, the plastic reception desk, the five hookers and the slightly older receptionist.

Six pairs of shocked eyes fastened on Fizz like vampire bats.

'Can I help you?' barked the receptionist in that tone people in authority use when they mean 'Shove off!'

She was about thirty and her face was caked an inch thick with make-up like those clowns you see behind the make-up counter in Boots. In fact all the women were wearing the full slap: pancake foundation, thick eye-liner and lipstick, blusher, eye-shadow, false lashes, cake mix, the lot. Fizz found this interesting and wondered if it was intended to convey some sort of sexual over-eagerness to their deluded clients.

She smiled at the receptionist and looked nervous, which was no true test of her acting skills. 'Is the boss in?'

'What d'you want the boss for?'

'I was wondering . . . I wanted to see him about a job.'

Her expression softened, but not a lot. 'Well she's not here tonight. You'll have to come back when she's in.'

'She?' said Fizz, aiming for a softly softly approach. 'I was told the boss was Mr Lamb.'

'Who told you that?'

'A girl I met at a party.'

The receptionist lifted a cigarette from the

ashtray beside her and took a drag. 'Well, he's away at the moment. You'll have to talk to Olwen, and not when we're open for business. She'll be in tomorrow about five.'

Fizz thanked her and took her time about getting to the door, smiling at the girls on the banquette and getting a good look at them at the same time so she'd know them again. Three of them were bored-looking and hard-faced but there were a couple of youngish ones who smiled back and looked like they might be amenable to being buttonholed. The youngest of these two was probably the best bet. She was one of those limp and spiritless losers that God made as the natural prey of people like Lamb and it was patently clear from the expression on her face that, given a few dozen more neurones, she'd be a half-wit.

Outside, the wind was still bitterly cold, nipping at Fizz's bare legs, but she sat at the foot of the stairs with her coat wrapped round her tightly until she heard the door open above her. Four times she had to nick out sharply and hide in a shop doorway while punters emerged and disappeared into the night. No one else went in, which was unexpected, but it was already half past midnight and also mid-week so maybe that was par for the course.

Round about one o'clock the girls started to emerge. The first two to appear were both hard-faced ones: miniskirted, spikey-heeled and unmistakably on the game. They were arm in arm and in such close and interesting conversation that they stepped into the doorway of the empty shop to finish what they were discussing. Behind them, on the window of the entrance, was a large notice which proclaimed 'We give green stamps' but it attracted no custom for either of them and in minutes they went their separate ways. Shortly thereafter, the tall, skinny girl that Fizz had chosen as her target sallied forth. Pausing at the foot of the stairs, she lit up a cigarette and crossed the road quite close to where Fizz was lurking in a doorway.

She jumped as Fizz came up to her but then relaxed and gave a short laugh. 'Oh, it's you! I thought I was being mugged. You get some weird characters around here.'

Fizz fell into step beside her. 'Sorry. I thought you'd seen me. I was waiting to talk to you.'

'What about?' Her mind laboured visibly. 'Working at Touch-and-Go?'

'Yes. Can I buy you a coffee? There's a late night place just across there beside Waverley Station.'

The girl shook her head. 'Actually, I'm in a bit of a rush.'

Fizz took a hand out of her pocket and showed her the two twenty-pound notes she was holding. 'I'm willing to pay for your advice.'

Hard cash, in Fizz's experience, simplified decision-making. Pictures speak louder than words.

They walked up the hill towards Princes Street and found a corner table in the café. Their only company was the guy behind the counter, two tipsy Italian tourists and a terrified-looking middle-aged woman with a pair of suitcases.

Fizz collected a couple of coffees and two chocolate muffins and sat down.

'My name's Judy,' she told her guest. 'What's yours?'

'Margaret . . . but at work I'm called Trixie. They choose you a sexy name when you start.'

Fizz personally didn't consider Trixie a particularly sexy name but decided it could hold connotations not immediately visible to the lay person. She said, 'How long have you worked at Touch-and-Go?'

'Since the Christmas before last.'

'What's it like?'

She shrugged and made a face. 'Not so bad when you get used to it. Better than going it alone.'

'But the money's good?'

It took her a few seconds to answer and, when she did, it wasn't all that convincing. 'Oh, sure,' she said and then picked up her bag from the seat beside her. 'Must go to the loo. Won't be a minute.'

She was, in fact, several minutes during which Fizz withstood the speculative gaze of the two Italian guys and absentmindedly ate both muffins. Trixie, on her return, looked comparatively bright-eyed and bushy-tailed which led Fizz to the conclusion that she had either achieved a particularly satisfactory evacuation or had been shooting up.

'The girl who told me about your place said Mr Lamb wasn't bad to work for,' she said, when Trixie had settled down again. 'But I don't think she worked there for very long.'

Trixie turned sideways on her chair and crossed her legs well above the knee. She was obviously aware of the attention of the Italians and not averse to encouraging it. 'Who was she? Did she tell you her name?'

Fizz looked at the ceiling for a moment and then said, 'Something like Collette, I think.'

Trixie's eyes bounced back from the two drunks and fastened on Fizz's with sudden interest. 'Colleen? Colleen Wilson? I knew her. Did you know she died?'

'What?' Fizz looked indescribably shocked. 'What of?'

'Somebody bashed her on the head and left her in a rubbish skip. It was horrible. We were all scared stiff. I wanted to pack in the job before the same thing happened to me.'

'Why didn't you?'

She dropped her eyes and fiddled with her coffee cup. 'It's not that easy. Terence didn't want us to make too much of a drama about it. Bad for business.'

'Did they get anyone for it?'

'No.'

'Any ideas who might have done it? One of her johns, maybe?'

Trixie's eyes darkened. 'She wasn't turning tricks then. She was Terence's current girl.'

Fizz got the picture. She said, 'He takes his pick, does he?'

'Every few weeks, usually, but Colleen lasted quite a bit longer than that. I think he really liked her.'

'And what about Colleen,' Fizz asked, wishing

184

she'd stop sticking her boobs out for the boys. 'Did she really like him?'

'Couldn't stand the sight of him.' Her eyes brightened at the sight of one of the Italian tourists pushing back his chair and approaching their table.

He was good-looking, like most Mediterranean types: big brown eyes, jet black hair, golden skin, but a bit on the tubby side.

'My friend and I were wondering,' he said in carefully rehearsed English, 'if you ladies would care to join us.'

Fizz gave him an acid little smile that should have raised a weal and spoke in the dialect she'd picked up during her two years in Perugia.

'Take my advice, sweetie, and stick to your own class. There's plenty of poxy old slappers around.'

'What did you say?' Trixie asked when he had limped back to his friend.

'I said, perhaps later.' Fizz finished her coffee, got a couple of refills, and returned to the fray. 'You were saying Colleen didn't like Terence.'

'Loathed him.' She lit up a cigarette, relaxing now in the knowledge that the johns weren't going to disappear. 'She wanted out but Terence wouldn't let her go.'

'How could he stop her?'

Trixie passed on that one, clearly wishing she hadn't let her tongue run away with her.

'Well,' said Fizz, soothingly, 'at least you know that Terence wanted her around so it wasn't him that bumped her off.'

'Right.' Trixie drank some coffee, her eyes

sliding away sideways in the forlorn hope that
Fizz wouldn't notice the lack of enthusiasm in
her agreement.

'He's in jail for murder just now, didn't you
know that?' Fizz said, making her eyelids flutter
nervously.

'We're not supposed to talk about that.'

'It's no secret. It's been in all the papers,' Fizz
told her. 'Besides, who's to know? I bet you're
not supposed to moonlight either, but you're
going to, aren't you? I won't tell if you don't tell.
Go on, tell me why you think he had something
to do with Colleen's death.'

Trixie's vapid face took on a chummy
expression. She smiled and took a long drag on
her cigarette. 'She knew something about him
that he didn't like her knowing.'

'What was it?'

'Haven't a clue, but she seemed to think she
could use it to make him let her go.'

'Did she tell him she was in possession of this
information?'

She shrugged, her attention returning to the
Italians who seemed to be having a debate about
leaving. Giving them a smile, she re-crossed her
legs and opened her mouth to let her tongue run
suggestively across her bottom lip.

'Where did she get the information?'

'From one of her regular clients.'

'Know his name?'

Trixie flashed her a scornful glance. 'Like he'd
tell her his name.' She picked up her bag and
slung the strap over her shoulder but Fizz hung
on like a pit bull.

186

'Don't you know anything about him?'

Meaningful eye contact had now been established between Trixie and the Italians and they were calling for their bill. She said, 'I think he told her he was a soldier, but that was probably a lie. Are you ready to go? I don't think they'll wait forever.'

'Just a minute, there's another thing I want to ask you.' Fizz put out a hand to hold her in her seat. 'Have you ever come across Amanda Montrose?'

'The woman Terence is supposed to have murdered? How would I have come across her? She was from Inverness, wasn't she?'

She had thrown off Fizz's hand and was already on her feet so, seeing no way of holding her, Fizz let her go.

'Aren't you coming?' she asked when she saw Fizz was making no move to follow her.

'No. I've done my quota for tonight. I'm for beddie-byes.'

Trixie staggered away on her spikey heels, no doubt happy at the thought that she'd soon have the price of another fix.

13

Buchanan and Justin were just about to sit down to their meal when Fizz turned up.

One could have foretold her coming without the aid of a star in the east, Buchanan reflected as he let her in, since she had a nose for the scent of cooking food that operated competently over a radius of several miles.

'What,' she said as she stepped, nostrils flared, across the threshold, 'is that? Roast chicken?'

One could scarcely deny it since there were two heaped plates lying there in full view on the kitchen table.

'Yes, but I'm afraid there's only a scrap left, Fizz.'

Justin leapt to his feet like a gentleman, all smiles. 'Don't worry. We haven't started yet. I can redivide the portions.'

This would not have been Buchanan's first response because he'd been drowning in his own saliva in anticipation of gorging himself, and his stomach was rumbling like Mount Etna approaching a critical state. However, it was Justin's shout due to the fact that he'd made Buchanan a present of the ingredients and talked him through every step of the cooking procedure. He'd have relented in the end, of course. Fizz had, after all, been the one to provide sustenance on more than one occasion recently and, while it would be a long time before she got herself out of the red in that field, one could scarcely see her starve. Besides, as the sole architect of the repast before them, he was prey to the artist's longing for recognition.

'Buchanan cooked a meal?' she said, when Justin appraised her of that fact. She chewed a forkful. 'An edible meal?'

'All with my own dishpan hands,' Buchanan replied, faking a wholly genuine conceit. 'Justin wouldn't even peel the garlic. I've been sweating over a hot stove for two hours.'

Fizz tested the stuffing. 'Mmm. That's good.'

'One of these days he'll make a wonderful wife for some lucky girl,' Justin told her, grinning like Jack Nicholson in *The Shining*. 'I'd grab him while the going's good if I were you.'

'How is he on ironing?' she asked with her mouth full.

'We haven't started work on that area yet. I don't want him to peak too soon.'

Fizz chewed busily. 'How's your wife's diet going?'

'Great. She says my amazing resistance to temptation is an inspiration to her. She lost four pounds last week, three the week before.'

'Brilliant. If she keeps that up you'll be rid of her completely in a few months.'

'Were you out last night?' Buchanan inserted into the conversation, in an attempt to divert it onto less personal channels. 'I drove past your flat on my way back from my parents' place and it looked like there were no lights on.'

'What time was that?' she asked with a little curious frown.

'Elevenish. Maybe half past.'

The frown cleared. 'Oh, right. Yes. I was over at Touch-and-Go.'

For a micro-second Buchanan's brain refused to accept that she had just said what she'd just — so matter-of-factly — said. No, no. She hadn't really said she'd *been* there, or he was momentarily mistaken in thinking Touch-and-Go was the name of the massage parlour. He'd got it all wrong.

But he hadn't; and as the realisation hit him he was swept by an anger that was as much disappointment as true annoyance. His voice shook with the effort of keeping it level.

'I understood you to say you had decided not to go.'

She waved her fork. 'I thought I'd suss out the exterior but once I got there I thought, what the hell, I'll just take a quick peep at the set-up and see if there's anyone likely to have a chat with me.'

'You talking about the massage parlour?' Justin asked as Buchanan knuckled his brow and tried to visualise a tropical beach with waves beating softly on the shore. 'You don't want to be hanging around places like that.'

'It goes with the job,' Fizz smiled, visibly charmed by exactly the sort of friendly concern for which she'd have slammed Buchanan. 'We have the craziest case on our hands at the moment: an old lady who claims to have done a murder that someone else has been jailed for committing.'

Buchanan coughed. 'Er . . . client confidentiality, Fizz.'

'Oh, pooh! I haven't mentioned any names, have I? And it's all in the public domain anyway.'

She carried straight on putting Justin in the picture but it was pretty obvious that she was merely using the guy as a barrier between herself and Buchanan's wrath. Fat chance. He was determined to have it out with her properly once they were on their own and sat glowering and reminding himself of her appalling gall so that he wouldn't cool down too much in the interim.

'What did she say to you last night, Buchanan, when you asked her what she has that's worth someone breaking into her flat to obtain?'

'There's nothing,' Buchanan growled, striking a fine balance between righteous fury and adult restraint. 'She swears she has absolutely no idea why someone should do that. She's sure it was the boys who were responsible for the broken pane.'

'Did you believe her?'

'I . . . I'd have to say yes to that, I suppose. She was determined to convince me once and for all that she's told us the whole truth. She actually swore to it on her eternal soul, would you believe? And we know how religious she is.'

Fizz turned back to Justin. 'You see? She could be giving us the authentic facts or she could be mentally ill. It's impossible to tell.'

'Or,' said Justin, 'she could be spinning a complete tissue of lies for some objective that she considers worth the risk of her eternal soul. I mean, even her show of being religious could be a fake. She may not even believe she *has* an eternal soul.'

Buchanan had already given that possibility some thought but hearing it voiced by an independent assessor gave it added weight. 'It's possible she doesn't,' he said, 'but it's not something a lot of people would take a chance on.'

He got up and took the baked bananas out of the oven. There were four of them, which didn't divide easily by three, but he took pains to make Fizz's portion smaller than the other two. Not small enough to give grounds for complaint but sufficient to communicate the fact that he was still mad at her. Her ball of ice cream, likewise, although it looked comparatively generous, was hollow in the middle.

He saw her dig her spoon into it and then glance appraisingly at Justin's plate and his own. She said nothing but a flicker of wry amusement shimmied across her face like the glint of sunshine on water.

'Anyway,' she said, as though he had voiced his displeasure aloud, 'you haven't asked me whether my visit to Touch-and-Go was a success or not.'

Buchanan positively did not want to discuss the matter in front of Justin — which was, beyond a doubt, why she had chosen this moment to bring it up. Thwarted in his desire to speak frankly, and probably loudly, on the subject of her demented conduct, he had no recourse but to listen calmly to her report. His only other choice would have been to refuse to listen to her altogether but that would make him look huffy and pettish, traits he considered despicable in a grown man.

'One would hope you gained something worth the risk you took,' he said levelly.

'What risk? It was just a massage parlour, for Pete's sake, not some depot for the white slave traffic. Anyway,' she rushed on when he opened his mouth to argue that point, 'I'd say it was very much worthwhile. I caught this girl as she came out and we went for a coffee together.'

'How do you *do* that?' Buchanan had to ask, his anger fading just a trifle as he realised she hadn't actually entered the brothel. 'How do you get perfect strangers to enter into a conversation with you?'

She tipped her head modestly. 'I'm multi-talented. Anyway, I asked this girl — Trixie, she's called — if she knew Colleen Wilson, and she did. Told me quite a lot about her in point of fact.'

Justin scraped the last spoonful from his plate and pushed his chair away from the table. 'Sorry. Have to rush. The wife'll have my clear chicken soup and salad waiting for me. See you tomorrow, squire. Bye Fizz.'

He let himself out, whistling contentedly as he passed through the lounge, and Buchanan's attention returned to Fizz, who said, 'Colleen was Terence's special girlfriend. His normal habit was to choose a different girl every few weeks — evidently they have a pretty regular turnover in hookers or he'd soon run out of fresh talent — but Colleen lasted longer than the average so she must have had something special. She, however, couldn't stand the sight of him.

Loathed him, so Trixie says, and wanted out altogether, only Terence wouldn't let her leave.'

'How would he stop her?'

'Trixie declined to say but I reckon physical violence would come into it somewhere along the line, don't you? Or maybe she needed him to keep her supplied with drugs. Who knows? In any case, it turns out that Colleen had something on him. Trixie doesn't know what it was but it seems likely she tried to use the knowledge as some kind of lever.'

'Blackmail, you mean?'

'That's my interpretation, yes, and it must have been based on something fairly heavy — don't you think? — since he considered it worthwhile to shut her up permanently. Someone in his position — already on the CID's most-wanted list — doesn't go out on a limb like that unless it's really worth his while.'

Buchanan absorbed this information with a certain amount of gratification but could see no way of taking it any further. One could question the other employees of the massage parlour, of course, but even if he managed to psyche himself up for that endeavour, he wasn't confident that he shared Fizz's talent for worming her way into people's confidence: not as long as there was any danger to their supply of drugs. And the idea of letting Fizz penetrate any further into that murky region — that was simply a non-starter.

He said, 'Did you believe . . . um, Trixie . . . when she said she didn't know what Colleen had against her boss?'

Fizz considered that and then nodded, pursing

194

her lips. 'Yes. She's pretty dim, actually, and I could've told if she was lying. All she knew was that the guy Colleen got the information from claimed to be a soldier.'

'Pity,' Buchanan said and then realised Fizz was looking at him quizzically. 'A soldier? What regiment?'

'She didn't know,' Fizz said, smiling at his sudden interest. 'She didn't necessarily believe he was telling the truth: it could've been nothing but the sort of misinformation the johns frequently hand out. All the same, it makes you think, right?'

Buchanan was indeed thinking, his mind dashing from Ewan Montrose's military background to Terence's alleged heroism and wondering if there was something more in that story than met the eye.

'How do we check that out?' he wondered aloud.

'Well, if you're asking me, the first thing I'd do is establish exactly when Lamb and Montrose were in Northern Ireland together. I'd bet his solicitor could tell you. Give him a ring.'

Buchanan looked at his watch. It was getting on for eight, not intolerably late to phone a guy he'd known for years, but he cavilled anyway.

'He'll be in the middle of his dinner.'

'Rubbish. Give him a ring. It's his bloody client we're trying to clear.'

'It could wait till tomorrow morning.'

'Oh, get on with it, Buchanan, it could be important.'

It was difficult to perceive just how it could be

so important but procrastination had cost Buchanan dearly in the past and he was now somewhat superstitious about putting things off till tomorrow. He went through to the lounge, got out his address book and dialled the number. By the time he put down the receiver Fizz was beside him trying to hear both sides of the conversation.

'So? He had a note of the date?' she demanded as he started to hang up.

'Dates. Montrose and Lamb were in Crossmaglen from 1988 to '89. The shooting happened on Christmas Eve 1988.'

'Right. So, now we know the date to concentrate on all we have to do is to find someone who was in Belfast at the same time. Who do you know in the Royal Scots?'

Buchanan was touched by her assumption that he had friends in every walk of life. 'Surprisingly enough,' he said, 'no one.'

'Well, do you know anyone who might know someone?'

'Sorry.'

She nibbled her pinkie nail and appeared to subject her list of acquaintances to a prolonged mental scrutiny. 'Okay,' she said at last. 'I suppose we'll just have to brass neck it. Where's their HQ?'

Buchanan had no idea. He looked her very firmly in the eye and said, 'What are you thinking, Fizz?'

'The same as you, probably: that we'll have to go in the front door. Or rather you will because you have a little more clout than I do, if only in the eyes of military top brass. You'll have to march in with your advocate's hat on and ask to be put in touch with anyone who was in the same section or platoon, or whatever, as Lamb and Montrose. We need some eyewitnesses to the incident that crippled Lamb.'

'I should've thought about checking out that incident right at the beginning,' Buchanan said, annoyed at himself, but Fizz, for once, was uncritical.

'It's the sort of thing anyone would take at face value,' she said kindly, as she got up and went through to the kitchen for her jacket and shoulder bag. 'After all, the army must have conducted their own inquiry and if they found nothing iffy about the shooting it's unlikely we will. But all the same I'm betting that there's something connected with that business that reflected very badly on our friend Lamb. Something he'd kill to keep hidden.'

Buchanan wished he had her infallible optimism but he spent the best part of the following day trying to locate the right man to talk to. It was a frustrating business and he was heartily sick of talking to machines and pressing button one, two or three before he found himself, at last, dealing with the Military Police in Belfast. It turned out that they were able to access military records and, once Buchanan had established his credentials, they were perfectly willing to do so on his behalf.

It took them till five in the afternoon to fax Buchanan the details, by which time Fizz had phoned him three times to inquire what was taking him so long to come up with the answers. In the meantime he had made a pork Stroganoff with fluffy rice and petits pois which he and Justin had scoffed as soon as it was ready and, incidentally, before the arrival of Fizz, straight from the office.

'Greedy bastards,' she commented, and phoned down for a pizza. 'Okay. Where's the fax? I want to read it for myself.'

Buchanan handed it over and she scanned it rapidly, her eyes zigzagging down the page.

'They don't give away much, do they? Just the bare facts you asked for. Four witnesses including Lamb himself — and one of those is dead. Is that all you could get out of them?'

'So far,' Buchanan admitted. 'I could try getting a warrant, I suppose, if they're not willing to part with the whole story in the absence of one, but I suspect the version of the truth they were given is likely to be much the same as we got from Montrose.'

Justin leaned a hand on Fizz's shoulder to steal a look at the fax and she said, pointing at it, 'We know this Terence Lamb, and we know the second lieutenant, Montrose, so if the lance corporal was shot and killed there's only one other person left to talk to and that's this guy. Dougal Kershaw. Private.' She turned to Buchanan. 'Where do we find him?'

Buchanan twirled a finger to draw her attention to the second page of the fax. 'Currently stationed at Redford Barracks, Edinburgh. C company, in charge of stores. Should be quite easy to locate.'

'You mean, you haven't contacted him yet?'

'Dammit, Fizz, it was five o'clock when the fax came through.'

'And you thought the army was only open from nine to five? You could at least have tried phoning. Give them a ring.'

Buchanan sighed and went to the phone without argument. One could hardly admit that, since the fax arrived, his entire concentration had been focused on making sure the cream didn't curdle. Fortunately Fizz's pizza arrived while he was making the call so he didn't have to suffer her supervision. There was the usual buck passing operation to go through, then he had to convince the adjutant that his business was urgent, and finally, when he eventually reached C company's stores, he learned that the man he wanted to talk to was off duty.

By that time Fizz's pizza was reduced to a small rectangle of crust and she was engaged in using it to scrape the last traces of Stroganoff from the unwashed pan.

'Just testing,' she said when he caught her at it. 'It's pretty good. Did you manage to reach Private Kershaw?'

'Colonel Sergeant Kershaw now. No, he's off duty but I know where he can be found. He'll be at the Quick Fit gym in Colinton till about seven.'

Fizz sucked a trace of Stroganoff from her index finger and looked at her watch. 'Nearly six o'clock. Bags of time, then. We can catch him as he leaves.'

Buchanan had been entertaining self-indulgent thoughts of a round of golf but now saw that possibility fading into the sunset.

'Six o'clock?' Justin drained the dregs of his coffee and scrambled to his feet. 'Hell! I'm in the doghouse tonight. My steamed fish will be like blotting paper.'

Buchanan went with him to the door and, since the work on the lounge was almost completed, gave him the cheque he'd already made out. He felt rather sorry to see Justin go since he had been good company and the food had been a distinct improvement on past cuisine. He said, 'Any time you feel like joining me for dinner, Justin . . . '

'How about tomorrow?' Justin grinned, half in fun, wholly in earnest. 'Fried haddock and chips?'

'You're on. We'll split the cost.'

Justin laughed, gave him a high five and clattered away down the stairs.

Back in the kitchen Fizz was making a fresh pot of coffee. 'You two are getting quite pally, aren't you? What was all that about?'

'Mind your own business, Miss Nosey.' He was still a bit peckish but he knew that if he opened his only packet of chocolate chip cookies Fizz would finish it.

She sat down sideways at the table and crossed her legs. Smoothly curved calves and frail ankles in sheer black tights . . . or maybe stockings . . . skirt almost short enough to ascertain which . . . almost . . .

'Have you seen Mrs Sullivan today?' she asked.

'No, but I spoke to her on the telephone.'

Buchanan snatched his eyes away and stared blandly into hers. 'She called about lunchtime to ask if there was any progress to report. I said we were pushing ahead and still had possible leads to pursue but I didn't give her any details. It's better for her not to be too involved. She starts building up her hopes too much and then she gets upset when we hit a blank wall.'

'How did she sound? Normal?'

Buchanan waggled a hand. 'Hard to say, really. I thought her speech sounded a little slurred once or twice and maybe her responses were a bit on the slow side but, then again, that could have been my imagination.'

Fizz pursed her lips doubtfully. 'We should try to see more of her, really, so that we can get a better idea of her mental state. If she's unbalanced and imagining things we might as well cut our losses and back out gracefully.'

'Absolutely,' Buchanan agreed. 'I'm seeing her tomorrow anyway but, you're right, one of us should check up on her every day if at all possible. Maybe we could call in on her after we've talked to Kershaw.'

'Good idea,' Fizz said kindly. 'I could murder a sherry.'

It was starting to rain outside, not heavily but enough to clear the tourists off the streets. They got to the gym about twenty to seven and, after asking the receptionist to alert them when Dougal Kershaw emerged, retired to the refreshment bar and the therapeutic effects of a tomato and celery cocktail with basil.

'This,' said Fizz, after sinking half her glass in

one gulp, 'is boggin'. I can feel it melting my fillings.'

'That's how you know it's good for you,' Buchanan assured her, moistening his lips with his own sample, to show how stoic he was.

They waited quarter of an hour before Kershaw came looking for them. He was a fit-looking man who could have been anything between thirty-five and fifty. Short sandy-coloured hair that was lightly frosted with grey, a hard body with no spare flesh, tattoos showing on both forearms above the rolled-up sleeves of his shirt.

'Frankie says you're waiting to see me, sir.'

Buchanan stood up and offered his hand. 'Tam Buchanan, and this is Miss Fitzpatrick who's assisting me on a case. Would you have a few minutes to talk?'

'What about?' he asked without taking the seat Buchanan pulled out for him.

Buchanan gave him a quick résumé of his dealings with Mrs Sullivan none of which appeared to carry much weight with Kershaw, or, if it did, it didn't show in his face. 'I haven't seen Terence Lamb for something like twenty years,' he said with the sort of finality that didn't encourage debate. 'There's nothing I can tell you about him that would be of any help to you.'

'Let me put you more fully in the picture,' Buchanan urged him, again indicating the empty seat. 'There are aspects to this matter that make it quite crucial that we get it cleared up one way or the other.'

Kershaw shifted from one foot to the other

while he considered that proposal. Finally he said, 'I'm going for a walk. If you want to come with me that's okay by me, but I'm not promising anything.'

'No? Why not?' Fizz asked artlessly as she gathered together her belongings and stood up. 'Are there things you'd rather we didn't enquire into?'

He looked at her with narrowed eyes, clearly wondering if that guileless baby-doll face and golden-capped head could possibly be the seat of some low, animal cunning. 'There's military secrets, miss. Things were rough in Belfast in '88, not like they are now, and there's things the army doesn't like talked about.'

'This is a murder case,' Buchanan said bluntly. 'I've had clearance from the Military Police at Aldegrove, and from your adjutant as well so I don't think you have much to worry about.'

He gave a non-committal grunt and led the way out into the low evening sunlight. They headed uphill through the fringes of Colinton village and out onto the track that led to Bonally Reservoir. The pastures at either side were swept by a light breeze that rippled through the long grass like waves.

Buchanan put forth his case again, this time in more detail, stressing Mrs Sullivan's angst and the danger of allowing Amanda Montrose's real murderer to walk free and possibly to kill again. This time Kershaw listened with more attention and, when he had heard everything he needed to, said, 'There's no way I'm going to give evidence in court. You can forget that. I don't

203

care who murdered Amanda Montrose.'

'It's unlikely we'll need your testimony,' Fizz assured him with absolute but totally unjustifiable confidence, so that Buchanan had to say, 'We can't be certain of that, of course. However, if there is any aspect of your evidence that could cause you embarrassment at a later date we can take steps to protect you — even from criminal prosecution.'

Kershaw walked on in silence communing, one supposed, with his conscience. He was setting a brisk pace and, the incline being considerable, both Fizz and Buchanan were beginning to puff a bit.

'Okay,' he said, coming to a decision. 'I don't mind telling you what happened, just to set the record straight, but I'm putting nothing on paper, I'm signing nothing, and I'm not going to court whatever protection they promise me. I've got my pension to consider. I'll talk to you in confidence — right? — but if the MPs come round I'll deny it till I'm black in the face.'

'That's no problem,' Fizz got in quickly, with a little flutter of excitement in her voice. 'Like I said, it probably won't come up in court.'

He looked from her face to Buchanan's and his mouth twisted wryly. 'Okay. I must be nuts but I'll trust you.'

'Before you start,' Fizz breathed, 'could we sit down for a bit? Just so I can concentrate on what you're saying and maybe take a few notes.'

They found a convenient wall, shaded but still warm, but Kershaw spurned such wimpish self-indulgence, preferring to pace up and down, talking largely to the ground.

'Right. We're talking about the winter of 1988 when we were at the security force base at Crossmaglen. I'm, like, nineteen or twenty, first time at the sharp end, don't know my arse from my elbow. Christmas Eve, we're out on foot patrol. It's getting on for midnight and freezing hard and there's the four of us: two jocks, namely me and Terence Lamb; the lance-jack who's a big Aberdonian called Sean Whiteford, and Second Lieutenant Ewan Montrose. Montrose is much my own age but even greener than I am, a matter of months out of Sandhurst and none too bright at the best of times.'

He halted his pacing to pluck a stalk of grass and stick it between his teeth. For a moment his eyes rested on the distant panorama which stretched from the Forth road bridge to Leith docks, but they were half-closed and unfocused. He shook his head at some thought and muttered, almost as though he'd forgotten their presence, 'Not a bad bloke, Montrose. No worse than most of them, just inexperienced. They fill their heads with such crap at Sandhurst: the glorious history of the regiment, the importance of its good name . . . '

Fizz and Buchanan, sitting on the wall like two green bottles, watched him in rapt silence as he brooded.

Then he resumed his pacing and went on. 'Anyway, there we are in the pitch dark working our way through the Drumintee Bowl — that's a rural area that used to be full of old barns and deserted farm buildings, the sort of place you get

205

players holing up in or using as arms dumps.'

'Players,' Fizz mumbled as though she were considering the word.

'Terrorists, miss. That's what we call terrorists. The place was crawling with them at that time so we were fairly jumpy. Okay, so round about midnight we come up to a derelict farmhouse. It's just the sort of place to appeal to a player: inconspicuous, not overlooked, backed by a large area of woodland so they can come and go without attracting too much attention. We move in for a closer look. Terence is lead scout followed by the lance-jack, then me, with Montrose as tail-end Charlie. The field all around the building has great holes and ditches dug out of it, probably, to slow down anyone approaching at night and they slow us down real good, I can tell you. First thing we see is wires snaking across the hoar frost by the back door so we know we're looking at some kind of IED. That's an improvised explosive device, miss, or a bomb if you prefer to think of it like that. So we take a good look round the outside and see nothing. Everything silent as the grave. It looks like there's nobody home so Sean Whiteford decides we're going in.'

'Not Montrose?' Buchanan said.

Kershaw waved a dismissive hand. 'Montrose was only there for experience, Sean Whiteford was team commander.' He chewed his lip briefly and then went on, 'Lamb kicks in the door and whips back against the wall and, before anyone knows what's happening, there's a hail of bullets all round us. LSW fire like we use ourselves. I hit the ground and wriggle into one of their defence ditches which gives me some cover but, through the yelling and gunfire, I hear Whiteford start screaming and I know he's been hit bad.'

He took time out to stare at the view again, this time with his back to his audience, and Buchanan suspected the memory of that night still had the power to affect him. His voice, when he continued speaking, was less forceful than it had been.

'It was the worst noise I ever had to listen to in my life and it went on for — God knows how long, could've been five minutes. I still wake up in the night hearing it in my head. Anyway, we start to return fire. I set up my LSW on the tripod and manage to get a line of fire straight through the front door but Lamb — he's like a raging lion: standing up and firing indiscriminately, getting in my way and trying to work his way round to where Whiteford's still lying on the ground screaming and wriggling around like a scalded snake. I can hear Montrose yelling, telling Lamb to get the hell down, but I can't see him in the dark. Then there's a second or two of silence and I hear him bellowing, 'Hold your fire, Lamb, for chrissake!' over and over.'

A low shaft of sunset-pink light pierced the high bank of bushes behind the wall and spotlit his face as he turned round to face them. He seemed to have difficulty in meeting their eyes.

'Right away, a guy appears in the doorway, hands up and waving a white T-shirt. He starts to call out something but Lamb doesn't wait to hear it. He opens up with his SA80 and damn near cuts him in half. Then he steps up to the doorway and starts spraying the interior with bullets. Montrose is up like a flash and running after him, ordering him to stop firing, but Lamb's beyond listening. He's completely lost it. Could've been Whiteford's screaming set him off. Maybe it was just a reaction to being scared shitless, I don't know, but he's doing this maniacal bellowing and swearing and shooting, roaring mad like some wounded animal or something. I don't mind telling you it did my head in. I never saw anything like that in my life, before or since. There was no way anybody could have stopped him without doing what Montrose did. He put a bullet through his knee.'

Fizz let go a deep breath as though she'd been holding on to it for some time and turned shining eyes on Buchanan. 'Not quite the heroic tale of derring-do we were asked to swallow.'

Buchanan nodded but forbore to answer because he suspected, judging by Kershaw's body language, that there was more to come. He was right.

'We find six players inside, all well dead, plus a collection of arms and ammunition and a completed explosive device that looks like it was going to be used as a booby trap. Whiteford has also given up the ghost, but that's a blessing in disguise because he's messed up something terrible. We leave him there and I get ready to carry Lamb who's bleeding like a stuck pig and in terrible pain. Montrose gets the radio off Whiteford's body and retreats to a safe distance so that we can notify base that there's been an incident. I'm trying to get some morphine into Terence but I'm shaking so much I drop my first aid kit and it falls into the ditch behind me. I dive down to get it but, just as I stoop to pick it up, there's one almighty thump that knocks me tits over arse and the farmhouse goes up.'

'The bomb?' Fizz whispered.

'They must have had it on a timer. I whack my head on something on the way down and pass out for a minute or two, maybe longer. When I come to Terence looks like a blob of strawberry jam and Montrose is back beside me, putting a field dressing on the back of my head. He says, 'Dougie, are you a man who can keep his mouth shut for the sake of the regiment?' Well, I'm not going to say 'no', am I? So he says something like, 'You know what would happen if this cock up gets into the papers? The Royal Scots would be disgraced, that's what. So we keep shtumm about it. There's no witnesses except us three so when we report back say we took a burst of hostile fire and, as we retreated, the farmhouse blew up'.'

He spread an expressive hand and hooked an eyebrow at them as though to say, What would you have done? But getting no reply, he gave a small shrug and went on with his story.

'Well, that's the way we played it. Forensics pieced together what they could and decided the shootings had been the result of a falling out between different factions. The bullet in Terence's knee could have come from any of the weapons found in the house and Ewan Montrose footed the bill for his convalescence et cetera.'

As Kershaw stopped speaking Buchanan became aware of the singing of a skylark so high up above his head that it was a mere speck against the blue. He looked about himself with eyes that had been seeing the blackness of a winter's night and realised with a second's confusion that the hills were glittering gold with sunlit gorse and a family of rabbits had stolen out of the hedge for supper a mere five yards from where he sat.

Fizz said, 'And after that? Did either Montrose or Lamb put any pressure on you to stay silent?'

Kershaw shook his head. 'We never spoke of it again. In fact, I've never seen Terence Lamb from that day to this. He was in hospital for quite a while and then got a medical discharge and a pension, jammy bastard. The wicked shall flourish like the green bay tree, right?'

'Right.' Fizz's face became even more angelic. 'Have you ever mentioned or even hinted about this matter to any of your mates?'

'Never. I'd be in the clag as much as the other two of us if the truth came out. That's why you have to keep this to yourselves. I've my pension to consider.'

Fizz was voluble with reassurance but Buchanan could discern by her smug expression that she was pleased with herself for establishing that it was Kershaw himself who had been Colleen Wilson's informant. One could easily conceive of his making reference to the incident during a drunken romp, possibly after hearing that the establishment he was patronising was owned by his old comrade-in-arms.

Whoever said 'the truth will out' certainly got it right. The only surprise, given Lamb's willingness to silence any potentially troublesome witness, was that Kershaw had lasted so long.

14

It started to rain on the way home. Buchanan drove in silence for much of the way, probably because he was thinking over what Kershaw had told them. He was one of those people who had to have peace and quiet while cogitating deeply whereas Fizz didn't know what she was thinking until she heard herself say it aloud or, in extreme circumstances, wrote it out on a piece of paper.

She tried to keep silent because she wanted Buchanan to pursue his own line of thought before comparing it with hers but that lasted about three minutes, then she said, 'What d'you think, amigo mio, is it another blackmail thing?'

'Mmm.' He slowed for a traffic light and sat drumming his fingertips on the driving wheel, keeping time with the windscreen wipers. 'Could be, but who's blackmailing whom?'

Fizz was about to say that Montrose was possibly blackmailing Lamb but then realised it could be the other way round. The charges, if the truth came out, might not be as severe for the officer as they'd be for the private, but Montrose sure as hell wouldn't be too happy to have it known that he had covered up Lamb's private massacre.

'One thing we do know,' Buchanan said, 'is that while Terence is screaming about being framed he's also being very careful not to point the finger at Montrose. He wouldn't want his past history coming out right at this moment in his life.'

'Actually, Montrose could be just as likely as anyone else to have framed Lamb,' Fizz mused. 'Imagine what he would do if he found Amanda was having it off with Terence. The obvious plan would be to bump off Amanda — thus inheriting all her money — and frame Terence for the job. Two birds with one stone.'

'Uh-huh. I thought of that, but there's one snag. Terence says he got nowhere with Amanda and I have a gut feeling that he's telling the truth. The way he spoke about her, calling her frigid, et cetera. That's exactly the way he'd react if he'd tried it on with her and been slapped down. Besides, he doesn't strike me as the type to admit to a failure in that field if it's not true.'

'Right,' Fizz had to agree. She considered the implications for a minute and decided that if Lamb had, in fact, been having an affair with Amanda he'd immediately have suspected her husband of framing him for her murder. The mere fact that he still trusted Ewan was proof enough that his conscience was clear, as far as breaking up the happy home was concerned. She said, 'I reckon there's no way Terence would keep his mouth shut about the massacre if he thought Montrose was setting him up to take the rap for Amanda's murder. He'd blow the whole story and take Montrose down with him. So he must really believe Montrose innocent.'

'That's the way I see it,' Buchanan nodded, 'but that's just his opinion. Maybe Montrose is cleverer than we think. I wish I knew if the police found anything suspicious about that guy. He's definitely iffy.'

Fizz looked out of her window and discovered they were passing through Glenlockart en route to Mrs Sullivan's house. 'Five minutes and we could be down at Tollcross.'

'What's at Tollcross?'

'Charlie Vivers's local, that's what's at Tollcross. Barclay's bar. I bet he'll still be there.'

Buchanan looked at his watch, patently hoping it would tell him it was too late, but it let him down. 'I suppose it wouldn't do any harm to pop in.'

Fizz was relieved to hear him acquiesce with so little argument since their brisk walk had left her parched right down to her belly button. No doubt his acceptance derived from the fact that he was suffering from the same symptoms.

They found Charlie ensconced at the bar, just finishing what he had probably intended to be his last pint of Guinness. However, all thoughts of departure were quickly forgotten when he saw the Last of the Big Spenders push through the throng and he accepted a double malt with very little persuasion. They retired to a table that was comparatively private and Buchanan got right to the point, probably to save on expenses.

'We've made very little progress this week,' he said frankly, 'but we're both of the opinion that Ewan Montrose would merit a closer inspection. I get the impression that his marriage was not the closest of relationships and, that aside, there's no denying that Amanda's death left him a wealthy man. I wondered if you felt, at any

214

time — or if your Inverness colleagues ever felt that there might be some reason to suspect his involvement in the case?'

'Well, obviously he had to be the prime suspect right from the beginning. Nine times out of ten it's a close family member who turns out to be the perp, but Haig never managed to get anything on him that would stand up in court.' Charlie stuck his fag in his mouth so that he could use both hands to open his packet of crisps. With his eyes screwed up to avoid the smoke he looked a little like a fat Clint Eastwood. 'What makes you think he wasn't happily married?'

'Nothing specific. I could be way off the mark but I can't help thinking there's something not quite genuine about Ewan's grief. Also I get the picture that Amanda had her own interests and was away from home quite a bit.' Buchanan sipped his tonic water, regarding Charlie hopefully over the rim of his glass. 'And then there's Marcia.'

That brought a grin to Charlie's face. 'Ah, yes. Marcia. You think there was a bit of hanky-panky going on between Ewan and her? Wouldn't be a bit surprised, but we weren't able to establish any proof of that. They both denied it and nobody else admitted to knowing anything to the contrary.' He turned his glass slowly on the table top, his fingers delicately placed at its base. 'I can tell you Haig and his team checked out Montrose pretty closely. You're right when you say he inherited a fortune. Amanda left him everything she had — didn't have anyone else to leave it to as far as we could discover. No,' he corrected himself, one finger raised, 'I lie. There were small bequests to Oliver and Marcia.'

'Were those three the only suspects?' Fizz asked. 'Ewan, Oliver and Marcia?'

'Those three and Lamb were the main suspects, yes, but Haig took a long look at some of the people in the village. There had been some ill feeling a few years back over a right-of-way that Amanda tried to fence off. Totally illegal, of course, but landowners are still trying that one on and hoping to get away with it.'

'What about Chloe Miller?'

'The journalist?' He raised his brows at her as though surprised that she knew the name. 'She may well have been somewhere on the list, but pretty far down, I'd imagine. You know something I don't?'

'No, no,' Fizz said, trying not to look too disappointed. 'I just thought, when I spoke with her last weekend, that she wasn't a big fan of the Montrose family.'

'You got that right anyway, lass. Montrose said she was always snooping around Breichmenach House hoping to dig up some dirt she could cause trouble with. He claims he once found her upstairs in a bedroom during a garden party. I believe Inspector Haig asked her about it but she just laughed it off. Said it wasn't anything personal, she was just hunting for something to write about like she did all the time.' He finished his packet of crisps and upended the packet to tip the crumbs into his mouth. 'That's what she claimed, anyway, but I think you could find a bit of a grudge between them if you looked hard enough. Nothing more than the typical village backbiting, more than likely, but you only have to read the articles Chloe Miller wrote after the murder to see she was delighted to put the knife in. If you read between the lines you'll see what I mean.'

'We've tried speaking to her once or twice,' Buchanan admitted, 'but she doesn't give much away.'

Charlie was stubbing out his fag but paused to look at him as though his interest was suddenly aroused. 'Really? That's interesting.'

'Is it? Why?' Fizz asked, but he seemed unwilling to say more.

'Oh, I dunno.' He consulted his watch as though suddenly worried about the time. 'I just wondered why she should have anything to hide, that's all.'

Fizz would have liked to pursue this matter a little further but Buchanan forestalled her by saying, 'I found Oliver extremely reticent also. Maybe it's a Highland trait — not talking with strangers.'

Charlie seemed more than willing to accept that explanation, so willing, in fact, that Fizz's suspicions were aroused. She was certain he knew something about Chloe that he didn't want to share and she couldn't help but wonder what it was. She glanced at Buchanan's face and thought she could discern a certain closeness of gaze as he looked at Charlie, an expression that told her he had noted the policeman's reaction and was as curious as she. There was no point in trying to return to the subject. Charlie was no half-brained hooker, like Trixie, and wouldn't spill any information he didn't mean to part with, so if he gave her any answer at all regarding Chloe's integrity, it was likely to be an invented one.

They took their leave after one drink, citing their rendezvous with Mrs Sullivan as an excuse, and hurried out into the rain.

Buchanan didn't start the car straight away. He said, 'Did I imagine it or did Charlie clam up there very suddenly?'

'That's what it looked like to me,' Fizz told him. 'He was talking about Chloe and then he backed right down. I reckon he's torn two ways: he'd love to see his mate Haig shown up for having arrested the wrong man, but he also has his own reputation to consider. After all, it was he who was able to confirm Haig's suspicions about the guy. So, if he's beginning to wonder if Chloe is somehow involved he must be hoping we don't uncover it and set the cat among the pigeons.'

'He seemed quite happy to talk about Chloe at first,' Buchanan brooded, 'but something must have occurred to him. Was it something we said?'

Fizz cast her mind back but could remember nothing significant. Neither could Buchanan. He started the car and drove sedately across town to Joppa where, parking at the side of the house, they spotted Mrs Sullivan in the back garden. This came as something of a surprise since the rain was now falling steadily and she was wearing nothing more appropriate than a thin summer dress. She was walking slowly around a lilac tree, touching the trunk and staring up through the leaves with an expression on her face of complete bliss. Were this not strange enough, Fizz then realised that the silly old thing was, in fact, barefoot.

The old lady was too engrossed in what she was doing to notice the sound of the car drawing up and too far away to call to, so they went round to the front door and started ringing the bell. It took several attempts to finally attract her attention and, when she at last opened the door, she looked fairly normal apart from the fact that her dress was soaking wet. She had obviously taken the time to dry herself as much as she could and to don a pair of slippers and her voice when she greeted them was, if understandably breathless, low pitched and matter-of-fact.

'Sorry to keep you standing there in the rain, my dears. I was out in the garden. Isn't it miserable, after all this good weather we've been having? It must have come on so suddenly. I was having a little nap after my dinner and when I woke up it was pouring. I had to rush out and bring in the washing so you find me looking like a tsunami victim! Come away in and find yourselves a seat and I'll change into something warm before I get pneumonia.'

She shepherded them into the lounge and then fluttered away into her bedroom from where snatches of quickly stifled song emerged to entertain them for the next five minutes or so. Fizz listened, wide-eyed, to this performance.

'She's flying,' she whispered to Buchanan who

appeared to be taking the matter very much to heart. 'And, what's more, she knows it. You can see she's trying to cover up.'

Buchanan flapped a restraining hand and shook his head at her to indicate that they'd talk later, but Fizz didn't do polite silence.

'We'll have to confront her with it. What's the point of going on like this, not being sure whether we're dealing with a drug addict or a senile old woman who can't tell fact from imagination?'

'I don't think she's taking drugs,' Buchanan hissed. 'And, if she is, there's no point in challenging her about it. She'd deny it like mad.'

'Not if you ask her nicely. You could put it to her like . . . '

The sound of faint footfalls in the hallway silenced her for the moment but she had time for a really pointed look at Buchanan before the door opened. His answering glower was even more pointed and he underlined it by showing her his fist which she read as a hint to mind her own business. His way was not her way and never would be but she had to admit that, from time to time, he appeared to know what he was doing. Well, she thought, he can handle this client as he chooses, but she's not as sweet and uncomplicated as he thinks she is. Not by a long chalk. That lie about taking in the washing had come rather too blithely to her lips.

Mrs Sullivan, as she came back into the room, seemed to be entirely back to normal. She had swapped her damp dress for a long woollen housecoat that looked like cashmere and had even taken the time to apply a touch of pink lipstick to her withered lips. Fizz watched her closely as she bustled about pouring out sherry and tonic water but could detect no unsteadiness in her gait. Her hands were deft on the fine glasses and her voice as she chatted politely was just as brisk and steady as it usually was.

'And so,' she said on a sigh as she sank into her chair, 'what have you been up to today, my friends? Have you made any progress, or is it too soon to hope for that?'

'At this stage in the game,' Buchanan said, smiling gently, 'it's difficult to say if we've made progress or not. We're still at the stage of gathering information, speaking to anyone concerned with the Montrose family, checking out their evidence as far as we're able, weighing one statement against another. We've certainly uncovered one or two possible leads which may merit further scrutiny, but as yet we don't have any specific suspect in our sights.'

'What sort of leads?' Mrs Sullivan leaned forward in her chair. She seemed to be very alert but, to Fizz, that alertness of body was just a trifle forced. Nor was it matched by her eyes which, though fully open and intently fixed on Buchanan's face, gave the impression of being widely out of focus. It was fairly obvious that the woman was making a supreme effort to overcome whatever symptoms she might be suffering and to present the appearance of normality.

'Nothing very exciting,' Buchanan said. 'I don't want you to start getting your hopes up just yet but it does appear to me that, if Terence Lamb was indeed framed for Amanda's murder, as he maintains, the best place to seek the culprit is at Breich. I want to take another look at Ewan Montrose and also at the journalist, Chloe Miller. I don't have any evidence against either of them yet but I'm afraid another visit to the area is on the cards.'

'I'm not at all surprised to hear it.' Mrs Sullivan tossed back her sherry in one swig and then looked shiftily at her guests as though hoping they hadn't noticed. 'Amanda Montrose was an evil woman and evil breeds evil. God knows her wickedness infected me. It taught me to hate. I have not the slightest doubt that it had the same effect on all of those around her and if that is the . . . if that is the . . . '

Her audience waited for her to continue. And waited. And waited, while she remained frozen as though turned to stone, her wide-eyed gaze directed so fixedly across Buchanan's right shoulder that he turned his head and glanced behind him to see what she was looking at.

'Mrs Sullivan?' he said finally, and she blinked rapidly for a few seconds before her eyes slid round to his.

They sat looking at each other in silence, she looking extremely wary, he bland and faintly questioning. Then she forced a little smile, the sort you'd see on a torture victim, and said, 'Sorry, did you say something? I'm afraid I was off on a train of thought just then.'

He paused, carefully not looking at Fizz, and then gave a little cough and murmured, 'May I ask, Mrs Sullivan, if you are on any medication that might cause drowsiness?'

She didn't answer immediately but continued to meet his inquiring gaze while she thought it over. 'I am on medication, yes Mr Buchanan, but not the kind that I'd have expected to make me sleepy. My doctor prescribed a daily calcium tablet — it appears I have a touch of osteoporosis in my spine — but he didn't warn me to expect side effects. I must read the information leaflet again.' She passed a hand quickly across her forehead and eyes. 'I must admit, I haven't been feeling quite myself for some days now, but it never occurred to me that it could be caused by an adverse reaction to the medication. Dear me, how very strange.'

'Would you mind letting me have a quick look at your tablets?'

'Not at all. I'd be very grateful if you would.' She hauled herself out of her deep armchair and exited, closing the door behind her.

Fizz immediately leaned forward to whisper her opinions to Buchanan but he scowled at her and shook his head so she muttered, 'Sod you then' and looked for something to nose into while she had the opportunity. There was a red leather photograph album among the books on the shelf beside her, which was better than nothing, so she picked it up and riffled through a few pages of unremarkable scenery, groups of unidentifiable people, and the odd badly exposed snap of a middle-aged man with a fishing rod, probably Mrs Sullivan's deceased husband. One face, however, smiled out at her, halting her flicking finger for some reason which she was slow at identifying. She lifted the book higher to catch the light and studied the young man who formed the centre of a small group. He looked intelligent and supremely happy, his arms encircling two young children and a laughing woman who was obviously his wife.

Fizz studied the picture carefully, curious to know what had prodded her subconscious, but it was only when she gave up and started to turn the page that she got another flash of recognition and realised that she was staring at Mrs Sullivan's male counterpart. This guy didn't just resemble her, if you'd shaved him a bit closer and stuck a white wig on his head you'd have had two Mrs Sullivan's for the price of one.

Hurriedly, she thrust the book at Buchanan, but he had no time for more than a single glance at it before Mrs Sullivan was back amongst them flourishing a small white box.

'Adcal-D3,' she fluted, giggling like a school-girl. 'I couldn't have told you the name to save my life but that's what it says on the label. Two per day, with food.'

Buchanan took the box from her, extracted the information leaflet and started to study it. While he did so Mrs Sullivan noticed Fizz fiddling with her empty glass and replenished both it and her own, topping up Buchanan's tonic water without disturbing him to ask if he wanted it or not.

'I hope you don't mind,' Fizz mentioned with her most innocent smile, 'but I stole a little look at your photograph album. I love looking at photographs.'

She leaned over to lift the album from the coffee table where Buchanan had laid it but Mrs Sullivan, being closer than she, forestalled her and took it onto her own lap. 'Nothing but very boring old snaps in this,' she said with flat finality. 'I'll show you my other one.'

'There is one that caught my eye though.' Fizz held out a hand and, after a second's hesitation, Mrs Sullivan relinquished the book. 'This one here. I wondered if this young man were a relative of yours.'

'Ah . . . yes.' She donned the reading glasses that were swinging from her neck as usual and gave the photograph a long appraisal, almost as if she'd never noticed it before. 'That's my nephew, Nigel, with his wife and daughters. I haven't seen them for quite a few years now. They emigrated to New Zealand, I believe. Or was it Tasmania?'

Fizz was aware of Buchanan's eyes on her. She couldn't tell without looking directly at him whether he was furious with her or not and she didn't much care. 'He's very like you, isn't he? Facially, I mean.'

'You think so? I can't see it myself.'

'I'd say it was quite a marked resemblance. More striking than that between you and your son.'

Mrs Sullivan remained bent over the book on her lap, her face hidden from Fizz, and quite simply let the matter drop. It was only when she began turning over the pages to look at the rest of the photographs that Fizz realised she had no intention of elaborating on what she'd already said. It could have been a deliberate evasion on her part, but it could just as easily be a symptom of her current confused state.

Fizz was thinking about enforcing a return to the topic when Buchanan said, 'I don't see any likelihood of this medication causing side effects. Perhaps you're still tired after your trip to Inverness last weekend. I'd try to have a few early nights if I were you.'

'I feel sure you're right, Mr Buchanan. I'll take your advice and cosset myself for a few days. You won't require my presence at Breich again this time, will you?'

Buchanan put her right on that score and he and Fizz took their leave, squabbling spiritedly all the way back to town.

15

Buchanan had plenty of time for contemplation during the drive to Inverness. The traffic was light and sheets of heavy rain veiled the normally distracting views of mountain and loch, reducing his awareness to the routine of driving and the pictures inside his head.

Mrs Sullivan figured largely in his thoughts: her bizarre behaviour, her forgetfulness, her propensity for bending the truth. He was now fairly sure she indulged in recreational drugs, but probably nothing harder than the occasional joint and, according to Fizz, who was considerably better educated in these matters than he was himself, hashish was unlikely to persuade a person she was a murderer. One could easily understand her reluctance to admit to anything like a drug habit, since she was at pains to establish her complete and uninterrupted rationality, but it was a little worrying all the same. What caused him even more disquiet, and a certain amount of soul searching, was the question of why he was still on the case. Specifically: was he bending over backwards to give Mrs Sullivan the benefit of the doubt simply because he was enjoying all the side benefits that came with the job? Would he otherwise have been more willing to conclude that she was wasting his time?

It was something he'd have liked to discuss

with Fizz but there was no way she could be objective about something connected with moral values. He could already hear her derisive laughter ringing in his ears. She would never writhe under the claws of conscience as he frequently did, nor would she ever empathise with his recurrent attacks of remorse. It was enough for her to do what seemed best at the time. Which, when you thought about it, was all you could ask of anybody.

Thus comforted, he allowed himself a small glow of anticipation at the thought of an excellent dinner in the company of Chloe, who he'd had the foresight to telephone earlier in the day. Poor old Justin, by comparison, was going to be stuck with salad and cottage cheese tonight after all and hadn't sounded too thrilled about it when Buchanan had cancelled today's cooking lesson. Which was something else to feel guilty about.

A large Glenmorangie on arrival at the hotel, however, made these qualms a trifle easier to bear and by the time Chloe showed up an hour later he was primed to enjoy a pleasant and, hopefully, informative evening.

She'd taken a taxi, which was a good sign because it showed that this time she was going to drink more than a couple of glasses of white wine. Admittedly, she looked like a girl who could handle her liquor but if there was any chance at all of alcohol loosening her tongue he felt confident that Mrs Sullivan would be happy to foot the bill.

They had, accordingly, a very nice Sancerre

with their main course and a slightly less gratifying but still excellent Riesling with their dessert, before retiring to the lounge for coffee and liqueurs. It couldn't be said that Chloe gave any sign of being befuddled by these libations but she was unquestionably more relaxed than he'd seen her previously.

He sat down facing her across the corner of their coffee table so that he could enjoy the picture she made in her little black dress and waited for her to ask if he had anything to report. Both of them had studiously avoided the subject of Amanda's demise while they ate but they both knew they weren't here purely for the pleasure of each other's company. It took a minute or two before she broke.

'So tell me,' she said, making it look as though she'd exhausted every alternative subject for conversation, 'have you turned up any interesting clues in your murder inquiry?'

'One or two,' Buchanan told her. 'What about you? Made any progress?'

She shook her head, making two wings of black hair dance about her cheeks. 'Nothing new, I'm afraid. All my leads have dried up. If I worked full-time for the *Inverness Courier* people would be more willing to talk to me but they won't open up to a freelance. I'm relying on you to point me in a new direction. Who've you been speaking to?'

Buchanan tasted his Glayva. 'I had a few words with Sergeant Vivers, last night,' he said, watching her face for some response that might hint at a reason for Vivers's interest in her.

She looked dubious for a second and then said, 'Vivers . . . I've heard the name but I can't place him. One of the coppers investigating the murder, right?'

'That's right. A middle-aged bloke, slightly tubby. I think he spoke with you.'

'Right,' she nodded, wrinkling her brow uncertainly. 'I think I know the one you mean. Was he from Edinburgh?'

'That's the one. He seemed quite interested in you.'

That startled her. 'Me? Why?'

'I got the impression he was curious to know if you had something personal against Amanda and Ewan. Something more than just a general dislike. Apparently Ewan told him that he'd found you exploring upstairs in Breichmenach House during a garden party.'

'Oh, really, what a fuss that man makes about nothing!' She pursed up her lips and stared angrily out at the drizzle for a moment and then said, 'I was looking for the loo, that's all, and took a tiny peep into Amanda's bedroom as I was passing. It was just bad luck that he caught me there but I wasn't up to any mischief, as he insinuated, I was just admiring the furnishings.'

Yeah, right, said Fizz's voice inside Buchanan's head, for all the world as though he were wired up to her. Or was he just becoming as cynical as she was? 'When you say Amanda's bedroom,' he said, mildly intrigued, 'd'you mean they had separate rooms?'

'Oh, unquestionably. All frilly and feminine. Perfumes and make-up on the dressing table. A magnificent satin housecoat over the end of the bed. It was Amanda's room all right and I bet Ewan didn't get to see much of it.'

Her confidence, Buchanan surmised, was consistent with having established that there were no men's garments in the wardrobes and probably no shaving gear in the en suite bathroom either. 'You mean . . . they weren't all that close?'

'That's what I hear.'

'From Terence?'

'No, not Terence. He never told tales out of school, but Marcia once insinuated that Amanda was frigid and I got Oliver to more or less confirm it, later, when he was drunk and trying to chat me up.'

So that's what she'd been trying to verify when she was caught snooping during the garden party. A right little dirt digger. One had to wonder why such a fact would have interested her. He said, 'Was their estrangement due to his supposed relationship with Marcia?'

'No.' She gave a cynical little smile. 'Marcia's only been around for about eighteen months and she wasn't the first of Ewan's sexy little 'helpers'. Amanda and Ewan hadn't slept together in years. At least three years if my suspicions are correct.'

Buchanan found this surprising. Somewhere along the line he had formed the opinion that Ewan and Amanda's sex life was pretty active. It was hardly a fact that would have been important to him so it had to have come, gratuitously, from someone else. Then it came back to him.

231

'The first time we spoke, Chloe — at the garden fête, you remember? — didn't you tell me that, whatever their differences, there was no trouble in the bedroom? Something was said about Ewan getting as much sex as he could handle.'

He had no particular reason for pursuing this topic, other than to get the facts straight, but the quick flush that swept up from the low neckline of her dress alerted him to the fact that she was either embarrassed or extremely annoyed.

He said, 'If he wasn't having an affair with Marcia and his wife was giving him the elbow, who was the lady in his life?'

She finished off her liqueur and set the glass down on the table with a click. It was quite clear that she was furious. With him? With herself? Buchanan waited to see which of them would get the blasting. Then she turned her head to give him a level look and said, 'God knows how that slipped out. Listen, Tam, it's not that I don't want to level with you, but this thing is important to me. There's a story in it: a story that could get me a permanent post on the *Courier*. Can you understand that? There's money in it — there's maybe even a book in it — but, if the facts leak out before I can sell it, you can see for yourself that it won't be worth a button.'

Buchanan felt both elated and depressed: elated by the hint that there was something cogent to be learned about the Montroses, depressed by the certainty that Chloe wasn't daft enough to share it. She had to know as well as he did that he couldn't guarantee to keep secret any facts she might divulge to him. If he needed to disclose information to free Terence Lamb or to bring a different perpetrator to justice he'd have no choice but to do so. For a moment he wished he had Fizz's conscience.

'I see your point,' he said, and was rewarded with a glowing look that wasn't so much a smile as a facial hug.

'You're a nice guy, Tam,' she said.

He was inclined to agree with her but not enormously cheered as being a nice guy had earned him very little in life, other than derision.

'How close are you to writing up your story?'

Her bosom rose and fell in an interesting sigh. 'What I know is already written up, so I'm not too worried about that, but there's more to find out and that could take me months. Obviously, the story wouldn't have half the impact if it came out piecemeal. Consequently I'm now working against the clock to complete my research in case you beat me to it.'

'Okay.' Buchanan nodded his acceptance of that and decided to try a shot in the dark. 'But as it happens, I think I may already know the first part of the story. Would I be right in assuming that it concerns Amanda's involvement with Terence Lamb's vice racket in Edinburgh?'

She took a moment to decide how to handle that question and then smiled. 'You're a fast operator, Tam. It took me months to sniff that one out. How did you get on to it?'

'I still don't have any proof,' he admitted, softening the blow with his most bashful smile.

'How did you find out?'

For a moment he thought he'd blown it. Her face hardened visibly as she realised she'd been more forthcoming than necessary but then she gave another delicious sigh and said, 'I watched Terence, that's how. I knew there had to be some reason for his frequent visits other than his supposed love of fishing, so I simply watched him from the moment he arrived till the moment he left. It cost me a packet, I swear to God: first class binoculars, a sound enhancer, night vision goggles.'

'You were that sure there was something to uncover?'

'I was certain. Terence is a dyed-in-the-wool crook. He couldn't hide it if he tried and he didn't try very hard. He had a cushy life up at Breichmenach House: free board and lodging, no boss breathing down his neck, and money in his hand at the end of the week, but that wasn't enough for him. He was always on the lookout for a scam, always boasting about hitting the big-time one of these days. Definitely not the sort of guy who'd take a weekend off from his so-called security business for a cast or two in the Blackwater. Okay, I'd seen him fishing once or twice before he left but that was because there was nothing else to do, so I was absolutely certain that he had a better reason for visiting Breichmenach House on such a regular basis.'

'How often did he turn up?'

She tipped her head to the side uncertainly. 'Difficult to be sure, because he tried to keep a low profile, and I know there were plenty of times when he managed to avoid my attention, but I reckon it was around once every month or six weeks.'

'So you suspect he was handing over Amanda's share of the takings?'

'I know he was,' she said, and her eyes shone with a self-satisfaction she was unable to hide. 'Not only do I know it, I have a photograph to prove it.'

The words 'and you don't' were as audible as if she'd spoken them aloud. A good point. This information was of little use to anybody without proof and if he tried to subpoena her she'd deny everything she'd told him.

'You have evidence of money changing hands?'

'I have. Stacks of it. They had it spread out on the kitchen table one dark night last January and I caught the whole scene. I reckon Amanda gave him the money to start the business and it turned out to be a very nice little earner.'

Buchanan leaned back in his chair and looked around him. Most of the guests, the vast majority of whom were middle-aged or older, had toddled off to bed and the waiter was wilting visibly behind the bar.

'Let's have a nightcap, shall we?'

He ordered the drinks and waited till she'd started on hers before he asked the obvious question. 'So, if that partnership was your first area of research, I assume you're now looking into Amanda's background. If you have any leads at all to follow that may be something I could help you with. You spoke of your difficulties as a freelance journalist: maybe an advocate would have more clout, more strings to pull, better means of accessing information. I have an adequate expense account to draw on and money can make all the difference in this sort of situation.'

After a moment's consideration she shook her head. 'I don't think so, Tam. It's too important to me.'

Buchanan had been wondering if she had either certain knowledge that Amanda's past was interesting or had discovered any lines of inquiry worth pursuing, so this reply was encouraging. He sipped his drink and said, 'If we are sharing our information freely there may not be any problem. You'd be ready to publish at the same time as I decide to take my evidence to the police, which would be well before they could slap an embargo on you. But, even if you were unable to publish before or during the trial, your story would still be the first — and the most informed — account to reach the media and would surely have more of an impact than if it came out before the trial.'

That appeared to have only a moderate effect on her resistance. She sipped her drink and had a good look at her fingernails and seemed to be giving the matter her consideration but Buchanan could see she was by no means enthused by the suggestion.

Finally he had to say, 'I suppose it's a gamble whichever way you look at it. You could confide in me and I could double-cross you — which I think you know is not on the cards — or you could decide to go it alone and chance my beating you to the post by being forced to reveal Amanda's murky past before you do.'

'No, it's not that I don't trust you, Tam. I know you're not the type to go back on your word.' She thought for a moment, the tip of her tongue moistening the corner of her mouth. 'But, as you say, the truth could come out before I'm ready. I'd be silly not to accept any help you can give me.'

'I honestly believe that would be your best course,' Buchanan told her, holding his impatience in check so as not to appear too voracious, 'particularly if you have any leads that are proving difficult to research.'

'I have,' she said with a wan smile. 'That's the only kind, isn't it? However, I can tell you one thing for sure, Tam. Amanda Montrose was poison.'

'How do you know that?'

'Because — and I'd really like this to stay confidential if at all possible — she brought about the death of a girl I roomed with at university.'

'She killed her?'

'As good as. Edith was doing the same course as I was. She was a darling girl and I loved her to bits but she was very young for her age — silly, really. She didn't know what day it was. And so, naturally, she overspent her grant and was scared to admit it to her parents. I gather they were pretty tough on her, particularly her father. She was the only one in the family to get the chance of doing a degree and there was a lot of pressure on her to do well, et cetera . . . I was scraping the bottom of the barrel myself and couldn't be much help to her so, as time went on, she worked herself into a state of panic. She wasn't eating, she wasn't paying her share of the rent, she was just hanging on, waiting for the axe to fall. So what happened — although I didn't know this till much later — was that someone told her about Amanda. Only she wasn't calling herself Amanda — not to Edith anyway. She was just plain Jean.'

'The massage parlours?' Buchanan hazarded.

'No, apparently not. It turns out that Amanda had a charming little business of her own: she ran an international 'escort agency'.' Chloe supplied the inverted commas with twiddled fingers and her lips twisted in a humourless smile. 'You and I would have known exactly what that meant but to Edith it conveyed a picture of being pleasant company for visiting business-men, accompanying them to nice restaurants or to the theatre, laughing at their jokes and making interesting conversation. I don't know whether that was the picture Amanda painted for her but that's certainly what she understood to be the job description.

'And, actually, Amanda broke her in very patiently. Edith's first 'client' was a lad not much older than herself: so sweet and gentle, so 'suddenly carried away', that he was almost certainly in Amanda's pay. Edith was pretty shocked at 'going too far' — her own words, by the way — but the money she got in the post the next morning solved at least one of her problems. I can just about imagine what a relief it must have brought her. So, when Amanda gave her another client a week later she fell for it again, only this time it was made clear to her at the last minute that mere conversation wouldn't earn her enough to finish the term. Once again, Amanda had chosen her a personable partner, so she went through with it. I suppose she'd been in heaven for a week and now couldn't bear to plunge back into the mire.'

She broke off and circled a hand to indicate a continuing state of affairs. 'So, you can guess the rest. The following week another man, slightly older, slightly less fanciable. Soon it was more than once a week and the customers were frequently pretty gross and had strange tastes. Somewhere along the line it was suggested to her that a line of coke would make the job a trifle less distasteful and after that there was no turning back. By that time I could see there was something nasty going on but she wouldn't talk to me about it and I convinced myself that she was just worried about her exams. She pretended she had finally managed to get a late-night job stacking shelves at Safeway's and it wasn't till just before she died — of a heroin overdose — that she told me the truth.'

It was a common enough story, Buchanan supposed. He'd certainly heard it many times before but it saddened him all the same. He said, 'So you decided to hunt down the madam . . . Amanda?'

'No, not really.' She lifted a self-deprecating shoulder. 'I was too busy getting myself a job,

239

first on a free-advertising rag and then a local paper. I did find out who'd been the 'friend' who'd recommended Edith to contact 'Jean'. A certain Pam Cooper. She did well for herself after leaving uni, did Pam. When I ran across her again three or four years back she'd opened a pricey little private art gallery and was hauling in the cash, driving a Porsche and nicking off to Malaga every other weekend.'

Buchanan returned her cynical smile. 'Having earned enough through Jean's agency to get herself started?'

'That's what it looked like to me and I can tell you, Tam, it made my blood boil to see her so smug after what she'd done to an innocent like Edith. That's when I decided to put an end to 'Jean's' operation altogether.'

Once again, it was easy to hear more in her words than she intended to impart. No doubt she had been genuinely wounded by the way her friend had been used, no doubt she would have welcomed an opportunity to avenge her tragic death, but the fact that there might be money and/or promotion in an exposé must also have weighed with her.

'I imagine Amanda wouldn't be so easy to locate,' he murmured. 'She was a lady who knew how to cover her tracks.'

'She certainly did. She also trusted nobody. As far as I've been able to discover, nobody but she knew about the escort agency. It's possible even Ewan himself was in the dark though you'd think he must, since her death, have found some trace of her activities. Amanda did all the recruiting herself, made all the appointments, took all the money, paid all the bills. All I had to do was hint to Pam that I might be interested in moving up into the money bracket *she* was currently enjoying and all was made easy for me. Within a week I had an appointment with the lady herself.'

Buchanan managed to nod sagely but he found this crazy plan so uncannily like something Fizz would think up that he was astonished. My God, he found himself thinking, there's two of them!

'Of course, I had no intention of actually keeping the appointment, but I was staking out the hotel room where we had our rendezvous, ready to clock Amanda and follow her home to Breichmenach House.' She smiled vivaciously for the first time since they'd left the dinner table, every inch a newshound thrilled by the excitement of a successful chase. 'Halfway there she pulled off the wig she'd been wearing and discarded her heavy-rimmed glasses.'

You had to hand it to Chloe, Buchanan thought, she didn't mind putting the work in. One of these days, given a decent break, she'd be a first class investigative reporter. 'So, you actually moved to Breich for no other reason than to study her operation?'

'To be honest Tam, no, not entirely. I'd always wanted to get out of Edinburgh. I'm not a city person and I hated the job I was in but around that time I'd been doing well with placing my freelance stuff. So, when my dad passed on two years past at Easter and I inherited his house I realised I could sell it and move up north where property's cheap, give myself a few years to see if I could earn a living wage. Amanda was still very much on my agenda at that point and Breich looked as good a place as any to settle so I decided to go for it.' She regarded Buchanan's face with eyes that betrayed, just for a second, an unsuspected vulnerability. 'So you see, Tam, I have a lot invested in this story. If things pan out the way I've gambled they will I've made my career: if I'm pipped at the post I . . . I don't know what I'll do. The bottom will fall out of my world.'

Buchanan would have been one hundred per cent sympathetic to her plight had he not detected a certain similarity, in those final phrases, to the sort of balderdash Fizz could come out with in a similar situation. It appeared there were indeed two of them and neither was as vulnerable as they'd have him believe. However, he couldn't find it in his heart to blame either of them for exercising their wiles, especially as he was now much wiser to that type of manoeuvre than he had once been.

It seemed he had much to thank Fizz for after all.

16

Fizz always found it difficult to settle to anything when Buchanan was out of town. She couldn't have said exactly why this should be but it had something to do with the suspicion that he was having more fun than she was. Breich, obviously, was where it was at, but it was also where Marcia was at, not to mention Chloe, and those two together spelled more fun than was good for Buchanan. It also irritated her that he might progress faster with the case than she, over the next few days. Okay, it was, officially at any rate, his case but one had one's pride in such matters and it wouldn't do to let his already intolerable hubris get out of hand.

She forced herself to put in a good morning's work, ate her usual fruit and yoghurt lunch, and then fell into a bored lethargy with her feet on the desk and her brain on auto-pilot. It was still raining outside, the trees in the green square outside dripping on the lunchtime shoppers. If it was raining this hard in Breich there was a good chance the salmon would be coming up the Blackwater. Maybe that would keep Buchanan out of mischief.

The picture of Mrs Sullivan swam into her mind. What was the woman up to? It was obvious she hadn't actually murdered Amanda but the more one saw of her the surer one became that there was something fishy about her that couldn't be explained away by either senility or a drug habit. That snapshot of her nephew, for instance. How come he looked infinitely more like her than her son did? When you thought about it rationally the guy in the graduation photograph displayed on her coffee table looked nothing like her at all.

She sat half-dreaming about that anomaly for a couple of minutes and then wondered how she could check up on it. The records office, presumably. That would have been no trouble at all had Mrs Sullivan been Scottish, since the Scottish Records Office was only a few doors away from the premises of Buchanan and Stewart, but doing that sort of research by telephone was virtually impossible, especially the way telephones operated these days. It could take all afternoon pressing buttons and talking to machines to even get connected to the right department.

She dawdled around for another half hour, knowing she was going to do it but hoping vaguely that something more important would sidetrack her so that she could pass the task over to Buchanan. He would balk at the suggestion since, basically, he had every confidence in his client but there was a good chance she could talk him into it. In the end it was the thought of — just possibly — being able to phone him with news of a breakthrough that made her go for it herself.

It turned out to be not quite as bad as she'd expected. The first guy she spoke to tried his best to be discouraging but Fizz hung on in there, pleading and schmoozing, till she wore down his endurance and drove him, in desperation, to pass the buck to someone else. She was, by then, prepared for a similar battle with the second guy so she brought out all her best weaponry right away, a sexy voice à la Marcia, a description of her need-to-know as not just a murder case but a matter of life and death, plus as much flattery as she could ladle on without going totally over the top.

From the outset he gave the impression of being not too unwilling to help. It took a scant three minutes to get on first name terms and less than another five to win him over completely. Whether this was due to her tactics or simply to his having as boring a day as she was, Fizz could not say, but she was gratified to have achieved her objective so quickly.

'Just give me all the details you have,' he said, 'and I'll get back to you tomorrow.'

'Oh, gee, Robbie, I'd hoped it wouldn't be too long a job. We have a murderer on the loose here and it would be terrible if he killed again.'

Robbie hummed and hawed a bit but finally said he'd get on to it as soon as he had a minute.

'And you'll check up on anything you can find about Mrs Sullivan's son? His marriage, his death certificate? Anything at all, really?'

Some of the enthusiasm had drained from Robbie's voice as he said, 'Like I said, I'll do my best.'

Fizz cooed her thanks into the receiver and hung up, feeling she'd at least moved forward an inch or two today. If Buchanan should phone she'd show him a shining example of industry and creative thinking. Thus revitalised, she got on with her work and kept her head down for the rest of the afternoon.

Robbie phoned back just as she was thinking about packing in for the day. He sounded less than excited by his findings and spent the first few minutes going on about what a tough time he'd had and how he should have been getting on with other things. Fizz made appropriately sympathetic and grateful noises and told him what a star he was and finally he got round to reporting the results of his gargantuan labours.

'Your Mrs Sullivan's well documented,' he said. 'Born Eleanor Dixon in 1934, married in 1956 to a Frederick Henry Sullivan of Wimbledon. I have his death certificate here, dated 1983, cause of death myocardial infarction — that's a coronary to you and me. Fortunately, she was an only child and her husband had only one sibling who died of diphtheria at the age of eight, so that saved me from having to check up on whether she had a nephew or not. She clearly hadn't.'

Fizz was speechless for a few seconds, torn between shock and elation. 'That's very helpful, Robbie,' she breathed shakily. 'I can't thank you enough. And, did you manage to check up on her son, William?'

'U-huh. He's registered here as being born at Cornwood nursing home on 27th February 1959. I've also got his marriage certificate dated 2nd August 1985.'

'His wife's name?'

'Julia Mather, aged twenty-six.'

Fizz, scribbling the dates on her scrap pad, did a double take at the receiver. 'Julia Mather? You're sure you've got the right William Sullivan?'

'Yes, yes,' he said showing signs of testiness. 'This is Eleanor Sullivan's son all right. I have all his papers here.'

That threw her for a second. Did it mean that Amanda had been using a false name and reverted to her real identity only when it came to getting married? Or was it her new name that was the fake?

'There's something funny there, Robbie,' she said, loading her voice with excited adulation. 'In fact, you may have hit on the very fact that will help us catch our killer. The name Julia Mather could be a pseudonym. Does she have any previous documentation?'

'Hang on and I'll see,' he muttered over the sound of tapping keys, all reticence forgotten. And seconds later, 'Yes, here's her birth certificate with the names of both her parents. I could check them out tomorrow if you like, but we're closing up now and — '

'No, don't bother with that right now,' Fizz told him, her brain buzzing. 'I'll get back to you if it turns out to be necessary, but tell me about William before you go. What does his death certificate give as the cause of death?'

'Ah . . . crushing injuries. Thirteenth November, 1992.'

Fizz was totally confused. 'The information I've been given is that he committed suicide in

247

1987,' she muttered, her mind still struggling to come to terms with this information.

'Well, you've been misinformed, lady. At that point he still had another five years to live. Crushing injuries. Not a nice way to go.'

There were still questions she wanted to ask but at that point in time she couldn't think what they were. Robbie was now working overtime and patently not amenable to hanging around while she groped her way forward so she had to make a date for another chat tomorrow morning and hang up.

She was still sitting there as though turned to stone, with her eyes locked on the wall in front of her and her mind in turmoil, when the Wonderful Beatrice walked in.

'Hello-ho,' she sang, waggling her fingers in front of Fizz's blank gaze. 'Anyone at home?'

Fizz blinked and looked at her. 'Unnh?'

'Are you planning to work late, or what, because the rest of us are leaving.'

Fizz looked at her watch but a second later couldn't have said what the time was. 'I'm leaving, Beattie. Buchanan didn't phone today, did he?'

Beatrice gave her the dead eye. 'When you were asleep, you mean? No, of course not. I'd have wakened you.'

'You malign me, Beattie. I've had a busy and productive day.'

'I'm glad to hear it. Would you mind going home now so's we can lock up?'

Fizz blew her a noisy kiss and hurriedly packed her bag, her entire concentration on the facts she'd just been given. It was a fifteen minute walk up to the High Street and, for most of the way, she kidded herself on that she was going to spend the evening in front of a friend's television watching a history programme they'd been looking forward to for a week. What she really wanted to do was to confront Mrs Sullivan with her findings and demand to know what the hell she was playing at, but that was out of the question. Buchanan would be in anger-management therapy for the rest of his life if she took a step like that without consulting him first and, even if she did consult him, he'd only ban her from going anywhere near Mrs Sullivan till he could accompany her. There had been times in the past when she had barged ahead and to hell with what he thought, but she flattered herself that she had changed, matured, learned patience and discretion.

But what was wrong with just dropping by to check if the old dear was *compos mentis* and to maybe see what came out in an ever-so-slightly steered conversation?

She found Mrs Sullivan just clearing away a late dinner, having been at the supermarket doing her weekly shopping till after six. She seemed relaxed and cheerful in her cashmere housecoat and ushered Fizz into the lounge as though pleased to see her.

'It's extremely kind of you and Mr Buchanan to keep me so well informed. I feel I'm quite *au fait* with everything you're doing. Have you heard how Mr Buchanan is progressing in Breich?'

249

'No, he hasn't phoned today. I think he planned to visit Breich House and have another few words with Amanda's husband but I'm sure he would have let me know if there'd been any major breakthrough, so I think we just have to be patient.' Fizz chose the same chair she'd occupied on her previous visit, casually sliding it an inch or two closer to the bookshelf just in case an opportunity should arise to grab another look at the photograph album.

'Now, my dear, what can I offer you? Sherry again? Or would you care to join me in a peppermint tea? I always have a cup of peppermint tea after my meals. Wonderful for the digestion.'

'Sherry please.'

Fizz's hand was drifting out towards the bookshelf before Mrs Sullivan was out of the room but the album wasn't where she'd seen it last. It wasn't on the shelf it had occupied and, it soon emerged, it wasn't on any of the other shelves either. Nor was it lying around the room.

She took a quiet walkabout with her hands clasped behind her back, pretending to be looking at the paintings or the view from the window but, in reality, hoping to see a red leather corner sticking out from behind a cushion or from under the pile of magazines. Zilch. If she wanted to see that snapshot again she was going to have to ask for it.

'Right then,' said Mrs Sullivan comfortably, as she handed Fizz her sherry and settled back into her chair. 'Tell me what stage we're at today.'

'Well, I've been stuck in the office all day,' Fizz

waffled. 'Unfortunately, I don't have the same amount of free time as Buchanan has at present, but I did a bit of thinking this afternoon. Just collating the information we already have, actually, and trying to identify any avenues we've not yet explored. Did you manage to locate any of William's friends who might help us?'

'No, I'm afraid I didn't, my dear. Not one. I'm almost sure I had some addresses in my old address book but I can't set my hand on it. I must have thrown it out. If I could just call some names to mind you might be able to trace them but, really, my memory is appalling. Of course, I rarely heard their surnames. William simply referred to them as Andy from the office, or James the dentist, or more often just Andy or James. I'll be honest with you, I wasn't sure who he was talking about most of the time and I rarely caught more than a glimpse of them.' She sipped her mint tea and set the cup and saucer down on the table beside her. 'It's most irritating but, really, I can't imagine their being a lot of help, even if we were able to locate them after all these years.'

'Possibly not,' Fizz agreed, 'but we've been trying to look into Amanda's past and it turns out to be very difficult. We know she was in Brighton some ten years after her marriage to William but prior to that she could have been dropped from a spaceship for all the trace she's left. It would be nice if someone who knew her back then had heard her mention where she'd been or what she'd been doing.'

'Yes, I can see now how important that could

be. I wonder if that address book could be up in the attic? I have tea chests up there that haven't been opened since I moved here. Perhaps Mr Buchanan could climb up for me.'

'I could do it now,' Fizz offered, swiftly finishing her sherry, but Mrs Sullivan waved a restraining hand.

'I don't have a ladder dear. There used to be one in the garden but someone made off with it. Terrible, isn't it? You can't leave a thing outside these days.'

Fizz let her replenish their drinks before she said, 'What about university friends? Did William stay in contact with any of his fellow students?'

'Well now, let me think about that for a minute, because I think he did.' She laid a forefinger to her lips and was silent for a moment. 'The name Duane Ellsworth rings a bell but where he came from I cannot tell you. Of course, William took his degree in Canada, I did mention that, didn't I?'

Fizz's hopes of accessing university records took a hammering. She could still do it, eventually, but it would be a slog.

'Which university was that?'

'Queens University. I can't remember the name of the town it was in — could have been Winford . . . Whinford . . . something like that — but it was in Ontario.'

Things could only get better.

'What year did he graduate?'

'Oh my goodness, now you're asking, Miss Fitzpatrick. I'd have to work that out. You see, he worked in Canada for quite a few years before he went back to his studies and I'm not sure how long that was. It's so long ago now.'

She gave a sudden loud trill of laughter that made Fizz jump.

'You'd think the Fates were against us, wouldn't you dear? You must be thoroughly frustrated, trying to investigate things that happened so far in the past that . . . that no one . . .'

She seemed to forget what she'd intended to say — or, more precisely, to have forgotten she was even speaking. She sipped her tea and regarded Fizz with bright eyes as though waiting for her to instigate a fresh topic of conversation.

'Um . . . what did he study?'

'William? He studied medicine, like his father.'

'Was medicine in his blood, so to speak, like law is in Buchanan's?'

'Yes, dear, it was. His grandfather was a doctor also, as was *his* father.'

'And your nephew, was he a doctor too?'

Mrs Sullivan's eyes gave a split second flick in the direction of the bookshelves before she answered. 'No. He went into business for himself. Something to do with computers.'

'What was his name again?' Fizz asked innocently.

Mrs Sullivan sank the last dregs of her tea, struggled out of her chair, and reached for Fizz's glass. 'Let me top you up, my dear. You're not driving, are you? Your nice Mr Buchanan is so particular, isn't he? Won't touch a drop when he has to drive home. I do admire that but, of course, being a lawyer he has to be whiter than white, I suppose. Such a charming young man. Such a gentleman. You don't meet many young men like that these days. I must say I've quite taken to him. Such beautiful eyes. Such a nicely pitched voice. My late husband had a voice like that, with the same hint of vibrato, the same . . . '

Fizz let her rabbit on, satisfied that she was doing so in an attempt to cover up the fact that she couldn't remember what name she'd given her fictitious nephew. It was a struggle to resist repeating her question but she knew Buchanan would go ballistic if she succumbed to the temptation and the thought muzzled her. One thing he could do better than she was rapping the knuckles of recalcitrant witnesses without spooking them completely and if anyone could get Mrs Sullivan to part with the actuality of whatever game she was playing it would be he.

She tried to imagine what possible reason there might be for her to display a false likeness of her son. She hadn't taken time to study the photo in the album but, apart from the striking resemblance of the young father to Mrs Sullivan herself, she had noted nothing particularly remarkable about it. So why was she so touchy about anyone seeing it? Why present a bogus son to the world? It was patently obvious that she had thought out the whole thing in advance, anticipating what questions she might have to answer and preparing suitably unverifiable answers. The only question she'd lost marks on was the one she hadn't expected — the name of the guy in the snapshot. What, in God's name, was she playing at?

Okay, give her a little more rope and see if she might hang herself.

'Would you feel comfortable talking to me about your son's death, Mrs Sullivan?'

'Certainly, certainly,' she said airily, presenting a full glass of sherry with a theatrical flourish.

Fizz saw immediately that her momentary lapse a few minutes ago had not been an isolated incident but an early warning that her secondary personality was starting to surface. Now she was visibly elated, glittery-eyed, exhibiting a strange bonelessness as she sank back into her armchair.

'Ask away, my dear. What would you like me to tell you?'

'I . . . uh . . . I just realised that you've never mentioned how it happened.'

'What method he used to kill himself?'

Fizz nodded dumbly having been, for the look of things, at pains to phrase her question with a good deal less frankness than Mrs Sullivan evidently thought necessary.

'He hanged himself, dear. With my washing line. I found him swinging from his bedroom window.' She rolled her eyes. 'Not a pretty sight.'

It was silly to be shocked by this response since Fizz knew as well as Mrs Sullivan did that the gruesome event had never taken place, but it was weird to hear such words spoken in a tone more in keeping with a humorous anecdote. In fact it was downright spooky. There was now very convincing proof that Mrs Sullivan's funny turns were not due to drug abuse: Fizz had the evidence of her own eyes for that. The old lady had been perfectly rational at the beginning of

255

the evening and had not smoked as much as a joint since then yet now she was acting in a manner that could only be described as scary. She was doing her best to appear normal, that was easy to see, but she couldn't hide her mood change and, although she remembered what lies to tell, she couldn't quite hack the grieving-mother impersonation.

And here I am, Fizz thought, all alone in this bloody house with a madwoman. Time for a swift exit.

17

The rain clouds drifted east overnight and Buchanan awoke to a sky dappled with high cirrus and to the faint scent of wood smoke drifting in at his open window. The water level in the Blackwater, according to the Web report on his laptop, had risen by two feet. Unfortunately he'd slept too long to make a pre-breakfast cast or two a possibility but plans for rectifying that mistake were uppermost in his mind as he made his way down to the dining room.

He made short work of a generous portion of grilled kidneys plus eggs scrambled to Justinian perfection and garnished with deliciously crunchy morsels of something distantly related to the potato and then sat dawdling over his coffee while deliberating on how best to spend his morning. Ewan, who was top of his must-see list, was unavailable till four-thirty in the afternoon since he was going off to a sale of farm machinery with Oliver and Marcia was also busy: attending to a customer who was bringing his mare to stud.

He reviewed the mental list of odds and ends he'd meant to clear up and finally settled on driving over to Moy, the little village where Mrs Sullivan had stayed during her allegedly fateful holiday last March. It was unlikely to prove anything more than that she'd actually been there at roughly the time of Amanda's death but it was one of the accumulation of minor chores, common to every case, that ought to be got out of the way while he was in the vicinity. He had forgotten to ascertain the address of her holiday house but in a village the size of Moy that was unlikely to constitute much of a problem. The tourist brochure for that area would list the available properties and a ten minute chat with the relevant proprietor would suffice to elicit all the necessary information. It was a perfect day for a drive, the route was scenic and interesting, and it appeared to be the best way of making use of the time available.

It took him the best part of an hour to get there, largely because he dawdled around admiring the scenery, shopping for the dental floss he'd forgotten to pack, and watching a couple of guys fishing for — and catching — trout. The village itself was harder to find than he'd imagined, being some miles down a badly signposted road, but it turned out to be a little gem. Thirty or so old stone cottages lined a central square of emerald grass, each one ablaze with colourful window boxes, hanging baskets, urns and troughs. A small whitewashed church could be seen beyond those, its miniature steeple outlined against the purple of the distant mountains, and the road led on towards a higgledy-piggledy scatter of larger houses, a couple of shops, and a market garden.

Buchanan consulted the tourist guide he'd picked up en route and scanned the brief entry for holiday lets. There were five houses listed but only three of them were of a size to interest a single lady. Two of those were in the village square so it took only a matter of minutes for Buchanan to ascertain that Mrs Sullivan had not stayed at either. At the third, which was at the end of the road, next to the market garden, he drew another blank.

A small itch of uneasiness was beginning to make itself felt at the back of his mind as he reread his tourist guide. The only other self-catering accommodation that was listed consisted of large houses more suited to families or groups; one offering four bedrooms, the other five. It seemed highly unlikely that Mrs Sullivan should choose to pay more than double the rental it would have cost to stay in one of the smaller properties, all three of which having been, as he had already discovered, vacant during the month of March, but as one of them was handy he decided to check it out, just in case.

It was set well back from the road, largely hidden from passing view by its elevated position and a screen of pine trees. The gardens stretched up the hill behind it in a series of broad terraces, some of them furnished with sunshades and benches, some in rough lawn with children's swings and chutes.

As Buchanan slogged up the steep driveway with the sun hot on his back he spotted an elderly man on a stepladder cleaning the downstairs windows and conversing loudly with a curly grey head emerging from the casement above him.

'Dirty devils!' he was saying, applying chamois

leather to glass with such violence that it squeaked in protest. 'What's their own home like, eh? That's what I'd like to ask them.'

'And the kitchen,' bleated the woman upstairs, 'I don't think they lifted a scouring pad the whole time they were — '

She broke off as she noticed Buchanan's approach and the man turned his head to see what she was looking at.

'Morning,' he said, with the super-friendly smile of a man with something to sell.

Buchanan returned the greeting and paused while the man descended to his own level, then he presented his card and said, 'I wonder if you can help me. I have a client who stayed in Moy for two weeks in March and I'm trying to locate the house she rented.'

'What's her name?' demanded Curly from just above his head.

'Sullivan. A lady on her own.'

'We don't ever have that kind of let,' she said flatly. 'We have five bedrooms so it's too expensive for single occupancy.'

Her presumed husband completed his scrutiny of the card and raised milky green eyes to Buchanan's. 'Sullivan?' he asked. 'The name's not familiar but we did have a let in March. I remember that because we don't often get bookings till after Easter. Come away in and I'll have a look at the book.'

The grey head was swiftly withdrawn from the upstairs window and was identifiable, as they entered the lobby, as belonging to the fat woman descending the stairs at a fast waddle. Her husband beat her to the hall stand and opened the visitors book.

'May . . . April . . . March. Here we are. Paterson. That's right, I remember now. The Paterson family from Edinburgh.'

Buchanan had been prepared for a no-win result and was drawing a breath to say, well thanks anyway, when the coincidence struck him.

'Edinburgh?' he said. 'You're sure it was a family?'

'Well, we assume it was a family,' put in Curly, still panting a bit from her exertions. 'Could have been two couples: we get that sometimes, or a party of hill-walkers, maybe.'

'Didn't you see them?'

She shook her cheeks. 'No, we live in Perth. We do all the arrangements by mail and just drive up between lets to do the cleaning and tidy the garden. That's why we're here today.'

Buchanan hesitated. He still had one house to check out and there was at least a chance that, regardless of its capacity, Mrs Sullivan had stayed there. Given her propensity for throwing money away, she might be capable of splashing out on more luxurious accommodation than that offered by the small cottages. Yet he found himself unwilling to move on without taking things one small step further.

'Do you have a contact address for the Patersons?'

Curly exchanged an inquiring glance with her husband and left it to him to answer.

'I suppose we'll have a note of it in the

261

bookings register. Want to take a look, Babs?'

'You look,' she said, 'and I'll put the kettle on. This young man looks like he could be doing with a nice cup of tea and a slice of my carrot cake.'

Buchanan protested politely while following her into a large and spotless kitchen and they made the usual sort of weather-related conversation while she rewashed the china, slandering her recent tenants as she did so, and produced what she called elevenses. As she cut into the promised carrot cake her husband returned and opened a hard-backed school jotter on the table.

'Here's what we're looking for. March. Fifteenth till the twenty-ninth. EM Paterson. Och, Babs, I wish you'd take time to write clearly. I can't make head nor tail of this address.'

She muttered under her breath and flounced around for a minute looking for her reading glasses while Buchanan resisted snatching the book and reading it himself.

'Here, let me see.' She screwed up her face and brought the book to the end of her nose. '21 Stevenson Place, Joppa. What's so unreadable about that? It's new glasses you're needing.'

Buchanan couldn't take it in till he'd requested a look at the book and read it with his own eyes. 21 Stevenson Road, Joppa. Mrs Sullivan's address. What in God's name had she been up to, renting a house under a false name? Why should she want to do a thing like that and, having done it, why had she not admitted it to Fizz and himself?

He ate his cake and drank his tea and avoided answering his hosts' questions with his usual, well-practised dexterity but his mind was on none of it. He couldn't wait to get back to the car and get peace to think. Even there, however, parked at the road end with neither pedestrians nor traffic to distract him, he found it impossible to weave what he'd just learned into the web of facts he'd already constructed.

On the face of it, one would have to conclude that if Mrs Sullivan had felt it necessary to act with such subterfuge, she must have been trying to cover her tracks and that led inevitably to the conclusion that she had indeed done Amanda Montrose to death. However, there was another way of looking at the evidence and that was simply that Mrs Sullivan had not been staying on her own during her time in the village. It was quite possible that she had come with a friend — or several friends — but had simply not thought it worthwhile mentioning that fact. One could envisage a scenario where a friend — EM Paterson — had visited her from, say, someplace abroad and they had decided to have a couple of weeks exploring the Highlands.

That would be infinitely easier to believe than the alternative explanation, but it constituted yet another complication which Buchanan felt he could well do without: he now had to decide whether to tell Fizz what he'd uncovered. To tell her everything was to risk her barging into Mrs Sullivan's house, demanding to know what she was playing at. To tell her less than everything could, if Mrs Sullivan was, after all, a vicious killer, put her life at risk. It wasn't actually all that hard a decision to make.

He drove back to the phone box he'd seen in the village square and got hold of the Wonderful Beatrice.

'Hi, Beatrice. Is Fizz around?'

'No, I'm afraid she's not, Mr Buchanan. She phoned in this morning to say she had something to do and would be in later but she hasn't shown up yet.'

'Okay. Will you ask her to phone me as a matter of urgency as soon as she comes in? And, just in case, you'd better tell her not to contact Mrs Sullivan till she speaks to me.'

'Actually, she did say she might be some time, but if she phones in I'll make sure I speak with her.'

'Cheers, Beatrice. Talk to you later.'

He'd have felt better if he could have spoken to Fizz himself but if anyone could be trusted to pass on a message it was Beatrice. All the same, it wouldn't do any harm to phone again in an hour or two if Fizz didn't get back to him before that. Truth to tell, he mused as he drove back to Breich, he was halfway to missing her on this trip. Discussing things with her seldom affected his own conclusions but just running the facts through her mind helped to clarify his thinking. Also, the whole exercise would be better fun with a bit of company.

The afternoon was half gone by the time he got back, ate a late and leisurely lunch and tried again to contact Fizz. This time Beatrice sounded, to his ear, somewhat less serene.

'No, not yet, Mr Buchanan. Not a sign of her.'

Buchanan hated the little worm of worry that wriggled in his guts every time Fizz did something like this. 'What time did she say she'd be in?'

'She didn't specify a time, just that she'd see me later, but I did get the impression it might be a good bit later.'

'Did she have any appointments today?'

'No.' Beatrice's voice took on the motherly tone that had irritated him beyond measure in the days when he had been her boss. 'Now don't you start getting in one of your tizzies, Mr Buchanan. You know what Miss Fitzpatrick's like. She hasn't fallen under a bus, you know.'

Buchanan ground his teeth. 'I'm not worried about Fizz, Beatrice, just impatient to discuss something with her. As soon as you get hold of her tell her to give me a ring on my mobile. Immediately. Okay?'

'Will do,' Beatrice cooed, 'but I don't expect she'll bother coming into the office at this hour of the afternoon, do you?'

There was, Buchanan accepted, little chance of that and it frustrated the hell out of him. Fizz was too mean to have a telephone in her flat and she switched on her mobile as rarely as he did himself, preferring, as he did, to be unavailable outside office hours. That meant that, unless she chose to call the office to pick up her messages, she might be out of touch till tomorrow morning. Damn the woman! Why couldn't she think of other people once in a while? He sent her a curt text message telling her to contact him

265

and tried not to worry.

As he passed through the lobby en route to his appointment at Breich House he was accosted by Arthur, one of the receptionists: a middle-aged guy with a bald head, a vast belly and, unaccountably, an earring. Fizz, on their previous visit, had been gagging to uncover the thinking behind this personal adornment (did he think it made him alluring? Cool? Piratical?) and it had taken all of Buchanan's eloquence to prevent her asking him.

'Mr Buchanan. Good afternoon, sir. This came for you this morning just after you left.'

Buchanan took the yellow slip of paper and discovered it was a telephone message form, timed at eleven-fifty a.m., from a Mr Townsley, no return phone number. The message read, 'Can we meet to discuss CM? Dovran pool, ten p.m.'

The name Townsley rang no bells in Buchanan's memory, nor could he remember speaking to anyone whose name had not come up in conversation but who might conceivably want to speak to him. 'Townsley?' he said. 'I don't know a Townsley. Do you recognise it as the name of anyone local?'

'I'm afraid not, sir. I don't think there's anyone of that name down in the village and there's certainly no one in the hotel. A holidaymaker, perhaps?'

'I take it there's no possibility of a mistake, Arthur? I mean, this Mr Townsley was quite specific about who his message was for?'

'I didn't speak to the caller personally, sir, but

266

there's no doubt he meant you. He asked if Mr Buchanan was still in the hotel and Alex tried your room but got no reply, so the caller said that wasn't a problem and he'd just leave a message.'

Buchanan thanked him and continued round to the car park wondering what to make of it all. There was something just a tad Hitchcockian about the message — even the receptionists appeared to have found it worth discussing — but that was easily explainable, particularly in a small village community where one might not wish it generally known that one had been willing to grass on a neighbour. Alternatively, it could, whatever Arthur thought, turn out to be a case of mistaken identity. Buchanan wasn't all that uncommon a name and it could also be confused with Buchan as he'd found often enough in the past. CM didn't have to refer to Chloe Miller, it could be an abbreviation for anything from carbon monoxide to Common Market. Even the supposition that the Dovran pool would be a suitable place to meet wasn't necessarily remarkable since, with the river in its present fecund state, there would be more than one angler on the lower stretches later on tonight in the hope of hooking a sea trout.

All the same, Buchanan found himself more than willing to disregard any possibility of confusion and take the message at face value. For one thing, the Dovran pool — which he was able to locate on the estate's map of their beat — was barely fifty yards downstream from the scene of Amanda Montrose's murder and that made him wonder if someone knew something about how her corpse had entered the river: someone who wanted, quite naturally, to remain anonymous. The name Townsley was probably a pseudonym, and that was a supposition that gave rise to a host of fascinating questions. Was it, for instance, a cover for someone he knew? Someone from Breich House? Marcia, maybe? It was certainly not impossible for a woman to lower her voice enough to sound like a man. The thought of meeting Marcia by moonlight on the river-bank had its attractions but one could try not to let that get in the way of logical thinking, and logical thinking led to the possibility of this rendezvous proving to be a trap.

He found himself smiling at the thought. He wasn't in some over-the-top B-movie with assassins lurking behind every bush nor was he playing a part in any way comparable to that of the archetypal private eye, intrepid but ultimately gullible. Certainly a murder had been committed and a murder implied a murderer but in this case, Buchanan reasoned, the murderer was almost certainly in jail and, even if he or she were still at large, why should that presage any danger to himself? It could definitely not be said that he was closing in on the guilty party or even that he was appreciably closer to doing so than he had been a week ago. If he'd had to put money on it he'd still have plumped for Terence Lamb as the killer and Terence at least was in no position to cause any more mayhem.

Not that any of that made a lot of difference. He could scarcely do other than keep the appointment with 'Mr Townsley' since it could turn out to be important but he would certainly be watching his back as best he could and making sure that he didn't get into any situation from which it was difficult to retreat at speed. It would have been nice to have had Fizz with him, if only to keep an eye on the proceedings from a safe distance, but in truth, even that precaution seemed a somewhat exaggerated response to a highly unlikely risk. Suffice, he thought, to send her an email before he set out, letting her know where he was going and what the circumstances were. That way, should he be dredged lifeless from the river she'd know it was no fishing accident.

In point of fact he was infinitely more worried about what Fizz was doing. His lunch lay like an anvil in his stomach as he drove to Breich House and at times he was within an inch of cancelling his meeting with Ewan and driving down to Edinburgh forthwith to check up on her for himself. The only thing that stopped him was the possibility that she might, at that moment, be en route to Breich. It was just the sort of thing she would do and, in point of fact, he had suspected that she would do her damnedest to think of an excuse to surprise him before the weekend. Obviously, since there was no real reason to fly into a panic, the sensible thing to do was to keep his two appointments and see what the morning might bring. But, if she didn't turn up in the office by nine o'clock he'd be in Edinburgh by lunchtime.

This decision did little to calm his uneasiness

but he gleaned a certain amount of satisfaction, as he drove, in mentally berating Fizz and rehearsing the bollocking he was going to give her when he finally had her ear.

He found Marcia lounging on one of the stone benches that flanked the front door, a large glass of amber liquid in one hand and a black cheroot in the other. She was wearing a loosely draped, silky sort of garment that made the best of her generous curves and increased her already marked resemblance to a plump, rosy and sweetly slumberous baby.

'Ewan is having a bit of a lie down,' she said, sliding along the bench to make room for him to sit beside her. 'According to Oliver, there was rather a generous buffet at the sale and he was taken suddenly drunk, poor lamb. Actually, I think he forgot you were coming.'

'No problem,' Buchanan said, dragging his mind determinedly away from Fizz's disappearance and trying to act like a professional. 'I'd just as soon have a chat with you if you have the time.'

'Time,' she said with an expansive sweep of the hand that held her glass, 'is a plentiful commodity around these parts. We could export it to New York.'

'I imagine such peacefulness could get to be very boring after a while,' Buchanan suggested.

'Boring's not the word for it,' she said, and smiled her slow, sensuous smile. 'There are compensations — once in a while — but living here permanently would drive me crazy.'

'You're not planning to stay, then?'

'No chance. I'm on a short-term contract. Another five weeks and I'll be on my merry way.'

'Oh, of course,' Buchanan muttered, unintentionally aloud, as a series of unconnected facts clicked together in his brain. Marcia's presumed relationship with Ewan was no fortuitous amour: she was one of a series of sexual partners provided by his frigid wife, and probably chosen by him from her stable of up-market 'escorts'. Normally he would have filed that information away for further perusal but tonight he was in a funny mood: angry, impatient to wind things up, and somewhat reckless. He said, 'Of course. I didn't realise you were one of Amanda's recruits.'

He knew at once, from her expression, that his assumption was spot on. Her eyes lost their come-to-bed expression and narrowed in sudden concern. 'What do you mean, Amanda's recruits?'

He smiled. Not a mocking smile, he hoped, but one that said, come on now, Marcia, don't be coy. We're both adults after all.

'One of Amanda's girls. From the agency.'

She stared at him for a moment then tore her eyes away, drawing deeply on her cheroot and then throwing it, with a furious overarm action, into the nearby rose bushes. 'Bugger,' she said. 'Who the fuck told you about that?'

The change in her persona was instant and unqualified. Exit the sloe-eyed houri: enter the pragmatic, self-centred working girl.

'Does it matter?' Buchanan hedged.

'Damn right it matters! Do you think I want

271

my face plastered all over the papers when this comes out? I have family, you know. I have another life.'

'The press will be more interested in the Montrose side of it,' Buchanan said, laying a hand on her arm in an attempt to calm her down before she attracted someone's attention, but she threw him off.

'Don't you believe it. That bitch Chloe Miller will suck out every speck of dirt like a vacuum cleaner. Bugger Ewan Montrose! He's not dragging me down with him.'

Her half-full crystal glass sprayed a golden arc of spirits as it followed the cheroot into the roses, probably doing wonders for the greenfly, and she started to scramble to her feet.

Buchanan caught her by the wrist.

'Take it easy, Marcia. It's not going to hit the headlines tomorrow, or even this week. Sit down and talk about it. If you can keep your mouth shut about my interest in the matter we can work something out.'

She turned her eyes on him and something of the houri began to peep round the curtain of her lashes. 'What do you mean?'

'I mean, there are only a few people who know about Amanda's operations and I control all of them.'

'So you could keep the story secret?'

'No,' he admitted, 'I couldn't do that. The police will have to know about it eventually, but I could sit on it till you have time to make your arrangements and exit gracefully. I could, that is, if you are able to give me something worthwhile

272

in return — and, no, Marcia, thanks anyway but I'm talking about information.'

She removed her hand from his thigh, with an engaging little pout, and nodded. 'What sort of information?'

Buchanan had been thinking merely of some details that would lead him to other 'escorts' or their customers, whom he could call as witnesses to Amanda's operation but Marcia's bright, confident gaze made him wonder if she had something else to trade.

'I don't have anything specific in mind,' he said. 'What can you tell me?'

She swung round and looked over her shoulder at the house, carefully scanning every window before she turned back to him. 'That sodding Oliver,' she said under her breath. 'He's a right creeping Jesus. Even now that he hasn't got Amanda to snitch to, you can't take a leak without him slithering after you to see what you're doing.'

'He was Amanda's man, was he?'

'To the back teeth. God knows how long he was with her but they went back a long way. Years and years.'

'Did he ever mention where they were before they turned up at Breich?'

'Never. He never said a word to me if he didn't have to and he didn't like it if you asked too many questions.' Her face brightened. 'But, I'll tell you what, I reckon they were in Greece at some point. Maybe a long time ago.'

'In Greece?' Buchanan tried not to look too interested. 'What makes you think that?'

'Naxos,' she said. 'That's one of the Greek islands, isn't it? Well, I heard Amanda mention it once when she was speaking to Oliver and I walked in on them on my bare feet. She said something like, 'You know I can't do that, Oliver, not after what happened in Naxos.' I wouldn't even have registered it if she hadn't looked so livid at seeing me there. Oliver was mad too but he covered it up better.'

'Mmm.' Buchanan found this piece of news very strange since it drew the spotlight firmly back to Breich House. His suspicions were now swinging backwards and forwards with such pendulum-like regularity that he was starting to feel seasick. If Oliver and Amanda shared a guilty secret — evidently about some incident that had taken place in their shared past — the finger of suspicion was now swinging round to the faithful henchman himself.

He continued quizzing Marcia on the subject of her co-workers and their customers and managed to get a list of contacts that was pretty well guaranteed to get a result. Few of them would be happy to speak out but he had every faith in the persuasive talents of the Lothian and Borders police.

The matter of the Greek connection could well be the missing link to the whole mystery of Amanda's death but, with any luck, he'd have Fizz's help in sussing it out. Greece had been one stop in her seven year odyssey so she probably had at least a smattering of the language. She'd enjoy schmoozing the Greek police for information.

If she was okay.

18

Fizz's day had started well enough. She'd left home a little earlier than usual in order to swing by Buchanan's place, having promised to check his mail, feed his cats, and let Justin in to complete his transformation of the living room. It was a lovely fresh morning with just enough wind to blow the cobwebs from her mind and give her an appetite by the time she reached Buchanan's mews, so she selected a handful of nuts and fruit out of his packet of muesli and ate it while she performed her chores.

Justin arrived minutes later, lugging dust sheets, paint cans and an aluminium stepladder.

'How's it going, dollface?'

Fizz rarely responded to this form of address, at least not in a positive way, but Justin was a nice guy and unlikely to play a permanent role in her life so she let it pass.

'Hi, Justin. Just let me zap through this pile of mail and I'll be out from under your feet.'

'No rush, sweetheart,' he said, producing a large packet of sausages and a can of beans from the capacious pockets of his overall. 'I'll just have a bite of breakfast before I start. There's only a couple of hours' work left to do so I've an easy day of it. Fancy a roll and sausage?'

Fizz did fancy a roll and sausage but doubted her ability to do it justice so she concentrated on the mail while he clashed pans in the kitchen. As she read, however, her eye was repeatedly drawn to the stepladder Justin had propped against the wall and, iota by iota, a tiny seed of potentiality grew into a resolve.

'Justin,' she called. 'Could you fit in an extra hour's work this morning?'

He appeared in the doorway, chewing, an oversized mug barely visible in his oversized fist. 'Whassat?'

'Can I hire you for an hour before you start on the walls? I want to borrow your stepladder and you'd need to transport it for me and pick it up later. Just over to Joppa. You could be back here by ten at the latest.'

'Sure. No problemo. I won't need the steps till I start on the ceiling and that won't be before lunch. When d'you want to leave?'

'Finish your breakfast. I've things to do before we go.'

It was not yet nine o'clock but she knew the Wonderful Beatrice would already be at her desk.

'Buchanan and Stewart,' came her clipped Edinburgh accent, worthy of Miss Jean Brodie at her most genteel.

'Top of the morning to you, scrumptious. This is your captain speaking.'

'Good morning, Miss Fitzpatrick. What can I do for you?'

'Not a thing, Beattie. Just stay as sweet as you are. I'm just letting you know I've got things to do this morning but I'll be in later — maybe quite a bit later. You will manage without me, won't you?'

'I'll do my best, Miss Fitzpatrick.'

That was as close to humour as you were likely to get out of Beattie and it showed she was in a good mood this morning. One could hope for the same cheerful reaction from Buchanan. She dialled the number of his mobile but drew a blank, probably because the reception among the mountains was inadequate. The hotel reception desk was able to tell her he'd just left the premises and she couldn't break into his computer to send him an email. Not that it really mattered, she supposed. There was no real rush to pass on what she'd discovered from the records office, she could do that from the office this afternoon when time wasn't so pressing.

Justin was ready to leave before she'd got her head in order so she hurriedly locked the upstairs and downstairs doors and handed him the key. Buchanan was choosy about who he left his keys with, mostly because he didn't trust anyone but himself to lock up securely, but Justin was okay and anyway, she'd be back well before he'd finished what he had to do.

She could be sure, as they drew up outside Mrs Sullivan's house, that the old lady was up and about since the downstairs windows were open and the sound of a vacuum cleaner could be heard from within, so she sent Justin on his way and toted the stepladder up the path herself.

'Morning,' she sang gaily as the door opened, and warded off Mrs Sullivan's dumbfounded expression with a 250-watt grin. 'Sorry to surprise you so early in the morning but I didn't want to phone earlier in case I woke you up.'

'What . . . ?' Her voice wavered on the word

and she made a vaguely bewildered gesture in the direction of the stepladder.

'I thought we could have a rummage in your loft and see if we can find your old address book,' Fizz chattered, edging nimbly past her into the hallway. 'It's the only way we're going to be able to trace any of William's friends.'

'But I'm not at all sure that it's up there. Dear me, what a lot of trouble you've put yourself to. How on earth did you get here? Surely not by taxi?'

Fizz forged ahead, answering her questions while she discarded her jacket and mounted the stepladder. 'You don't have to worry about a thing, Mrs Sullivan. I'll just whizz through your boxes and be finished in a couple of hours at the very most. This isn't locked is it? Ah, no, I see how it unfastens. My word, you have plenty of space up here, don't you? You could turn it into an extra bedroom.'

There was no window in the roof space but a light switch operated by a cord illuminated a promising collection of tea chests and cardboard boxes stacked tidily against either gable. She hauled herself through the opening, aware without looking at her that Mrs Sullivan was not entirely pleased at the intrusion. There was a noticeable coolness in the voice that drifted up from the hallway saying, 'Very well, dear, if you feel it's necessary. I'll just put the kettle on, shall I?'

'Lovely.'

The loft was beautifully finished in the manner of most of Edinburgh's pre-war housing:

solid-looking roof timbers and comprehensive hardwood flooring currently covered with a layer of sooty dust that spoke of years of coal-burning fires. Much of the space was taken up by water tanks and chimney breasts and she could hear the muted cooing of pigeons filtering through the roof tiles. From the kitchen below came the rattle of Mrs Sullivan making the coffee, clattering stuff about as though she were raking through cutlery drawers with angry impatience.

Fizz could feel a possibly imaginary twinge of sympathy for the old dear but, after all, she only had herself to blame for not trusting them with the whole story at the outset. If she had come clean before now — or if Buchanan had just brought himself to be tough with her — none of this would have been necessary. What was really needed at this point, failing her compliance, was a complete search of her entire house but the attic was as close as they were going to get to that and, at first glance, it looked promising.

Most of the boxes contained china and glassware, books, gardening tools or picture frames, but at least two of them were untidily crammed with notebooks, documents, photographs, and a variety of small objects which commonly have no real home around the house other than, maybe, a jug on the mantelpiece. The sort of junk you'd never in a month of Sundays have the patience to sort through but don't dare throw out in case there's something important amongst it.

She worked fast, half-expecting Mrs Sullivan to return with some reason for halting the search, but the sound of continued clattering and banging from downstairs gave her temporary assurance. The coffee was a long time coming but the longer the old dear continued to search for whatever was eluding her the less likely she'd be to make a nuisance of herself in the attic.

Among the junk there was a mass of fascinating material she'd no time to dwell on: letters from an American friend written at the time of the Cuba crisis, photographs of a girlish Mrs Sullivan in ankle socks and bunchy skirts, Christmas cards, old chromium cigarette lighters, yellowed sheets of quarto typing paper, newspaper cuttings and theatre programmes from the nineteen fifties. When she heard a rasping noise behind her she assumed, vaguely, that it was the arrival of the promised coffee but when she looked up from the notebook she was scanning she discovered that the trap door had closed.

'Mrs Sullivan?' she called, but there was no sound from below other than a faintly metallic scraping which she interpreted as someone moving the stepladder. 'Mrs Sullivan?'

She scrambled across to the opening and tugged at the piece of dirty rope that was tacked to it as a handle, and a bolt of alarm shot through her as she discovered it was immovable. 'Mrs Sullivan? What's happening?'

'Oh dear,' said a faint voice. 'I do wish it hadn't come to this, Miss Fitzpatrick. But, really, I don't know what else to do, just at the moment. You'll have to stay there till I think of something.'

Fizz instantly leapfrogged the preliminaries and lost her cool. 'Get me the hell out of this, you crazy old bat!' she screamed, half-deafening herself in the process. 'Buchanan will be here in half an hour and he'll have your guts for braces!'

'I doubt that. He's still up north, isn't he, dear? I don't think we'll see him till at least the weekend.'

Fizz threw herself at the rope and started frenziedly yanking on it, yelping with the effort like she was on the Centre Court at Wimbledon but, though the trap door rattled a bit, she couldn't raise it enough even to afford her a glimpse of her captor through the crack.

'Please don't upset yourself like that, Miss Fitzpatrick. I couldn't find the padlock but I've put a poker through the hasp and I don't think you have any chance of dislodging it.'

'Why?' Fizz said, panting with frustration but somehow managing to get a precarious grip on herself. 'Why are you doing this to me, Mrs Sullivan?'

She heard a sigh.

'Because you are becoming too close to wrecking all my plans, dear. I'm terribly sorry, truly I am, but I can't allow you to spoil it all now.'

'Uh-huh,' Fizz returned in what she hoped sounded like a reasonable kind of voice. 'And how long do you propose to keep me here?'

It appeared Mrs Sullivan didn't have a ready answer for that one. Fizz could almost hear her thinking through the trap door. Finally she said, 'Oh dear, I just hate it when innocent people get in the way. So distressing. All I can tell you, dear, is that I'll do my best for you. You are a sweet little thing and I've become quite fond of you — and of Mr Buchanan too. It's quite clear that he adores you and I wouldn't like to break his heart.'

Fizz could have put her right on that score but didn't see how it would do her any good: quite the opposite in fact.

'And how are you going to shut him up? He knows everything I know — a lot of people do.'

'Yes, I imagine he does.'

'He'll know where to look for me.'

'Perhaps, but he'll believe me when I say you found the address book we were looking for and went off with it.'

'The guy I borrowed the ladders from will be back to pick me up.'

'Yes, I've thought about that, Miss Fitzpatrick, but I'll watch out for his return and take the ladders out to him so that he won't hear any noise you might make. I'm sure he'll accept that you finished your business quite quickly and didn't want to wait.'

Fizz lowered herself to the grimy floor and leaned back against a handy tea chest. She could feel her heart hammering at her ribs and realised with a sense of unreality that she was actually as scared as she'd ever been in the course of an abnormally scary life. Silly, really, because all she was dealing with here was a feeble old lady, but the thought that the same old lady could be a homicidal maniac was a hard one to put to the back of her mind. Actually, she was quite a big and heavy woman and might not be as feeble as she'd pretended to be. Furthermore, the old darling could be seconds away from announcing that she was going to have to take a hammer to her skull because God told her to.

She started scrabbling around in search of something she could use as a weapon but stopped when she heard, 'I'll leave you now, dear. I'm just going to have a little sit down at the window and watch out for your friend coming back. What time did you expect him?'

The sheer insouciance of that question, the bloody cheek of it, only confirmed Fizz's worst suspicions regarding the woman's mental condition. In a minute she'd be asking her prisoner to listen out for Justin's van and give her a shout when she heard it. She declined to answer and, in a minute, heard the stepladder being carted away and propped against the wall by the front door, after which the sound of Mrs Sullivan's soft footfalls retreated to the front bedroom.

It became very quiet in the attic. The pigeons had stopped cooing and even the water tank had fallen mute, it's intermittent dripping and gurgling subsumed in a suffocating silence. Fizz's thoughts went darting about like sparks above a bonfire, unable to rest on any single concept for more than a split second. What was she doing down there? Could that nail there constitute a weapon? Could she break through the roof? The floor? How long did she have? Would Justin . . . ? Would Buchanan . . . ? Would Beatrice . . . ?

She fell blindly on the piles of junk, raking

through tea chests, upending boxes in search of a blade or a club and began, marginally, to calm down only when it occurred to her to smash the glass in one of the empty picture frames and arm herself with one of the longer shards gripped in a leather gardening glove. That made her feel a good deal happier. She sat next to the trap door, breathing deeply and saying 'okay . . . okay . . . it's okay' to herself till she started to believe it.

Finally rational thought stole back into her consciousness like blood returning to a cramped limb and she tried to decide what to do next. She'd got herself a weapon. Okay. That was good. Now what? Keep Mrs Sullivan out. How? Nail the trap door shut. There was one rusty nail right beside her, lightly wedged between two floorboards, so there might well be others.

She subjected the floor to a close scrutiny, crawling through soot and pigeon shit and getting herself filthy in the process, and found one further nail plus half a dozen that were protruding far enough above the wood to be prised loose with a pair of pruning shears she found among the gardening tools. The same tea chest yielded an unidentifiable metal wedge, possibly part of a lawnmower, which might, if used with sufficient desperation, serve as a hammer. Great.

There was one snag with this plan, of course, and that was the problem of hammering home sufficient nails to secure the trap door before Mrs Sullivan twigged what she was up to and arrived to do a bit of her own brand of hammering. This would, of course, cease to be a problem after Justin's arrival since he would take the stepladders away with him and, even if Mrs Sullivan was lying about having none of her own, it would take her a minute or two to fetch them from wherever they were hidden. Until then matters were in the lap of the gods and if the gods chose to stand up it was just too bad.

She returned to a further perusal of the tea chests, searching for she knew not what — anything, really, that might ease her situation. There were stacks of curtains which she piled up to give her something to sit on while she worked. There were bits of string that looked encouraging but in what specific way she'd have been hard pressed to have said. There were several ballpoint pens and an antique cycling helmet which was something of a godsend, given the propensities of her hostess. There were also four or five ancient cigarette lighters, some of them beautifully enamelled and probably worth a bob or two at an antiques fair. They were all devoid of petrol but the flints were intact and produced sparks that looked a good deal more promising than the problematic two-stick efforts demonstrated in Ray Mears's survival programmes. Toying with the idea of starting a fire and alerting the attention of the neighbours, she started experimenting with different kinds of tinder: torn up newspapers, slivers of old wood shaved off a rafter with her shard of glass, a little stuffing material ripped out of a tea cosy, only to prove that Ray Mears was a hell of a lot smarter than he looked.

She was trying to coax a flicker of flame out of some shredded cotton fibres when she heard Mrs Sullivan rushing to the front door and knew that Justin was only a few yards away. Grabbing her bit of lawnmower, or whatever it was, she scrambled to the front section of the roof and started belabouring it with all her strength, yelling at the top of her voice, and generally making the sort of noise guaranteed to infuriate the neighbours and attract every emergency service in the city. She couldn't hear a thing over the racket but when she paused for breath she discovered that Mrs Sullivan was tapping on the trap door with what might have been a broom handle.

'He's gone, dear. I don't think he'll be back.'

Fizz tried to tell herself that she had expected this blow but it stung, all the same, to realise that she'd seen the last of Justin. He'd have finished his work on the flat well before Buchanan came home and no one would think to ask him if he knew where she might be. Buchanan would send him a cheque in the post and that, failing a miracle, would be that.

'Mrs Sullivan?' She crouched at the trap door and spoke in tones that were as non-contentious as could be expected of someone in her situation. 'Don't go away, Mrs Sullivan.'

'What is it, dear?'

'Please tell me what you're planning to do with me.'

'Oh heavens, don't ask me that right now. I really don't know what I'm going to do with you. I never thought it would come to this.'

'Are you going to kill me?'

'Now you're being silly, dear,' she replied, sounding like a tender mother reassuring a needlessly nervous child. 'That's the last thing I want.'

That closing remark did little to slow Fizz's heartbeat. She'd have been happier had Mrs Sullivan used a slightly more positive turn of phrase. Preferably one containing the word *never*.

'But I'm no danger to you, really I'm not. I've not a shred of proof that you killed Amanda Montrose — in fact I still don't believe you did it.'

'Oh dear, and I thought you trusted me, Miss Fitzpatrick. But, I assure you, almost everything I told you about that incident was the precise truth.'

'*Almost* everything?' Fizz had to query, even though the riddle of Amanda's death was not one she gave a hoot about right at that particular moment.

'Well, perhaps I have my little secrets but, really, they don't make the slightest difference to the facts of the matter. There was no need to tell you every minor detail.'

'But you can tell me now, surely? That wouldn't do you any harm other than land you in jail, and that's what you wanted all along, right?'

'Forgive me, my dear Miss Fitzpatrick, but all is not yet lost. I may still be able to do what I set out to do so it would be silly to hand you the means of thwarting me, wouldn't it? But, I'll tell you what: if things work out I'll explain everything to you. The whole truth and nothing but the truth. How would that be?'

'If things work out?' Fizz returned, probably with a little more angst than she had intended to exhibit. 'You mean, if you don't smash my brains out?'

'Oh, that's a terrible thing to say!'

'It's a terrible thing to do, for God's sake!'

'Dear, dear me. I don't even want to think about it. I'm going now. I have things to do.'

And, in spite of all Fizz could say to detain her, she went. A minute later she could be heard opening and shutting drawers and cupboard doors, bustling about in a manner that was profoundly disquieting. She was bloody well packing to leave.

19

Buchanan had no appetite for dinner. He ordered sea bass but could do no more than pick at it and left his table having ingested very little other than a couple of breadsticks and a pot of coffee. He could have murdered a large Glenmorangie but couldn't bring himself to drive, having drink taken, even the short distance to the Dovran pool. The roads around Breichmenach might be virtually deserted but that only encouraged idiot locals and kamikaze youths on motorbikes to use them like racetracks.

He killed time, till his 10 p.m. appointment, by reading over his notes on the case and trying to make some cohesive story out of what were, essentially, unrelated facts. It wasn't easy and his worrying over Fizz's whereabouts didn't make it any easier.

What it all boiled down to in the end was that Amanda had appeared on the Breich scene some five years ago with her henchman, Oliver, in tow, married Ewan, moved into Breichmenach House with him and Terence Lamb, and continued to run her international escort agency from there. Shortly afterwards she had set up the string of massage parlours in Edinburgh with Lamb as manager or, perhaps, as her partner. Lamb was a good choice for the job because Ewan had enough dirt on him to keep him under strict control: no worries about him dipping his fingers too deeply in the till and, even when he was arrested for Amanda's murder, little danger of his talking out of school. He might claim to have been framed but, even if he suspected he had Ewan to thank for that, it would have done him nothing but harm to reveal the truth about either the Belfast massacre or Amanda's main source of income.

Whether Ewan knew from the start where her money came from or discovered its origins only later was a moot point, but if he didn't like the idea there were certainly plenty of compensations, not only financially but in the form of an abundant supply of sexual partners.

And Mrs Sullivan? Where did she fit into the picture? There was still no clear indication of whether she was guilty of Amanda's death, imagining things, or lying — perhaps to protect someone else. And if that last eventuality were the case, then who was she trying to protect? Obviously, she was risking a good deal by playing such a dangerous game, so it had to be for someone very close to her. Her son, perhaps? Could he, in spite of what she claimed, be still alive?

Buchanan's mind jumped to Terence Lamb — his bleached hair — his doctored face. He didn't look much like Mrs Sullivan but then, neither did the photograph of the young graduate on her coffee table. Good God, how could he have been blind to that possibility for so long? How could Fizz have missed it? It was only a theory, he reminded himself, but it did appear to tick all the boxes and he was eager to embrace it since, if Terence was the real culprit and Mrs Sullivan nothing more dangerous than a protective mother, Fizz was, at this moment, less likely to be getting herself into trouble. The irony of a degenerate like Terence Lamb having a devoted mother like Mrs Sullivan was a poignant comment on the unfairness of life in general.

There were a few less significant loose ends to be tied up, not least the question of who really rented the house in Moy, but it did appear to Buchanan that he was getting somewhere at last. It could now, he felt, be a matter of checking Terence Lamb's blood group against that of Mrs Sullivan and that could possibly be arranged through the Inverness-shire police. He'd phone Inspector Haig first thing in the morning. He and his team might be crabby about his interference but would surely be interested to know if Mrs Sullivan could be done as an accessory. That charge, if it could be made to stick, might not satisfy her need for redemption but it was better than nothing.

He was still annoyed at Fizz for disappearing without warning like that, but by the time he set out for the Dovran pool he was in a considerably better mood than he had been earlier. He loved this stage of a case: it was now starting to look like the mists were beginning to thin considerably, allowing tantalising glimpses of the truth to shine through. With a bit of luck his mysterious informer would possess the necessary information to help him tie things up in a couple of days.

When he reached the river there was still

enough light to see where he was going and it was unlikely to get much darker for at least another hour by which time, he reckoned, he should be on his way back to the hotel. He had to leave the car about a mile from the pool and approach it along an unfamiliar track worn by the feet of generations of anglers. This led him through head-high balsam that filled the air with its pungent perfume as he crushed it underfoot and permitted only fleeting views of the river some twenty or thirty feet below him.

This stretch of the Blackwater was very different from the run he had already fished. The estate's map of the river gave no more than a sketched outline indicating the different beats so it came as a bit of a shock to find the Dovran pool a vastly different entity to those on the upper reaches where the course was wide and level. Access to the pool itself was difficult and must at one time have been seriously hazardous but someone had cut rough steps in the rocks of the steeply sloping bank and these, while slimy with moss, made the descent somewhat easier.

He could see the pool below him as he scrambled down, dark as tar and fringed with jagged rocks that looked like teeth in the mouth of a carnivore, but the nearby bank was hidden by the slight overhang of the slope. If someone was waiting for him down there he or she would be invisible till the last few seconds. This thought gave him pause. He stopped and scanned what he could of the thicket around him.

He'd started out expecting to meet some local fisherman: someone who wanted to combine a cast or two with a certain amount of privacy, but this situation was iffy, to say the least. Had he realised just what a gloomy and dangerous spot he was being lured to he'd at least have brought along a golf club, if not a witness. However, it looked like he'd be able to get a clear view of the river-bank from a little further down. From there he'd still have the advantage of height, should he need it — which he couldn't really believe he would.

He set off down the steep incline as warily as he could manage. For the first dozen or so feet it wasn't easy to keep his eyes peeled for sudden attack since the going was too dicey to risk taking a pace without having the extra security of a handgrip but the steps started after that and he was able to keep a more careful watch.

Had he been less focused on the middle distance and more concerned with where he was putting his feet he might have fared better, but all his attention was on an adjacent clump of rhododendrons when everything went crazy. One foot locked hard to the rock half a pace behind him just long enough for his latent momentum to shoot him into space. Suddenly he was catapulting outwards from the face of the slope, falling, spinning, careering forward towards the hungry maw beneath him.

The fall seemed to go on for minutes. He hit the ground some fifteen feet from the river with a bang that should have knocked him out but the adrenaline had kicked in by that time and, as he skidded downwards, he was grabbing with every prehensile part of his body. Heather, wet grass and loose stones whizzed past his face in a blur. Gravel burned his scrabbling fingers. Fists of rock slammed into his body, batting it about like a ping-pong ball. At last one hand locked on a clump of something wiry and low-growing and a split second later his opposite elbow whipped around an angle of rock. Slowed only momentarily, his legs went into overdrive, thrashing like the blades of a helicopter and finally getting a boot onto firmer ground. A dozen accelerated heartbeats later he had hauled himself partly onto a wet ledge, to which he clung like a shy child in danger of being parted from its mother.

It made him dizzy to see how close to the pool he had come. The swirling blackness looked, at a distance of a few feet, like the mouth of hell, and the smell of moss and rotting vegetation that rose from it was like the foul breath of Satan himself. He liked to think of himself as a strong swimmer but he wouldn't have put a fiver on his chances of getting out of that maelstrom alive.

Almost immediately he heard, above the roar of the water, the sound of someone descending the bank, boot scraping on rock at a speed which was that of either a fool or of someone very familiar with the terrain. Hastily, he grabbed the biggest loose stone within reach and flattened himself back as far as he could against the slope at his back.

The figure that rushed past him to halt at the brink of the pool was small and bareheaded, clad in dark trousers and sweater and carrying a solid wooden staff. It was, incredibly, Chloe.

She stood panting and staring into the depths

of the pool for two long seconds, then she took a look up and down the river, and turned. The shock of seeing Buchanan crouched there, almost within arm's length, made her take a step backwards and for a second it looked as if it would be she who'd take early retirement.

'Oh, my God!' she cried, reaching out to him. 'Are you all right?'

He held up a hand to fend her off, not just because he was wary of her but — absurdly — because he didn't want her to discover how much he was shaking. Pride was probably the last function to pack in as life departed a stricken man.

'I'm fine.'

'You're not fine, Tam! You're bleeding badly. Here let me help you.'

He would infinitely have preferred her to keep her distance but, precariously balanced as he was, he could have done almost nothing to defend himself, anyway, even from a shrimp like Chloe. She proffered her stick with one hand, which was a good sign, and grabbed hold of his arm with the other, holding him steady as he regained terra firma. They retreated a few yards from the danger area and found a stable rock to sit on while she took a closer look at whatever wound was soaking him with an inordinate flow of blood. The blood could, as far as he was concerned, be coming from any part of his upper body, every inch of which felt as though it had been flayed to the bone, but it turned out that the worst of the damage was around his left eye which was deeply cut, both above and below, presumably by contact with some sharp and immovable object.

She chattered erratically while she dabbed at his cheekbone with something that felt like heavy-duty sandpaper and then wet a hanky in the river to clean away the worst of the gore. Her remarks dwelt largely on what a shock it had been for her to witness his apparent death plunge and not at all on what a traumatic experience it must have been for him. It was so like Fizz's normal reaction to such an incident that he found himself missing her almost unbearably.

'I must have told the Montroses a hundred times that they ought to make this place safer. What would it cost them to fix up a rope to hang onto? Why is nothing ever done about hazards like this till some angler — or some child — is killed? Those stone steps are death traps. You feel safer on them, coming down, but if you slip on the moss you — '

'I didn't slip,' Buchanan stated positively. 'I tripped. Hang on. I'm going to take a look.'

His head pounded as he scrambled back up the bank and he discovered that his hands were bleeding copiously from a collection of cuts that smarted as he grabbed handfuls of grass to assist his climb. Unsure precisely where he had been launched into flight, he took a close look at each step he came to but he was almost halfway up when the evidence emerged. A double length of heavyweight nylon fishing gut was looped across the path in an artful manner that could have just as easily been accidental as malicious. Palest green and translucent, it was almost invisible even at close range and each end was woven securely, yet possibly randomly, into the heather stems at either side.

'What is it?' Chloe asked, arriving belatedly and considerably out of breath.

He showed her the gut, watching her face for a reaction, but she only swung her hair in an angry flutter. 'People should be more careful with that stuff. It's lethal, and not just to people. Lots of animals die from swallowing it every year. You should complain very strongly to Ewan about this.'

She was completely convincing, furthermore she seemed willing for him to retain her stick, so he risked saying, 'Actually, it was probably deliberate. I think someone was trying to kill me.'

It took a split second for that to sink in, then her head whipped round like it was on a spring release system. 'You what? *Kill* you? You're not serious!'

'Totally serious. Someone left a message asking me to come here tonight at ten. Corny, isn't it? You'd think I'd have more sense, I know, but the fact is, I didn't realise till I got here that it was such a dangerous spot. Besides, the message could have been genuine.' He shook his head in embarrassment. 'I have to admit, I found it hard to believe that that sort of thing could happen in real life.'

'I don't blame you. I'm having trouble believing it myself.' She pressed a hand to her forehead and stared at him with round eyes. 'Do you know who did it?'

'Haven't a clue.' His legs were still shaking too much to make the further ascent to the path an attractive proposition, so he found another perch on a fallen tree trunk and Chloe sat uneasily beside him and subjected the surrounding greenery to an energetic scrutiny.

'He could be hanging around for another shot at you.'

'I doubt it,' Buchanan said, possibly swayed in his opinion by the fact that he didn't feel much like running away right at that particular moment. 'It looks to me like whoever laid that trap is too smart to take a risk like that in front of a witness. He — assuming it *is* a man — may be waiting to retrieve that fishing gut but he obviously took good care that, if for some reason he couldn't get back to remove it, it wouldn't raise any suspicions. If my body had ever come to the surface it would appear that I was fishing and fell in. No waders, of course, but I wouldn't have worn them to fish this pool: no rod, but that could have washed away downstream.' He grinned bleakly. 'Should have been the perfect crime.'

'Who would do such a desperate thing? Someone in Breich?' She gazed hopefully at Buchanan's face but got nothing but a shrug in response. 'But you must be getting close to fingering someone for something, Tam. Ewan, maybe? He could have discovered that you know more than is good for him about the prostitution rackets.'

'That's possible,' Buchanan admitted, wondering

if Marcia could possibly have been crazy enough to have warned Ewan that he was on the point of being exposed as a pimp.

'Who *else* would do such a thing? Marcia's a stupid cow but she doesn't have the bottle for direct action. Oliver has the bottle, but he wouldn't care if the whole vice business blew up in Ewan's face tomorrow and he has no other irons in the fire as far as I know.' Her dark eyes ranged over the hillside on the far side of the river, pausing for a few seconds, on the just discernible stretch of road where Amanda's murder had taken place. 'I've wondered if, maybe, Oliver wasn't convinced that Terence was the guilty party. The way he looks at Ewan behind his back makes me think he doesn't trust the guy as far as he could spit him. You'd think he'd have moved on after Amanda died, wouldn't you? He was her creature, and hers only. I suppose he could be just biding his time to see if Ewan makes a false move and gives himself away.'

Buchanan was in too much pain and mental anguish to subject the matter to the full force of his intellect. He had tasted of death for a couple of minutes back there and the flavour kept returning like a burp. He refolded his handkerchief to expose a couple of inches of its surface that were not entirely blood-soaked and dabbed gingerly at his brow. It seemed to him that he was becoming conspicuously accident prone in recent years. He'd suffered concussion, a broken arm and a broken leg, a deep wound — incurred in an incident horribly similar to the one he had just escaped — which had required stitching, and had also been hospitalised for the removal of an inflamed gall bladder. All of these ills, when he came to think about it, post-dating the arrival in his life of a certain Miss Fitzpatrick. Could there be some obscure connection? Yes.

'You're going to need stitches in that,' Chloe said, taking his swab from him and applying it with somewhat less tenderness but more efficacy. 'I'll come with you to the doctor's.'

'No rush,' Buchanan said. 'My cousin's a doctor and I'd rather have him do it.'

'His practice is around here?'

'No, back in Edinburgh, but I was planning to go back tomorrow morning anyway.'

She looked at him somewhat accusingly. 'You didn't mention that last night. I thought you were planning to be here for quite a few days.'

'I was, but something has cropped up.'

'What?' she demanded, eyes suddenly intent. 'A development in the case?'

'No, nothing like that. At least I hope not. It's just that I've been trying to contact Fizz all day and can't reach her. She called her office this morning to say she wouldn't be in till later but she didn't show. It's probably nothing, but it's bothering me.'

Chloe considered this information, possibly wondering if there could be a story in it. 'Does she do that sort of thing often?'

'She has done,' Buchanan conceded, 'but I could wish she wouldn't do it at a time like this. I mean, we're investigating a murder, for God's sake, and there has to be a certain amount of danger inherent in that. She ought to be as aware of that as well as anyone on the planet so you'd think she'd realise that I'd be worried about her.'

Her big brown eyes drifted speculatively across his face. 'You're very fond of her, aren't you?'

'Sure,' said Buchanan, with a touch of brusqueness. 'We go back a long way. I'd hate to see anything nasty happen to her, especially as this is my case and she's only tagging along out of interest.'

Chloe smiled: the sort of sad but sympathetic smile Mother Theresa might have bent on a devious beggar trying to put forward a case for an extra bowl of rice. She seemed disposed to discuss the matter further so he continued quickly, 'As I said, there's probably a perfectly innocuous reason for her taking the day off work but if she doesn't contact me before nine tomorrow morning I'll have to go and check out the situation.'

She hugged herself nervously, keeping a canny eye open for sudden attack. It was perfectly obvious that if it hadn't been for the commercial prospects of the situation she'd have taken off — with or without him — minutes ago.

'If there's any danger, Tam, don't you think it's more likely to be here in Breich rather than in Edinburgh? The person who just tried to kill you can't be in two places at once, can he? Or could there be *two* murderers on the loose?'

'The person who laid the trap for me could be well gone by now. He or she could already be halfway to Edinburgh, with similar plans for Fizz.' Still woozy from his fall, he had spoken almost without thinking but suddenly the truth of what he had just put into words hit him like a punch in the head. What was the point of his assailant trying to silence *him* without also ensuring that Fizz could not produce equally damaging evidence?

'I'm going,' he announced and was already three steps on his way before Chloe could gasp:

'What? Where?'

'Edinburgh.'

'Tonight? Now?'

'The bastard's after Fizz.'

'Why should you think that?'

'I just know it, Chloe.'

She came stumbling after him. 'But you don't know where she is!'

Aye, he thought, charging blindly onwards, that's the rub.

20

Fizz had no very clear idea of the time. She almost never wore a watch, largely because she found it an irritation but also because she rarely had need of one in a city replete with clocks. Normally she could have made a pretty accurate guess at both the hour and the minute from the instant she opened her eyes in the morning but this was no ordinary day and, although the minutes crawled by like hours, the hours seemed to have passed like minutes.

How long had she spent raking through the packing cases? How many hours had she wasted trying to start a fire, prising at the trap door, attempting to make a breach in the roof? How long was it since Mrs Sullivan's departure? Was anyone wondering where she was?

Although there was no skylight in the roof she could tell that it was dark outside and had been for some hours. There were one or two small openings under the eaves through which she'd been able to see daylight a few hours ago but now they were invisible against the blackness. It could be getting on towards dawn, for all she could tell. Dawn, and Mrs Sullivan had not yet returned.

That was quite a scary thought, Fizz had to admit. It conjured up pictures of future tenants of the house — God knows how far in the future — opening the trap door to find the attic already occupied: by a grinning skull, a scatter of bones, and a rat-nibbled pile of clothing. She tried to believe that Mrs Sullivan would not choose such a method of silencing her, and common sense itself told her that was true. It was too chancy. How could she be sure that Fizz would be unable to escape or that no one would come along and hear her cries for help? Or — and this was an even scarier thought — had the old witch left behind her some sort of time bomb which would put a more conclusive end to her prisoner? Had she left the gas on? Or set a slow smouldering fire which would burst into flame only when she was far enough away to be beyond suspicion?

But maybe murder was not on her mind after all. Maybe her intentions were only to keep her trapped here till she could 'do what she set out to do', whatever that might be. But how long would that take her? If she'd intended to return in a matter of hours, why had she packed a bag? A girl could be eating her own shoes before she came back. If ever.

It was all too easy to dwell on such corrosive thoughts but they occupied only the surface of her mind: deep down she was pretty sure that Mrs Sullivan would show up again before long. Just what she would find it necessary to do with her guest when she did so was another matter. If she was, after all, Amanda's killer the future looked black indeed. Having killed once she'd have little compunction in killing again, but if she were innocent of that crime and interested only in some subsidiary matter — covering up a past misdeed, for instance — it was yet possible she wouldn't feel the need to go that far.

Fizz sat back on her heels and drew a bare arm across her forehead. It was hot enough already in the attic, which had been absorbing the heat of the summer sun all day, and she had long ago discarded first her shirt, then her tight skirt in an effort to cool down and to gain some freedom of movement. Stripping to her bra and pants didn't make a lot of difference and so much sweat ran into her eyes as she worked that she had to tie her shirt round her forehead to dam it.

She tucked up a dangling sleeve and took a straight look at the four-inch-long hole she'd been working on with all her strength for hours. Hole? It didn't even deserve the name. You could call it a dent, maybe. The merest concavity at the join of two floorboards, but nothing more. There was at least another quarter of an inch to wear away before she could even determine what was underneath.

The first few shavings had come away quite easily, filling her with optimism, but once the edges of the two boards were carved off it became increasingly difficult to apply her successive splinters of glass to good effect. They were awkward to handle, they became blunt remarkably quickly, and they inflicted what wounds they could whenever her mind wandered. She'd soon become adept at breaking glass so as to achieve the shape of splinter she needed: not too big to fit into the space available, not too narrow to have the required strength, and it now seemed to her that she was getting into the rhythm of the task. With a bit of luck the next quarter of an inch would prove a little easier.

As she worked, her ears were open for any sound from outside. The soundproofing was poor enough to let her hear the buzz of distant traffic but the few cars that came this far along the dead-end road merely used the turning circle to change direction and were gone before she could hope to attract any attention. She had already exhausted all the other possibilities of escape available to her but her mind roved hither and thither like a questing bloodhound, analysing the situation, planning for every contingency, reviewing the contents of the packing cases, constantly searching for new possibilities of escape. Sooty sweat dripped off her chin, blood soaked into the wood she was working, making it harder to cut, but she didn't dare pause to wipe it away. Mrs Sullivan could walk in at any second and when she did the work would have to stop.

But where *was* Mrs Sullivan and what was she up to? Bringing her 'plans' to fruition, probably. That was, apparently, all that mattered to her. The way she'd spoken earlier, now that Fizz had a moment to think about it, had given the impression that, once she'd accomplished what she'd set out to do, nothing else mattered. She'd obviously been in no doubt that both Fizz and Buchanan would have disapproved of her intentions, which indicated that they were illegal. Not the sort of iniquity a humane lawyer might turn a blind eye to, considering her advanced age and mental ambiguity, but something exceedingly naughty. Something she was now attending to.

Not silencing some other witness, surely? What would be the point of that? Even if she *had* been the one to put a hammer through Amanda's skull, that matter was now closed and she was under no lingering suspicion. Besides, all she'd wanted from day one was to be proved guilty of murder and sent to jail. Unless, of course, she'd been lying in her teeth all along and had been using Buchanan and herself as pawns in a game of her own devising. If so, it was a very complicated game.

Some time later — impossible to judge how long — the last strands at the bottom of the hole parted, allowing her to poke the glass through and cut lengthwise instead of downwards. At last she was able to open the gap between the boards all along its four-inch length. That gave her a cleft wide enough to accept the long spar of hardwood she'd found under the eaves and allowed her to lever the floorboard upwards just enough to pass the spar completely underneath it. She was panting with effort by the time she reached that stage but she pressed feverishly on, wedging a saucepan under the spar and jumping on the free end till the nails popped out, giving her a free view of the space beneath.

There was a gap of some four or five inches, floored with gratifyingly flimsy strips of wood which appeared to cover the plaster of the ceiling below. Fifteen minutes and she'd be the hell out of here!

She grabbed her trusty piece of lawnmower and wedged it under a strip of ply which gave with the first furious wrench: so did a chunk of ceiling. There was a sharp clunk as it fell to the floor and, in spite of being certain she was alone in the house, she held still for a second.

And in that second she heard the faintest whisper of a key in the lock of the front door.

Not Mrs Sullivan. She knew that within the micro-second it took her brain to compute an array of small clues: the preceding silence which should have been broken by the sound of the approaching Hyundai, the soft and furtive click of the lock, the heaviness of the footfalls passing swiftly down the hall. With her mouth already open to call for help, she paused, overcome by a sense of inexplicable danger. She couldn't have said what was suddenly putting an unbearable strain on her already depleted adrenaline supply but something was telling her to hold her horses. It took seconds for her to realise that although she now had a good chance of breaking through the ceiling unaided, by alerting the intruder to her presence she could find herself out of the frying pan and into the fire.

Strange noises followed, one of which might have been that of a blind being lowered, and a moment later a tiny shaft of light rose like a laser beam from the opening she'd created only seconds before. A reflex action made her whip a hand over the hole. If light could shine upwards like that it could also shine downwards. She replaced her hand with her discarded skirt while she crept across the boards and, concerned that the click of the light switch might be heard from below, used the dangling sleeve of her shirt to protect her fingers as she removed the light bulb. More rustling noises emerged from the room beneath her as she lifted the skirt aside and leaned gently forward to bring her eye to the hole.

She was looking into the kitchen. She could see the refrigerator, a length of counter top and the bottom edge of the cupboards above it. The illumination was faint and shifting, evidently supplied by a torch, but she could tell by the shadows it threw that someone was moving around down there with purpose and with a certain familiarity.

A cupboard clicked open. It wasn't one of those she could see but she could hear jars clinking together as they were pushed aside, then a hand came into view. Her first impression was that it was the hand of a corpse — of a drowned man who had been in the water for many days: pallid, featureless, the skin almost transparent enough to show the blood vessels underneath. But that image vanished on the instant, dissolving into that of a strong fist clad in a disposable plastic glove. The small area of wrist visible above the curled-over cuff showed hairy skin and something black and polished just showing beneath the sleeve.

The hand moved about, partly out of range, whatever task it was performing hidden from Fizz's eyes by her restricted field of vision, but she could tell by the speed at which the intruder was working that he'd be finished in a matter of seconds. If she didn't immediately make a move to identify him he might disappear before she had a chance of enlisting his help.

Shaking with the need for delicacy, she pulled off her shredded gardening glove, inserted one forefinger into the hole and slowly detached a few loose fragments of ceiling adhering to the edge. Flakes of plaster drifted down into the shadows below but failed to attract the attention of the man she could now see clearly.

His hair was covered by a black hood which seemed to be attached to the sweater he wore below a long raincoat of some dark, shiny material. From this angle, Fizz couldn't see his face, but she could tell that he was not particularly tall. He was shorter than either Oliver or Buchanan, too thick set to be Ewan, and there was nothing about him that seemed at all familiar.

His hands moved quickly, in the manner of one who had done this job before, but they were big hands and they managed to conceal his manoeuvring as effectively as though he knew someone were watching. There was a packet of something involved, Fizz could see it lying empty on the counter, and he was evidently inserting its contents into what transpired, after a moment or two, to be peppermint tea bags: cutting them open along the seam, tapping in something — liquid, powder, or solid Fizz could not determine — and sealing them again with a tube of adhesive He had already completed two and as soon as the third was sealed he returned all three to the box, interspersing them with undoctored ones. As he carefully wiped the working surface a sleeve rode up a fraction and she was able to identify the polished black object at his wrist as a watch. A black-faced watch.

One that she had seen before.

She stared hard at the bulky figure in an attempt to confirm her suspicions but she was given only a second to consider. A quick turn of his head to left and right, presumably to check that he had left no trace, and the torch was extinguished.

Fizz became aware that her mouth was open, and closed it. She listened to the footfalls move along the passage and heard the click of the front door as it closed but she remained kneeling there, straining her ears till she felt confident that she was alone again. Already she was beginning to doubt that she had actually seen what she thought she'd seen. Had that really been a black-faced watch or had her eyes been deceived by the unreliable light? Was her brain making things up to account for the vague similarity between the intruder and the unimpeachable Charlie Vivers of the Lothian and Borders police?

Charlie! she thought. I mean, *Charlie*? No way was he the intruder. Plenty of people had black-faced watches. She was jumping to conclusions.

But, even as she shook off the idea, half-formed images were darting through her head like frightened bats: Charlie's willingness to be involved in the case; his determination to see Terence Lamb off the streets; his firmly stated conviction that Mrs Sullivan was delusional; the broken window pane in Mrs Sullivan's back door; her strange uncoordinated behaviour. Why, if she was jumping to conclusions, should all the facts click together so neatly?

Suppose, just suppose, Charlie wanted to discredit Mrs Sullivan's claim of having killed Amanda. For what reason? Well, maybe to save police time. No. That wouldn't hold water. He wouldn't take such risks unless the matter were personal. Okay then, what if he didn't want Terence Lamb's conviction quashed? He knew Terence was a bad lot and wanted him off the streets so he wouldn't have been too pleased when Mrs Sullivan came along claiming responsibility for his alleged crime. Maybe he was sure in his own mind that Lamb was guilty.

A beam of light similar to that from Charlie's torch suddenly lit her brain with a brilliance like Blackpool illuminations.

What, in fact, if Charlie Vivers had been the one to plant the spurious water weed on Terence's boots? Had he been so keen to see the guy under lock and key — so keen to make a name for himself as the one who put Inspector Haig and his team on the right track — that he himself had made certain of Lamb's conviction? And having got himself out on a limb like that, risked his pension and his reputation for the sake of some professional kudos, he must have nearly flipped his lid when Mrs Sullivan arrived on his doorstep demanding to have the case reopened.

It was so obvious now. He'd had no recourse but to make her look unreliable. He must have hoped that by moving her car in the hotel car park, by slipping some drug or other into the tea bags she habitually carried with her, he might cause Buchanan to have serious doubts about her mental agility. Indeed, he'd succeeded up to a point and could, had Buchanan not been so soft-hearted, have persuaded him to throw in the towel a week ago. Her house had been broken into the day before their trip to Breich — by Vivers, of course, and it appeared he'd managed to take a copy of her front door key at the same time. But it must have been clear to Charlie that more persistent symptoms would be needed if Buchanan were to be scared off, so he was continuing to doctor her tea bags. What could be easier for a member of the drug squad, who had access to — and probably comprehensive knowledge of — every mind-expanding substance in the British National Formulary? He could have been back several times since then, replacing only a few tea bags each time so that the advent of her apparent delusions would be spasmodic. Should there be any subsequent inquiry he could be sure of getting there first to remove any remaining evidence. Maybe his strange reaction to the mention of Chloe Miller had been nothing but an attempt to set Buchanan sniffing down another trail.

This revelation concentrated her thoughts to such an extent that she lost valuable seconds staring blindly into the darkness, the exigencies of her current plight, if not forgotten, at least put on hold. But only seconds. A minute later she was hammering into the kitchen ceiling, with all her remaining strength, using her piece of lawnmower, her hands and finally her feet to create a space between the joists large enough to drop through.

The edge of the cooker caught her a solid wallop in the kidneys as she fell, which slowed her down a bit, but with adrenaline pumping through her nervous system, a gallon a minute, she was above such minor details. Forget the urgent need for toilet facilities, forget phoning the police, forget the advisability of ransacking the house for clues while she had the chance: the time for a swift exit was right now.

She half-crawled, half-staggered through a drift of fallen plaster and made it to the passageway that led to the front door. There she paused, trying to clear her head and get a grip on the pain in her back. There were two suitcases parked beside the tall old-fashioned hall stand as though ready to be loaded into a car. So Mrs Sullivan was coming back after all. Maybe to kill her prisoner: maybe to let her go. As the thought occurred to her a beam of bright light swung across the glass panels and she heard the gravel rasp as a car turned into the drive.

Without waiting to see if this heralded the return of the Hyundai or of yet another intruder, she spun on her heel, stumbled painfully back into the kitchen and threw herself at the back door. Unfortunately, Buchanan had taught Mrs Sullivan too trenchant a lesson on home security. She had fastened the door securely when she went out and no longer left the key in the lock.

21

It was ten past three when Buchanan reached Fizz's flat in the Royal Mile and the city was still abed save for the occasional team of garbage collectors and an insomniac or two. He charged furiously through the tunnel-like entry, letting the wrought iron gate clang back against the wall, and leaned on the bell of her entryphone. That there was no reply, after a minute or two, worried him a bit but not to the point of giving up. Fizz not only slept like the dead, she woke like a hibernating grizzly, too bloody-minded to answer the door. It would take persistence to annoy her to the point of actually getting her out of bed.

He moved out along the flat roof of the ground floor shops which served the flats as a drying green and looked up at her living room windows. The bedroom was to the front of the flat, overlooking the High Street, but it was four storeys high and effectively out of range. Only from the back court would he have any chance of making her sit up and take notice. He scouted around and finally located a piece of broken tile which he chipped up at her window. It landed with a smack that should have been heard throughout her two rooms but brought no response. A second projectile, launched with less restraint, cracked the glass and woke the downstairs resident, whose curtains twitched back to reveal a fat man in a white vest, seemingly mouthing obscenities which one could only guess at. Buchanan was, however, well past caring about the sensibilities of Fizz's neighbours. He launched another stone, this one missing her window altogether, thanks possibly to the anguish that was playing cat's cradle with his giblets, at which the irate spectator threw up the window and delivered a pithy address on the evils of drink and the provisions of the Common Nuisance Act.

'I'm trying to contact Fizz Fitzpatrick,' Buchanan called. 'It's extremely important. Could I ask you to run upstairs and bang on her door?'

The reply consisted of only two words but they were delivered with so much violence and such a threatening expression that it seemed better to drop the subject. He returned to ringing the doorbell but that awoke more irate and voluble neighbours. Not one of them was either sympathetic to his plight or amenable to persuasion, and he was, at last, driven from the vicinity with harsh words and threats of police intervention, delivered with a pungency that made him wonder if this was a community suited to a young woman of Fizz's station.

By that time, in any case, he had come to the conclusion that Fizz was not in residence. Her curiosity, if nothing else, would not have allowed her to ignore the drama that was taking place beneath her windows. Somehow he had come near to convincing himself, on the drive south, that she'd be safe in her bed: unscathed from whatever mischief she'd been up to for the past several hours and blissfully unaware of the scare she'd given him. Reminded of how often she'd acted so selfishly in the past, he'd managed to divert much of his uneasiness into righteous anger and already had a robustly-worded speech in his head, all set to deliver when he had her undivided attention. The fact that she had truly disappeared, that his fears were not hysterical imaginings but based on a pretty accurate reading of the current situation, was a hard one to accept without flying into a panic. Where the hell was she? Was she already dead? Had the person who'd just arranged his own demise made sure, at some earlier date, that Fizz was out of the way?

He paced up and down beside his car, staring optimistically up at her windows while he tried to decide where to check out next. The police, he knew from past experience, were a waste of time in a situation like this. It was way too soon to expect them to do anything practical and the thought of endless conferring and filling-in of forms only to be assured that most missing persons turned up safe and sound, made him sick with impatience. Mrs Sullivan might, just possibly, know something useful but the office was a lot closer than Joppa and there was yet a chance that Fizz could be there at her desk. With neither telephone nor computer at home, he'd known her, often enough in the past, to clock-in whenever inspiration or impatience woke her up, and often at the oddest hours. He could drop by, check it out and be on his way to Joppa in ten minutes.

He made it to the office in under eight, largely by breaking every traffic regulation in the book as, indeed, he had done all the way from Inverness. The streets were still deserted so there was little chance he'd hit something and, in any case, bobbies were pretty thin on the ground at that hour of the morning. The outside door was locked but there was still a key for it on his key ring and it seemed only sensible to check inside, just in case Fizz had locked the door behind her when she went in. In fact, he knew as soon as he stepped into the hallway that the place was empty. Somehow he had a sixth sense where Fizz was concerned and fancied he could always tell, simply by measuring the quantity of disturbance in the atmosphere, whether she were in or out.

He took the stairs two at a time and headed straight for her office, which had at one time been his own. It was empty, which was no real surprise, but a forlorn hope held him there in the doorway. She might have written a note for himself or Beatrice. She might have left some clue as to where she was going. He rummaged among the papers on her desk thinking, as he did so, that it was unlike her to leave stuff lying around like this. Her years of carrying all she possessed in a backpack had made her neat. She never collected a single unnecessary item and those she had were unfailingly returned to their proper place the moment she'd stopped using them. In contrast to his own desk space at home, which was always disorganised, hers was left, each evening, barren of even the smallest scrap of paper. But for once she'd neglected to file away the papers she'd been working with — not many of them; indeed in anyone else's office this desk would have raised no eyebrows — but enough of them to bring an empty feeling to the pit of Buchanan's stomach. She'd obviously left in a hurry the evening before last. To go where? To meet with whom? To get up to what kind of criminally insane mischief?

He flipped open her scrap pad and tried to decipher the scribbled mess of numbers, characters and doodles that covered the top page. At first glance it appeared only a little more complex than Linear B. Fizz's handwriting was usually neat but her abbreviations would have been a challenge to the Bletchley cryptologists as, indeed, they were to herself, nine times out of ten. The name Ella Dixon, which rang no bells, was followed by what looked to be birth and marriage dates, a scrawl that appeared to read *fried hen*, and more dates. An unspecified Will was born on the second of February 1959, married in '85, evidently to a Julia Mather aged twenty-six, and died on 13th November 1992.

All this would have led him to assume that Fizz had been talking to someone about a will were it not for the doodles that wove around and between the notes like those on an illuminated manuscript. Spindly trees a-dangle with hanged men. A crosshatching of black lines that proved, on close inspection, to be a maze. And, half-hidden in a spray of flowers and leaves, a claw hammer. Buchanan had often seen Fizz's subconscious thoughts illustrated in her doodling and these intrigued him enough to read through the notes again. This time the name Ella caught his attention. He knew that Mrs Sullivan's first name was Eleanor because he'd read it on the cheque she'd given him and, although the second name was not her present one, it could well be her maiden name since the dates of both birth and marriage fitted in with his estimate of her age. The fact that there was also mention of a Will who was of an age consistent with being her son more or less convinced him that Fizz had been checking the register of births, marriages and deaths for details of the Sullivan family. Just what part the fried hen played in the scenario remained an enigma.

He pulled the chair out from the desk and forced himself to sit down. Every cell in his body wanted action but, obviously, the sooner he figured out what Fizz's research had produced the faster he'd be able to find her. He had no real confidence in learning anything of interest from Mrs Sullivan so his drive to Joppa could be put on hold for a few minutes at least. He bent his head over the scrap pad and tried to concentrate.

Assuming Eleanor Dixon to be Mrs Sullivan's maiden name, she had married in 1956 at the age of twenty-two. At this point the fried hen entered the story followed by the number 83 and the word 'coron'. 'Coron' could be an abbreviation for coronary but he couldn't see Fizz taking that much interest in a hen's medical problems, so the phrase had to indicate a name — Fred Henry? — possibly that of Mrs Sullivan's husband, followed by his date and cause of death. All of which was unsurprising and of little practical help.

William's history was, however, another matter. Fizz's notes seemed to state, fairly unequivocally, that the woman he'd married in 1985 was not Amanda but a certain Julia Mather. Of course, his marriage to Amanda might have come later but Mrs Sullivan had attested that they'd tied the knot when William was twenty-six which, according to Fizz's dates, would have been in 1985. There were bigamists and there were bigamists, Buchanan reflected, but two brides in one year seemed a bit excessive. Also his date of death was five years later than that attested by Mrs Sullivan. The abbreviations *Cr Inj* which followed the numbers conveyed nothing at all to him, construe them how he might.

Clearly, Mrs Sullivan had been weaving a complete tissue of lies all along except, it appeared, about such primary matters as might chance to be verified by the police. In the light of this new data one could be forgiven for assuming that, whatever her connection to Amanda Montrose — if in fact there were such a connection — it was not a family one, nor, since her son had evidently pre-deceased her, had it been through the close relationship to Terence Lamb that Buchanan had suspected. The most likely possibility for her bizarre conduct was that she was just plain pixilated.

The thought steadied him a little. There was no point in dashing off to interview a confused old lady: not, at least, at three-thirty a.m. A more direct route to where Fizz had hidden herself away would be found through the scribblings on her scrap pad. Clearly she had unearthed a fact or facts that had sent her hurrying off on some trail that had led her further than expected. If he could just put his anger and apprehension to one side for a few minutes he should be able to find some clue to her train of thought at the time.

He stared at the scrap pad till the markings swam before his eyes but could decipher no more meaning in them than he had already gleaned. It was way too early to reach Fizz's contact at the English Records Office and he couldn't imagine where she might have headed from that point onward. But something in the data had caught her attention and, since Mrs Sullivan had lied only about her son's details, not her own, that would seem to be the weak link in her deposition.

How had William died? Fizz had — if *coron* referred to coronary, as it appeared to do — taken careful note of his father's cause of death, so why not William's? *Cr Inj*? Could that be his cause of death? *Inj* might be Fizzhand for injury. *Cr* . . . crash . . . cranial . . . ? That didn't take him much further but there was at least a chance that, if William had indeed died of injuries sustained in an accident, the circumstances might have been reported in the press.

He booted up Fizz's computer and spent the next twenty minutes scanning both Edinburgh and London newspapers printed on the day after William's death. There was no report of any incident worth a second glance. Frustrated, he propped his elbows on the desk and cupped his hands over his eyes. Fizz, he thought, where are you, goddammit?

The word *Greece* appeared in his mind as though someone had spoken it aloud. What had led him to think of it must have been some train of subconscious thought that had included the guilty secret in Amanda's past but he had no recollection of that. The connection between that enigmatic incident and William's accident had to be, at best, a tenuous one but he was scraping the bottom of the barrel for ideas and it took only seconds to locate a certain Athens News Agency which had an English edition for Friday the thirteenth of November nineteen eighty-one.

That Friday thirteenth had been an unlucky day, not only for William Sullivan but for a lot of people, including the forty-three individuals who had died with him. The story filled the front page and spilled over onto page two in a flood of lamentation for the dead and in vitriolic abuse for those the publication deemed culpable.

The purpose-built Acropolis Holiday Apartments building on Naxos had been operational for only eighteen months when, at eleven forty-five p.m. on the thirteenth, the entire six storey edifice had caved in on itself, seriously injuring thirty-seven tourists of various nationalities, and killing eight residents, the concierge and two passers-by. Shoddy building practices were immediately denounced by the emergency services interviewed at the site of the tragedy and the writer of the report didn't pull his punches when apportioning the blame. AHA Enterprises, the builders, had been in similar, though less tragic, trouble before but had been permitted to continue trading on payment of a severe fine. However, the suspicion of bribery and corruption in high places, while never alleged in plain words, was writ large between the lines.

Buchanan skimmed both pages, uneasiness returning like a cloud across the sun. He googled in the name of the building firm and found references to a court case dated some months after the tragedy in which the firm had been found guilty — in the absence of the consortium of the four major shareholders — of criminal neglect. Only one report named those vanished shareholders: Haffner Ausferder, Alexander Sipavicias, Helena Petropoulakis . . . and a certain Mandy Wakefield.

A fast search on Mandy Wakefield's name produced nothing new but the others were interesting. Haffner Ausferder, a Swiss entrepreneur, had died in a house fire caused by an electrical fault. Alexander Sipavicias, a retired manufacturer of kitchen furniture, had committed suicide by ingesting poison. Helena Petropoulakis, the widow of a well-known Greek landowner, was still alive but had been convicted of company fraud in 2004 and was currently held in the only women's prison in Scotland: Corton Vale.

Buchanan's brain went into fast forward, images flashing rapidly before his eyes as though projected on the opposite wall.

Something not all that far removed from a scream started rising in his throat.

The chair went over backwards with a crash as he jack-knifed to his feet and ran for his car.

22

Fizz heard the slam of the garage door and knew she had a matter of seconds to act.

The glass panels on the back door were too small to be worth smashing, the windows wouldn't open, there was no place to hide. She tried two or three drawers in search of a weapon but found nothing more lethal than dish towels in any of them. At the last instant, just as a key rattled in the front door lock, she made a grab for a tall plastic dirty-clothes basket, and threw the switch on the electricity meter on the wall above her head, plunging the room into the almost-darkness of early dawn.

Above the sound of her own breathing, which was pretty damn loud, she heard a light switch being snapped irritably on and off.

'Dear heaven, what next?' muttered Mrs Sullivan's voice, followed by, 'Miss Fitzpatrick? Miss Fitzpatrick? Are you asleep, dear?'

Silence sang in Fizz's ears like the distant buzz of insects as she waited for what would come next. Now that her eyes had adjusted to the half-light she could pick out the shapes of the kitchen furniture and realised that, poised beside the doorway, she was not as well placed as she could be. Carefully moving one bare foot at a time, she drew a chair towards her and climbed onto it, managing to flatten herself against the wall just as heels clicked their way down the passage towards her.

It seemed, for a single heartbeat, that her heightened senses could discern the scent of Mrs Sullivan's talcum as she pushed the door open.

Fizz lunged at her like a cat, all her pent-up wrath and apprehension and pain and frustration and resentment and desperation and whatever finding expression in the act, and crashed the upended basket down over her head and torso. The force of the attack was enough to throw them both to the floor but Fizz landed uppermost and was astride her prey and holding the basket firm before the old lady knew what hit her. She herself was pretty shaken up by the fall, which had jarred her bruised back, but the old lady was worse, well beyond offering serious resistance. Face down on the tiles, with her arms trapped in the basket and Fizz's 115 pounds solidly across her pelvis she didn't have many options open to her.

'Okay,' said Fizz in a voice that was intended to sound similar to that of Schwarzenegger in a bad temper but came out closer to Tweediepie. 'We can do this two ways. Either you do exactly what I tell you or I stick this knife through your ribs. State your preference.'

'Miss Fitzpatrick, I don't — '

Fizz walloped the side of the basket close to her ear. 'I forgot to mention: you speak only to answer my questions. On your feet.'

She got off Mrs Sullivan's back and helped her up by hauling on the basket, then, before the old witch could properly catch her balance, she shoved her into a chair beside the kitchen table.

The laundry line that had fallen from the basket was, luckily, within reach so she was able to use it to attach the basket to the back of the chair. During the moments it took to perform this operation Mrs Sullivan made no serious attempt to hinder her, merely mewling a little and asserting a plea for a modicum of tolerance and understanding.

'There's really no need for this, dear,' she said as Fizz stepped away from her to switch on the electricity. 'I'm deeply sorry for treating you the way I did but, if you'd just let me explain what drove me to it, I'm quite sure you could find it in your heart to forgive me.'

Fizz examined the face behind the blue plastic grille and found it an unhealthy greyish-beige with splodges of hectic colour on each cheekbone. It occurred to her that perhaps she had been a trifle precipitate in her handling of such an elderly woman. The basket was a tight fit and must have hurt as it crashed over her, and it was sheer good luck that she hadn't broken a bone or two in the fall.

For the first time since the trap door had closed behind her she began to wonder if she'd been a trifle over-the-top in her reactions. What — specifically — did she have against Mrs Sullivan, other than that she'd told a few whoppers and detained a member of Edinburgh's legal fraternity in her attic for a few hours? Not a lot. In fact she could find herself in big trouble if Mrs Sullivan chose to bring a charge of excessive use of force. Perhaps one should discuss the matter before phoning the police.

'Would you mind,' she inquired, striving for a politeness that sounded ridiculous even as she spoke, 'if I had a drink?'

'Not at all, dear. You've had a very trying day, I appreciate that. The sherry's in the lounge.'

'You wouldn't have anything stronger?'

'I believe there's some brandy left over from Christmas. Try the cupboard above the fridge.'

Fizz was not fond of undiluted brandy but after a short search which disclosed, in full view, a collection of sharp knives, a meat cleaver and a lethal-looking mallet, any of which would have been useful earlier, she found some tonic water and a tall glass and carried them back to the table.

'You must be hungry too,' commented her hostess with an apologetic smile. 'Take a look in the fridge and see if there's anything you fancy.'

Buchanan was never going to believe this.

She chose a packet of smoked salmon — farmed, but it wouldn't kill her — and a carton of cream cheese.

Mrs Sullivan watched her tucking in for a few minutes, a gentle smile playing about her mouth like that of a proud chef. She must have been feeling almost as rough as Fizz herself, and just as apprehensive, but she was hanging on in there and managing to give the impression that, in spite of everything, the situation would resolve itself amicably. Fizz sure hoped she was right.

After waiting till her guest had dulled the sharper pains of hunger Mrs Sullivan said, 'I've made such a mess of things, I know that. I should have trusted you with the whole story,

329

instead of which I've alienated you completely and brought about this quite appalling state of affairs. I can't imagine what you think of me but, obviously, you suspect that I might hurt you physically, which is — I'm sorry, but it's simply absurd. I couldn't be more embarrassed or ashamed.'

Fizz didn't answer, her mouth being full and her opinion uncertain. Mrs Sullivan's eyes looked red and tearful, as well they might, but that didn't necessarily denote repentance. She could simply be doing what Fizz herself would do if she were immobilised by a malignant adversary i.e. playing for time and trying to talk herself out of trouble.

'I didn't have anything to do with Amanda Montrose's murder, you know. That was all invented. Well, let's call a spade a spade, my dear, it was a lie, plain and simple. A wicked lie, and just look at the trouble it's caused.'

'What made you do that?' said Fizz between mouthfuls.

'I felt I had to.' There was a pause while she seemed to be trying to get her voice under control. 'It was the strangest thing. You probably won't believe it, and I wouldn't blame you for that because . . . because basically it's unbelievable . . . but . . . but I had a most vivid dream. It began with my late husband's voice calling to me down a long tunnel. I could see nothing at first but there was a circle of light at the end of the tunnel and a little later the silhouetted figure of a man appeared, outlined against it a long, long way away. He started to walk towards me and it seemed to take ages for him to come close enough for me to see his face and, when I did, it wasn't my husband . . . it was my son, William.'

She stopped talking, seemingly overcome with emotion and Fizz could see her bosom heaving as she sighed. Then, closing her eyes, she said, 'He spoke to me — but not the way I'm speaking to you. His mouth didn't move but I heard the words clearly inside my head. He said, 'You've got to get me out of here, Momma'. That's what he always called me. Momma. He said, 'I can't stand being locked up'. I wanted to stay asleep . . . to be close to him like that . . . but I couldn't. Suddenly I was awake and terribly upset and I had no idea what could have brought on a dream like that. Then, when I was having breakfast, I opened the paper and there was a photograph of Terence Lamb . . . staring at me . . . with William's eyes.'

Fizz frowned at her impatiently. 'What, you mean he looked like your son?'

'No . . . no, not exactly, but it seemed to me that William was . . . oh dear, I don't know how to explain this to you but . . . it was as if William's eternal soul was there inside him, as though he had somehow been reincarnated in the body of another man. It was such a shock to see him there — particularly right after the dream — that I almost fainted. And then to read that this innocuous young man had been jailed for a crime he insisted he had not committed — it all tied in, you see.'

Batty as charged, Fizz thought, wondering what she could reasonably say in reply to such a load of codswallop other than, Really, Mrs Sullivan, you should try to get out more. She tried to collate this version of the facts with those she had brought to light from other sources and found nothing that clashed too suspiciously. Had she gone a little lighter on the brandy she'd have felt more confident but, all in all, things looked a lot less alarming than she'd allowed herself to believe.

'Oh, I know how it must look to you, Miss Fitzpatrick, but I knew — I *knew* — that I had to do something even if it meant sacrificing my own liberty.' She tried to make some sort of gesture with her arms but had room for only a small twitch. 'What difference could it make to me where I spent my last few years? How indeed could I live, free and happy, knowing that my son was trapped in some kind of hell, inside another man's body?'

'He'd still have been inside Terence Lamb's body even if he were released from jail,' Fizz pointed out, quite reasonably, she thought, but Mrs Sullivan shook her head impatiently.

'It was the incarceration that troubled him, not the transmogrification,' she retorted, proving that she'd been reading up on the phenomenon. 'Terence Lamb was sentenced to thirteen years. William would have been terribly traumatised by that. It was insupportable. I had really no choice but to do everything in my power to take his place.'

Fizz ate the last scraping of cream cheese and smothered a burp. She'd have liked to help herself to another smidgen of brandy and tonic water but thought perhaps that wouldn't be too smart. Mrs Sullivan might be starting to appear merely doolally but until one were totally certain about that it was better to retain a modicum of rationality. She tried to think of some question she could ask that might clarify matters but Mrs Sullivan kept rattling on, giving her no peace to meditate.

'Perhaps I should have mentioned the dream earlier but, really, it did appear to me that it would only complicate matters if I did so. That dreadful Sergeant Vivers would have had me certified in a minute if I'd even hinted at such a thing. Men like that cannot even consider the possibility that there may be more in extra sensory perception than we currently believe. But I think you have a more open mind, Miss Fitzpatrick, and so has Mr Buchanan. One only has to look into his beautiful eyes to see that he's a thinker — a dreamer, possibly. I would have liked to be more open with both of you but I'm sure you will understand when I tell you I didn't dare. What I was trying to do was, however well-intentioned, breaking the law of the land and it would have been unreasonable of me to have asked either of you to ignore that.'

That, Fizz considered, was putting it mildly. It made her wonder just how estranged from reality Mrs Sullivan really was. She said, 'What was the point of locking me in your attic all day?'

This seemed to cause Mrs Sullivan a touch of embarrassment. 'Ah, yes, the attic. I do apologise about that, Miss Fitzpatrick. It was quite unforgivable of me but I simply couldn't think of any other way of stopping you. I knew, you see, that you . . . ' Her voice slurred a little on the last words and her head appeared to sag against the side of the basket. 'I . . . I . . . oh dear. Could you possibly take this thing off my head? Tie me up by all means, if you feel the need, but . . . if I could just get my head free. I'm like William, you see. A little claustrophobic.'

Fizz regarded her with the virtually imperceptible amount of sympathy she had at her disposal. The old witch could be hamming it up but, on the other hand, she could be on the point of keeling over stone dead, and that would just about put the tin hat on things. She stood up and went behind Mrs Sullivan's chair to loosen the knots on the washing line but, just as she bent down, the front door bell rang out like a klaxon making Mrs Sullivan start up in surprise, cracking Fizz across the bridge of the nose with the sharp edge of the basket.

There is something about getting cracked across the nose with something sharp and unyielding that makes a girl want to punch something, but Fizz was too shocked to relieve her feeling by such methods. It struck her immediately that Mrs Sullivan had been talking so volubly for only one reason: to keep her sitting there till help arrived. And here it was. The unceasing clangour of the bell betokened a visitor who knew that someone was within and wasn't going to go away till he or she got an answer.

'Who is it?' she barked, giving the basket a shake out of pure vexation.

'I . . . I can't imagine . . . it must be past four . . . '

The ringing went on and on and on while the two of them listened, frozen there, equally unable to move. Finally, Fizz glanced at the rope to see that it was secure and stole hurriedly down the hallway to determine what could be seen from the corner of the front bedroom window. Halfway there the ringing ceased and by the time she reached a viable viewpoint the front step was, as far as she could make out, deserted. Momentarily reassured, she darted back to Mrs Sullivan, who had apparently not moved a muscle in the interim.

'If you're lying to me — ' she was starting to say when the back door exploded inwards with a thunderous bang and there was Buchanan; his eyes blazing, his legs splayed and his jacket flying out behind him like Batman's cape.

Fizz was less surprised by his sudden arrival than by his amazingly compelling sexiness. It wasn't just the superhero entrance, it was something in his stern expression, in the way he held his hands and shoulders as though ready to meet any challenge, something akin to authority, strength, confidence maybe. Something, at any rate, that zinged across the room at her and hit her solidly in the solar plexus.

'What the hell,' he growled, 'is going on?'

For once Fizz found it impossible to put her thoughts into words. Those she was of a mind to voice were clearly unsuited to the occasion and anything approaching an explanation was, for the moment, beyond her.

'My goodness, is that you, Mr Buchanan?' cried Mrs Sullivan, trying to jiggle her chair around so that she could see him. 'Thank goodness you've come! I'm sorry to say Miss Fitzpatrick and I have had a little misunderstanding, but it's all sorted out now. She was just about to unfasten this basket. Perhaps you'd be so kind.'

Buchanan's face didn't change but Fizz could tell he was grinding his teeth. He kicked the door closed behind him but it swung ajar, askew on its hinges, lock dangling loose against the splintered jamb.

'I've had just about enough of you,' he said, blasting Fizz with the full force of an anger she'd not suspected him capable of. He had a black eye and a jagged cut on his cheekbone that was black with dried blood. 'I can't bloody take my eyes off you for a minute but you're running amok. What are you — suicidal, or what? D'you have a death wish, is that it?'

'Oh, behave yourself,' Fizz snapped back at him. 'What's suicidal about talking to Mrs Sullivan? She's not exactly a serial killer, you know?'

'Really? You've established that, have you?'

That snide remark didn't seem to Fizz to deserve a reply. She said, 'For God's sake come and sit down. Mrs Sullivan has a little confession to make.'

'Well,' he said, not at all pleasantly, 'that will be very interesting.'

He walked over to the table, appropriated Fizz's glass and poured himself an inch of brandy. Fizz had seen him furious before, but this was something else. Her response was to chatter, probably in the subconscious hope that the longer she could prevent him from voicing his anger, the more time it would have to cool down a little. She said, in something of a gabble, 'I'd have phoned you, Buchanan, but Mrs Sullivan has had me locked up in her attic since ten this morning — like she said, a bit of a misunderstanding, that's all. She's just admitted to me that her story about having killed Amanda had no basis in fact. It was all a concoction to divert the blame from Terence Lamb after she had a dream that her son was, somehow, trapped inside Lamb's body.'

'Ah,' said Buchanan with uncharacteristic sarcasm, 'why didn't we think of that explanation?'

He seemed to find some dark amusement in the situation and even gave a short bark of laughter, but Fizz felt no compunction to join in.

Mrs Sullivan said, 'I know it sounds unlikely but — '

'Unlikely, Mrs Sullivan? No, I wouldn't call it unlikely. Ridiculous, maybe. Insulting to the intelligence, certainly. But perhaps it would be best described as a deliberate untruth. But then, a small invention like that would scarcely be a challenge to your creativity, would it?'

'I don't know what you mean, Mr Buchanan.'

Neither did Fizz but she knew enough to shut up till she'd heard what Buchanan was getting at.

'Yes you do, Mrs Sullivan,' he said, 'You know

precisely what I mean. You are a very accomplished liar and a very dangerous and vindictive woman. Practically the only truthful information you've given me is that you did indeed smash a hammer through Amanda Montrose's skull. You tracked her down, you lured her into position on a lonely road and you murdered her in cold blood. I can prove that beyond doubt so, you see, you've got what you wanted, haven't you? You will be tried and found guilty of that murder — and for others — and you will go to jail for the rest of your life, just as you planned.' He ducked his head to get a clearer view of her face behind the plastic mesh. 'But, not necessarily the jail you hoped for.'

She began to cry, unable to cover her ravaged face with her hands, and Buchanan, big softie that he was, couldn't take it. He got up, untied the basket and lifted it gently over her head securing her loosely to the chair by passing the washing line around her waist. Some of his rage had evidently dissipated because his voice was somewhat less acerbic as he said, 'See if there's another glass, Fizz. She needs a brandy.'

Fizz complied, getting herself a fresh glass as she did so, and poured a generous measure into both. She wanted to press Buchanan for elucidation but couldn't quite get it together. He was different tonight, even in the way he addressed Mrs Sullivan. The gentle, almost affectionate tone of voice that was one of his more attractive attributes had been superseded by a much more aggressive approach. It might be a side effect of his anger but, equally, it might have something to do with his training as an advocate and, if that were the case, he was going to be hellish good at his job.

Mrs Sullivan's glass shook wildly in her hand as she raised it to her mouth. 'What are you going to do?' she whispered.

'I'm going to hand you over to the police, of course,' he said levelly. 'I really don't have any choice about that, do I?'

She dropped her head in her hands and did a bit more snorting and snuffling, but Fizz's patience had worn thin by that time.

'You've evidently had a productive time in Breich,' she said to Buchanan. 'How about bringing me up to date?'

Buchanan tossed down two thirds of his brandy and gave her a cool look. 'All I learned in Breich was that Amanda ran an international escort agency right up to the time of her death and that she and Oliver shared a guilty secret about some event that had taken place in Greece. Oh yes — and that someone wanted to kill me.'

'*Kill* you? You must be j — ! Who?'

He nodded in Mrs Sullivan's direction. 'Our friend here, I believe. She arranged to meet me at the river and laid a trap for me. It should have worked, Mrs Sullivan. Just bad luck that it didn't.'

'I . . . I hated having to do that.'

'That's a great comfort to me but, I must say, I'm surprised to find Fizz still alive. You've had her under your control all day. Why wait?'

She lifted her chin with a touch of her old

bravado but her eyes were tired and quite without hope. 'I knew I could silence her whenever I chose but I had to be sure I could silence you at the same time. To kill one of you and leave the other alive would have been asking for trouble.'

'And you never take chances, do you, Mrs Sullivan? In fact, I have to compliment you on your planning. It must have been spot-on all these years to permit you to escape any shadow of suspicion for the deaths of your other victims.'

'Unnh?' Fizz intruded. 'What other victims?'

Buchanan looked at Mrs Sullivan for a moment as though asking her if she wanted to take that question, then said, 'Mrs Sullivan's son was killed in the collapse of a jerry-built apartment block on the island of Naxos.'

'Not only my son,' she broke out, her voice shaking with passion, 'but my daughter-in-law and their three children — my only grandchildren. They were everything I had to live for. I couldn't stand the pain of knowing that those people — the builders — would buy themselves out of any repercussions, as they had done before, and go on living while my loved ones were lost to me.'

Sobs silenced her but after a minute Buchanan took up the story.

'She apparently decided to track down the four members of the consortium who ran the company responsible for the cut-price construction of the building and execute them one by one. Haffner Ausferder burned to death in his own home and Alexander Sipavicias was poisoned. The third member of the consortium was Mandy Wakefield who must have taken a long time to locate because she had, for five years, been Amanda Montrose and had taken the trouble to cover her tracks extremely well. But, you found her at last, didn't you, Mrs Sullivan? And you laid your plans well. You took a family house in Moy under an assumed name, hoping that anyone trying to retrace your steps would be looking for a woman on her own. You watched Amanda till you found a way of luring her to a place of execution. Did she recognise you? Did she offer no resistance?'

Mrs Sullivan had stopped weeping and her face was haggard but composed. 'She was afraid,' she said, with a certain grim satisfaction, 'as my darlings must have been.'

Fizz began to wonder if she'd missed something. If Mrs Sullivan had managed to escape prosecution for her first two murders, why should she confess to the third? If her mission to wipe out all four members of the consortium had been satisfactorily completed such reckless behaviour might be understandable, but there was surely another one to attend to?

'What about the fourth member?' she asked. 'Is she still alive?'

'The fourth member is a lady named Helena Petropoulakis,' Buchanan said, smiling. 'Care to tell us about her, Mrs Sullivan?'

'Helena Petropoulakis is a totally depraved woman,' she said. 'All four of that group were wicked, greedy, totally without morals or human

341

decency, but they were like babes-in-arms compared to Petropoulakis. It was she who was in charge of the firm's finances, she who proposed the use of shoddy materials, of seriously questionable building practices. She bribed officials — both with large sums of money and with girls supplied by Mandy Wakefield's agency. It was Helena, above all, whom I wanted to punish. In fact it was, latterly, only the hope of finding her and killing her that kept me alive.'

She gulped loudly at her drink and Buchanan watched her, his face pale and expressionless, Justice personified.

'I'd suspected for years that where I found Mandy I'd find Petropoulakis. They were close. Petropoulakis had once worked as a whore in Mandy's agency but it was her flair with money that had made them both rich. But it seemed for a while that I was wrong about that. I watched Amanda, both at home and in Edinburgh, but she didn't lead me to her friend. It was only a few weeks ago — months after Amanda's death — that I finally picked up her trail and, by that time, Terence Lamb had already been convicted of Amanda's murder. My luck had run out. Helena Petropoulakis was in Corton Vale Prison, serving a ten year sentence for a serious financial crime.' She looked at each of their faces in turn seeking, perhaps, some trace of understanding. 'Ten years. Too long to wait. I could be dead by then.'

Fizz found her mouth open and put some brandy in it.

'So, if I were ever to get to her, there was only one thing I could do, you see, and that was to get myself sent to prison too.' Mrs Sullivan seemed almost enlivened by the recital of her brilliant scheming. 'I would, of course, have to be charged with something serious so as to be sure of ending up in the same section as Petropoulakis and, as I'd already committed a murder I could confess to, that seemed to be the likeliest course to pursue.'

'But Charlie Vivers wouldn't listen to you,' Fizz murmured, nodding her understanding.

'I hadn't expected that,' she said. 'Of course, I'd done my best to make it a perfect crime because I'd no idea, at that point, that Petropoulakis was in Corton Vale, but I did think the police would check out my confession a little more carefully than they did.'

It occurred to Fizz that now was the time to mention Charlie's clandestine visits but she shelved that for the moment rather than interrupt Mrs Sullivan's flow of thought. Instead she prompted, 'So that's why you came to me.'

'I was desperate, dear. You were my last hope. Of course, I could have murdered someone else and made sure there was plenty of evidence against me but I would have hated to kill an innocent person.'

'But, if the worst had come to the worst, you'd have forced yourself, wouldn't you, Mrs Sullivan?' Buchanan's voice was like ice: it froze Mrs Sullivan into silence. 'How many other innocent people have you been forced to kill in all the years it's taken you to hunt down your

343

real victims? Would you class Miss Fitzpatrick here as innocent? You intended to kill her, didn't you? You had no hesitation in abusing her horrendously. Look at her. Are you proud of what you've done to her?'

Mrs Sullivan refused to raise her eyes but Fizz was made suddenly aware that she was sitting there in bra and thong, plastered with sooty sweat, bleeding quite copiously from a variety of cuts, and probably not looking her best. Curiously that seemed to be making Buchanan angrier than anything else.

She said tiredly, 'Well, it's all over now, Mrs Sullivan. You've rid the world of some nasty people, if that's the way you want to look at it, and three out of four's not bad.'

'It's all I had to live for,' whispered Mrs Sullivan, her face beginning to crumble again. 'There's no point in anything any more.'

She broke down completely, her body wracked with painful sobs, and Buchanan's no-more-Mr-nice-guy front crumbled to dust. He leaned over and patted her arm.

'You'll get over it,' he said gently, the old melted chocolate back in his voice. 'You should have had cognitive therapy way back in '92 and I'll see you get help to come to terms with all these painful issues as soon as possible. Finish your drink and let's get this over with.'

'You're going to let them take me away?' she whispered, her eyes pleading with him.

'I'll come with you and see you're treated properly.'

He got up and went through to the lounge

and, a moment later, Fizz heard him speaking on the telephone.

She looked at Mrs Sullivan and cracked a smile. 'It's a funny old life, isn't it?'

The thin, puckered lips curved a little in response and, after a couple of deep breaths, she said, 'It's a *short* life, Miss Fitzpatrick. Take care and make the most of it.'

'I do.'

'Do you? I wonder. You know that young man's in love with you, don't you? Oh, I think you do. I think you do. Take my advice my dear and don't make him wait too long. When you get to my age, it's not the things you did in life that you regret, it's the things you didn't do.'

Fizz tried for a careless laugh but had no time to pooh-pooh the idea before Buchanan returned.

'I'd better move the car before the police arrive,' he said, striding past them to the crippled back door. 'I left it in the middle of the road with the door lying open.'

Fizz had a sudden impulse to go with him: to step outside into the dew-wet garden and give him a hug. Just a friendly hug, like she'd give her brother if he'd suffered a traumatic experience.

But maybe that wouldn't be so smart.

She'd sleep on it.

We do hope that you have enjoyed reading this large print book.

Did you know that all of our titles are available for purchase?

We publish a wide range of high quality large print books including:
Romances, Mysteries, Classics
General Fiction
Non Fiction and Westerns

Special interest titles available in large print are:
The Little Oxford Dictionary
Music Book
Song Book
Hymn Book
Service Book

Also available from us courtesy of Oxford University Press:
Young Readers' Dictionary
(large print edition)
Young Readers' Thesaurus
(large print edition)

For further information or a free brochure, please contact us at:
Ulverscroft Large Print Books Ltd.,
The Green, Bradgate Road, Anstey,
Leicester, LE7 7FU, England.
Tel: **(00 44) 0116 236 4325**
Fax: **(00 44) 0116 234 0205**